P9-CKS-536

Also by Manda Collins

One for the Rogue

MANDA COLLINS

St. Martin's Paperbacks

This is a work of fiction. All of the characters, organizations, and events portrayed in this novel are either products of the author's imagination or are used fictitiously.

ONE FOR THE ROGUE

Copyright © 2018 by Manda Collins.

All rights reserved.

For information address St. Martin's Press, 175 Fifth Avenue, New York, NY 10010.

ISBN: 978-1-250-10992-7

Our books may be purchased in bulk for promotional, educational, or business use. Please contact your local bookseller or the Macmillan Corporate and Premium Sales Department at 1-800-221-7945, ext. 5442, or by e-mail at MacmillanSpecialMarkets@macmillan.com.

Printed in the United States of America

St. Martin's Paperbacks edition / July 2018

St. Martin's Paperbacks are published by St. Martin's Press, 175 Fifth Avenue, New York, NY 10010.

10 9 8 7 6 5 4 3 2 1

For Holly, who took a chance on an unpublished author and opened up a whole new world of possibilities.

Acknowledgments

No project of mine makes it to completion without an army of folks working behind the scenes to make sure every last detail is taken care of. Thanks to my fantastic and magical agent, Holly Root, who soothes my ruffled feathers and takes care of business (not necessarily in that order); to my friend, catcher of mistakes, and partner in mischief, Lindsay Faber; to my plotting buddies, Angela Quarles, Katie Reus, and Cynthia Eden; the amazing art department who never fail to outdo themselves with covers for my books; my marketing and promo whizzes, Titi Oluwo and Meghan Harrington; and last but not least, my editorial team of Jennie Conway and Holly Ingraham. You are all wonderful and I don't deserve you.

Chapter 1

The hushed sounds of the quiet house accompanied Miss Gemma Hastings as she crept from her bedchamber through the hallways of Beauchamp House.

She wasn't doing anything wrong. She was a woman grown and come the end of the year she'd be the owner of the estate on the south coast of Sussex. But her emotional memory of being chastised for her nighttime rambles as a child seemed to override her brain's sense of righteousness.

As one of the four heiresses named in the will of Lady Celeste Beauchamp, chosen for their intellectual capabilities to spend a year in residence at the house, which boasted one of the most impressive libraries in England, Gemma had enjoyed the freedom leaving her parents' house in Manchester had given her. But even so, she had moments when their expectations and mundane disappointments threatened to shadow her new life of independence.

Shaking off the anxiety, she pulled her dressing gown more tightly about her and lifted her candle higher to light the way to Lady Celeste's—now her—workroom and gallery.

Insomnia had been her constant companion from an

early age. One of her first memories was of lying beside her elder sister Sophia—whose skill with a paintbrush had earned her a place at Beauchamp House as well—and asking for one more story to relieve the desperation of sleeplessness. Poor Sophia had begged her to go to sleep, but Gemma knew that she asked the impossible. Her brain simply would not shut off no matter how much she wished it to. Unfortunately, it was still the case at times.

Now, of course, Sophia was likely fast asleep beside her husband Benedick, the local vicar. The thought made Gemma glance toward the windows overlooking the back gardens of Beauchamp House and beyond the winter-barren trees and shrubs toward the direction of the vicarage.

She'd expected pitch darkness, but to her surprise, she saw a light bobbing far beyond the area surrounding the house and near where she knew from frequent walks the bluffs overlooking the bit of shore belonging to the Beauchamp property lay.

"Who the devil is that?" she asked aloud, but the only response was the creak of a board beneath her feet. Not only was it two o'clock at night, but it was also a cold, bleak November night. No one of sense would be outside at that moment.

Her trip to the workroom forgotten, she quickly retraced her steps to her bedchamber and hastily pulled on the woolen gown she'd worn that day, her sturdy boots, and her warmest cloak.

Minutes later she was pushing through the kitchen door leading into the gardens with a lantern lifted from its hook on the wall. The cold struck her face like a slap. The wind had picked up since she'd dared to go down to the shore earlier in the day—or rather yesterday, she supposed.

It was darker than she'd first thought, but when the

moon came out from behind the clouds, it bathed the garden and the landscape beyond in light. And sure enough, she saw a dark figure carrying a light in the distance.

In the months since the heiresses—comprised of Gemma, Sophia, classics scholar Ivy and mathematician Daphne—had come to Beauchamp House, there had been several dangerous incidents, including murder and kidnappings, which should have given Gemma pause, but she had no intention of putting herself in danger. She would stay at a safe distance from whoever it was that trespassed on Beauchamp House land.

As the only one of the heiresses to have thus far been unable to interpret the letter Lady Celeste had left for her, she was eager for some sort of distraction. Her trek to the workroom had been intended as another search of the artifacts and fossils for some clue to the "greatest find" Lady Celeste had hidden away for her.

My own endeavors in geology were sadly lacking when compared with yours, but because I so admire your self-taught insight into the bone and stone remnants left to us by Mother Nature, I have in turn left to you my greatest fossil-hunting find. It lies where earth and sea and sky take hands and dance together in the wind, where once the terrible lizards roamed and giants walked amongst the—

Unfortunately, her benefactress had left the letter unfinished, no doubt because of the ravages of illness that had taken her life. So unlike the other heiresses, who had been left puzzles and quests to fulfill, Gemma had a half-finished letter alluding to a great find but giving only vague clues as to where it might be found. Gemma, who was not poetic at the best of times, had spent the months since her arrival at Beauchamp House staring at the inked lines, trying to make herself understand the hidden meaning there.

Thus far, she'd only managed to work out that the fossil was located somewhere along the shore. But the stretch of beach below Beauchamp House was too wide to dig up in its entirety, and besides that, why would Lady Celeste bury a fossil she'd already unearthed?

But Lady Celeste's fossil was not foremost in her mind as she hurried through the windy night. There was no reason for anyone to be on the Beauchamp House property in this weather and at this hour. She had to assume that they were here for nefarious purposes.

Wishing she'd brought some sort of weapon with her, she glanced around at the shrubs and trees of the carefully planned natural gardens and sighed at the fastidiousness of Jenkins, the gardener, who was far too conscientious to leave a convenient branch for her to use as a weapon.

The lantern would have to do.

Opening its window, she snuffed the flame and continued along the path toward the cliff's edge where she saw the dark figure step into the copse of trees near the sea stairs leading to the shore below.

When he emerged on the other side, he lifted his torch higher and she was able to see his face clearly in the light.

"Cameron Lisle!" she cried out in anger. "I should have known it was you."

Lord Cameron Lisle had done many foolish things in his lifetime.

There was the time he'd—on a dare from his brother Freddie—climbed onto the roof of the stables at Lisle Hall and removed the weather vane.

He'd also once ventured into a cave in Cornwall in search of what a smuggler had referred to as "odd bones" and almost been swept out to sea on the tide.

But wandering along the cliff's edge near Beauchamp House in the dead of night in pursuit of Sir Everard Healy was by far the most chuckleheaded endeavor he'd ever undertaken.

He tightened the scarf around his neck and lifted his lantern higher as he watched the other man—nimble for someone of his age and size—creep toward the sea stairs.

At the shout from behind them, from the Beauchamp House gardens if he wasn't mistaken, Cam stifled a groan.

He might have known Gemma Hastings would find a way to ruin this for him.

Secluding himself behind a tree, he watched his quarry glance over his shoulder in alarm before turning to run back in the direction of his carriage on the road beyond the wood.

"What are you doing here?" Gemma demanded, her tramping footsteps drowned out in the din of the wind. "At this hour, too?"

Turning to fully face his accuser, he saw that she brandished an unlit lantern like a cudgel, as if ready to swing it at his head at any moment.

"I might ask you the same questions," he said hotly. She'd very likely frightened Sir Everard so badly he'd not venture this way again, which meant Cam, in turn, would never learn what it was the man was after. "A lady has no business outdoors at this hour. And certainly not in this weather."

He'd hoped she'd rise to the bait and argue with him over the appropriateness of her presence here, but instead she *ignored* that and went for the thing he wished to avoid talking about.

"Who were you following?" Gemma demanded, her eyes narrow. "I saw another light near the stairs."

"That was likely a reflection," he said dismissively, hoping again that she'd get angry and change the subject. "You ladies are so fanciful."

On their first meeting, not long before her sister Sophia married his brother Benedick, she'd flown into the boughs when she learned he was the editor of the *Annals of Natural History*, and assumed it had been because she was a female. But, clever man that he was, he'd assured her it was only because her article was not interesting. Things had not gone well after that. Not only had Gemma ripped up at him, but so had Sophia and Benedick.

Now, however, she seemed determined to ignore his blatant misogyny in favor of pressing him for details he didn't wish to disclose.

Dash it all.

"Why are you here at all?" She demanded, pulling her cloak more tightly around her. "Sophia didn't tell me you were visiting them at the vicarage."

Recognizing that no amount of evasion would satisfy her curiosity, he sighed. "I'll tell you, but let's go inside. I don't want to be blamed for you catching your death."

She looked as if she'd like to argue, but finally nodded and began walking back in the direction of the house.

With one last glance over his shoulder into the darkness, he followed.

The drawing room off the terrace leading into the gardens was lit as brightly as a ballroom in the height of the season. Which should have been Cam's first clue that he'd made a huge mistake in following Gemma back to the house.

"I vow, you young people are far too spoilt with your blooming health and imperviousness to cold," Miss Dahlia Hastings said from her chair before the fire, where she sat with a book opened on her lap as if she'd just put it down. "Even sitting here near the French doors sent me scurrying for the fire. It is really too tiresome of you, Gemma, to make me do it."

The older lady, who had been paying an extended visit at Beauchamp House lowered her spectacles so that she might get a better look at Cam. When she recognized him, however, she gave a bark of laughter. "I thought perhaps you'd been up to no good, Gemma, but if it's young Cam you've been outdoors with in the dead of night I have no fear for your virtue."

Cam wasn't sure whether to be insulted or relieved at the assessment.

Beside him, Gemma unfastened her cloak and draped it over a chair before moving to stand before the fire.

"I didn't go to meet Cam, Aunt," she said over her shoulder. "I saw a light near the cliffs and went to investigate."

Deciding that silence was likely his best defense, Cam removed his greatcoat, gloves, and scarf and moved to stand as far away from Gemma as possible but still within the range of the fire's warmth.

"Your window doesn't overlook the cliffs, my gel." Aunt Dahlia fixed her niece with a speaking look. "You weren't in the collection rooms again, surely?"

At the mention of the collections, Gemma scowled at her aunt and tilted her head none-too-subtly in Cam's direction. Clearly she didn't wish to discuss the room where Lady Celeste's fossil collection was housed in front of him.

But Dahlia seemed not to have noticed. "You've wasted far too much energy searching for that blast—"

"Aunt," Gemma interrupted her. "We'll speak of it later."

Her aunt looked as if she wished to argue, but at Gemma's steely glare, she threw up her hands.

And, to Cam's dismay, turned her attention upon him. "So, what were you doing out on the cliffs at this hour of night, young Lord Cameron? For that matter, why are you in this county? I had it from Sophia only yesterday that you were expected to be away at a gathering of geologists for the next week or so."

"What?" Gemma demanded with a scowl. "She didn't tell me that."

"Likely because you wear that same expression whenever he's mentioned," Dahlia told her without any delicacy for either of their feelings.

It would appear, Cam thought, that Gemma still held a grudge over the rejected submission, then. Good to know.

"I do not," Gemma protested. Then, as if realizing that wasn't entirely believable, she corrected. "At least not anymore."

"Then who was it you were grousing about yest—?"

"Aunt."

To Cam's amusement, color rose in her cheeks.

"I have that effect on many ladies," he said with an attempt at levity.

As he'd hoped, it removed the sting of embarrassment and replaced it with annoyance.

She raised a brow. "That I believe."

Her honey blonde hair was mussed from where the cloak's hood had caught on it, and with her cheeks flushed from the fire she was in looks. It had never been Gemma's lack of beauty that made her the most frustrating female of his acquaintance. Her sister Sophia was probably the one who would be considered prettier. But he found he preferred Gemma's taller, more athletic build to her sister's petite one.

He let himself imagine what it would have been like if

they had been outdoors for lascivious purposes. Then, in horror, stopped. Clearly the cold had addled his wits.

Fortunately, Miss Dahlia Hastings was still bent on questioning them and since his thoughts had warmed him up, he was able to step away from the fire and proximity to Gemma and moved to the sideboard where he knew they kept a decanter of brandy.

"Well, young man?" the sexagenarian demanded. "What were you up to out there? Especially if you were meant to be somewhere else."

He used up as much time as he could pouring three glasses, then handing them round. It was cold enough he guessed that both ladies would appreciate the heat of the alcohol.

"I am . . . or rather, was, at a gathering of naturalists," he admitted. "But it's not in some far-flung locale, it's in this neighborhood in fact, at Pearson Close."

Both aunt and niece made noises of understanding.

"That explains why I wasn't invited," Gemma said with a shake of her head. "Is Pearson as violently distrustful of women as is rumored?"

This last she addressed to Cam, who shrugged. "I haven't seen him around any, but then again, he doesn't even have female servants, so there must be something to it."

"I suppose it's not that unusual to have an all-male gathering of fossil hunters," she continued. "The Royal Society doesn't admit women, after all. But even so, having such a gathering so close to home and not even being extended the courtesy of an invitation is quite angry-making."

"If it is any consolation," Cam told her, taking a seat opposite the chair she'd just dropped into, "so far the symposium has been quite dull. I had thought it might be entertaining since Pearson is said to know most of the major collectors, but most of the men there are only collectors with no real understanding of the science behind their finds."

"And was this meeting so dull that you were moved to walk along the chalk cliffs in gale force winds?" Aunt Dahlia asked, her expression revealing her skepticism at such a notion.

"Yes, you did promise to tell me," Gemma reminded him.

Both women sipped their brandy and turned similar, expectant looks upon him. If he hadn't known it already, their expressions would have confirmed their familial relationship.

"You won't like it," Cam said with a sigh.

But when no staying hand was raised against his speaking further, he knew he had to go on.

"I was following one of my fellow naturalists from Pearson Close," he told them. "And I have no notion of why he came here or what he was searching for. But I intend to find out."

Gemma wasn't sure whether she believed him or not.

It would be easy enough for Cam to blame his presence on Beauchamp property on following someone else. Especially if he wished to hide his own nefarious purposes.

Yet, Gemma was sure she'd seen another light beyond where he'd stood.

It was too much of a coincidence that she suspected Lady Celeste had left her a find of great significance on the very beach where this second man had been headed.

Could someone else know about the fossil her benefactress had left for her?

She studied Cam for a moment before she spoke. His looks were a bit more rugged than his brother—her brother-in-law—Benedick's. Whereas Ben's features were refined, almost ethereal, Cameron's were blunter, with less sym-metry. And his build was more solid, as if he'd spent more time physically laboring. Which, she thought, he likely had since he was rumored to prefer extracting his own fossils from the earth. Even without his brother's male beauty, he was still handsome—Gemma had to admit it—and to her mind, it was the slightly bolder, craggy ele-ments that made him the better-looking one.

Though she'd never say so.

Aloud she asked, "Who was it you followed? I—I mean we, all four heiresses, have a right to know who attempts to trespass on our property."

"So that you might go and confront him and make him flee the county before we even know what he's up to?" Cam asked with a raised brow. "I think not."

"You are the most infuriating man," she said crossly. "How are we to protect ourselves if we don't know why he was even here?"

"Might I make a suggestion?" asked Aunt Dahlia in a deceptively sweet tone.

Gemma knew her aunt far too well to believe that meek-ness.

But Cam was not so familiar with her wiles.

"By all means, Miss Hastings," he said with a nod of def-erence. "Perhaps you can talk some sense into your niece."

"I don't know about the two of you," the older lady said with a speaking look, "but I will be traveling back to Man-chester in the morning and I need my sleep. So I suggest you table this discussion until tomorrow. I will be sorry to miss your—no doubt, entertaining—argument over why and why not Gemma deserves to know this man's identity, but I am quite sure she'll send me an entertaining letter detailing all of it."

Gemma opened her mouth to object, but closed it when Dahlia raised her brows.

And to her disappointment, Cam seemed too well mannered to object to her aunt's suggestion.

"I am sorry to hear you're leaving so soon, Miss Hastings," he said over Dahlia's hand as he took his leave of her. "I wish you a safe journey. And I shall endeavor to make our row as colorful as possible so that you might be entertained by a missive about it in the future."

Gemma rose to see him to the door, but Cam shook his head, then shrugged into his greatcoat and pulled on his gloves and scarf. "I'll just go out the way I came in. I'll send word if I'm unable to call in the morning, Miss Gemma."

And with a jaunty salute, he stepped out onto the terrace and closed the French doors behind him.

"You might have allowed me to question him further," Gemma complained to her aunt after a minute. "I've all but convinced myself that whoever it was out there was searching for the fossil Lady Celeste left for me."

"If I knew Celeste at all," Aunt Dahlia, who had been well acquainted with the lady in their youth, said, "then I have little doubt that she hid it well enough that you need not fear someone stumbling over it in the dark. Or that she would breathe a word of it to someone else. If there was one quality Celeste was endowed with in large quantities, it was discretion."

"But that's just it, Aunt," Gemma protested. "The very fact that this man was trying to walk the beach in the middle of the night—and not just any man, but a fossil-hunter—must mean he knows something's there."

She crossed her arms against the sudden chill that ran through her. "Not to mention that for the past week or so I've had the distinct feeling of being watched."

Dahlia's dark brows—a contrast to her white hair—drew together. "You never said that. At least not to me."

Gemma shrugged. "I didn't wish to alarm anyone. And besides I've had no real evidence of anything. Just a feeling."

"You aren't prone to flights of fancy, my dear," her aunt said. "Promise me you'll speak to Serena about this tomorrow. And your sister. After what's happened to the other heiresses over the past months, it would be foolish to ignore your instincts."

Gemma nodded. Suddenly she wished Dahlia wasn't leaving. Having her here for the past month had been a great comfort in the wake of Sophia's marriage and Ivy and Daphne's absence. Once Dahlia was gone, there would be only herself and Serena. And as much as she loved the widow, Serena didn't enjoy spirited academic debate like the others did.

"You might also mention the matter to Lord Cameron," Dahlia said, interrupting Gemma's thoughts. "As much as you pretend to despise him, he's not as bad as all that. He did tell you he'd been following someone tonight. And he may have heard gossip amongst the gentlemen at Pearson Close about fossils hereabouts. Or perhaps the Beauchamp Collection itself. They might deny women the opportunity to join their clubs and societies, but they are happy enough to sweep in after the ladies have done the hard work and claim credit for it."

"In case you've forgotten," Gemma said wryly, "Lord Cameron is one of them. He's editor of one of the most important journals in the field of geology and has never once published more than a letter from a female geologist."

"I didn't say your objections to him were wrong," Dahlia said mildly. "Just that he may not be the worst of the lot. And he obviously has a great deal of affection for his brother and Sophia. That must account for something."

Gemma wasn't quite convinced but she didn't argue. "I will consider speaking to him about it. It's likely that whoever it was he followed tonight is the same person who's been watching the house."

"Good," Dahlia said with a nod.

Something in her tone made Gemma look closer. "Never say you're telling me to set my cap at him," she said with a horrified expression.

"Heavens no," Dahlia said with a laugh. "My opinion of marriage has changed not at all, despite the fact that your sister seems happy enough with her vicar. I want more for you, though, my girl. You have the potential to break down barriers. To succeed where those of us who came before you, like Celeste and I, failed."

It was something her aunt, who had been a part of the Hastings household in Manchester since both Gemma and her sister Sophia were small children, had told them again and again. She'd made sure her nieces, whose parents were loving but largely uninterested in their progeny, were educated and took them herself on outings to museums and the theatre and anywhere else she thought they might find food for the mind.

Her reaction to Sophia's marriage had been unexpectedly cheerful considering she had openly advocated against the institution for years. But, she'd decided since the deed was done—and she did like Benedick, Sophia's husband, a great deal—that she would not protest it.

And, after all, there was still Gemma to fulfill the spinster's dreams of the life of the mind.

Dahlia's own dreams had been crushed by the fact that her brother controlled her purse strings and had required her to live under his roof. But Gemma, as one of the Beauchamp House heiresses, had no such restrictions.

She was endowed with the funds and the independence that Dahlia had lacked, and Gemma felt the weight of her aunt's expectations upon her in a way that Sophia never had.

"I wasn't so sure when I first arrived," her aunt continued, "but now I'm certain that you've got the recognition we've always dreamed up within your grasp. Once you find whatever it is that Celeste left for you, I have no doubt you'll be able to show those closed-minded men of the Royal Society how wrong they are to deny you entrance. I can't wait to read the announcement in the papers."

Gemma wished she shared her aunt's optimism about her prospects, but decided not to air her doubts just now. It was quite late, after all, and they both had to rise early to get Dahlia on the road.

"Neither of us will do anything unless we get to bed soon," she said, helping her aunt to her feet. "I can't believe you're leaving us already. It feels as if you only just arrived."

Slipping her arm around Gemma's waist, Dahlia allowed her niece to help her from the room and up the stairs. "You must promise to write me as soon as Sophia is increasing. I know she'll want to wait but I trust you to keep me informed. And tell her I can be here in a week's time if she needs me."

For someone who was so against the notion of marriage, Dahlia was very much in favor of infants, Gemma thought with a smile.

Aloud she said, "I promise. And of course I'll write regardless."

They reached the door to Dahlia's bedchamber and she gave her niece an impulsive hug. "I've enjoyed these weeks here with you girls," she said. "I am so grateful to

Celeste for giving you this opportunity. I only pray you won't make the same mistakes I made and squander it."

Before Gemma could ask what she meant, she turned, and shut the door firmly behind her.

Chapter 2

Despite the lateness of his return to Pearson Close the night before, Cam was awake and dressed at a relatively early hour.

"I may be driving to Beauchamp House later this morning," he told his valet, Sims, who was arranging Cam's shaving things on the dressing table while Cam tied his cravat himself. "Ask James to be ready with the curricle."

"Yes, my lord," Sims said with a nod. The man had been with Cam since he was a youth, and though he may have wished for an employer who preferred a more flamboyant—or at the very least more fastidious—mode of dress, they rubbed along well together.

"Ask for some hot bricks," Cam added, remembering how cold it had been last night without them. Instead of bothering with the curricle he'd chosen to ride out to the cliff and had arrived back at Pearson Close shivering. "I don't think the cold will let up anytime soon."

Leaving the valet to finish tidying his bedchamber, Cam made his way downstairs toward the breakfast room.

Before he set out for Beauchamp House, he'd first question Sir Everard a bit to see if he could learn anything

more about why the man had been trespassing on Beauchamp House land last night.

So far the gathering of fossil hunters at the home of
Mr. Lancelot Pearson, a fossil collector known for his re-
clusive nature, had been less intellectually stimulating than
he'd hoped it would be.

For one thing, though there were a few collectors of
note among the guests, like Mr. Roderick Templeton, Viscount Paley, and Sir Andrew Reynolds, the rest were enthusiastic but not particularly knowledgeable about the
theories and science that tried to make sense of the origins and development of the creatures whose fossilized re-
mains they collected.

It would have been far more enjoyable if his own
friends in the collecting world, like Joshua Darnley, a phy-
sician who lived with his wife and children in Leaming,
or Adrian Freemantle, a Cambridge don, had been able
to make the journey. But both men were restricted from
such gatherings by the demands of their respective profes-
sions. He'd met both men through their membership in
the Royal Society and counted them among his closest
friends, aside from his brothers, of course. Adrian would
have made quick work of the worst offenses against logic
and sense at the current gathering. Sir Everard Healy,
whom Cam had at first thought was one of the more
thoughtful men at the meeting, would have infuriated
his scholarly friend. Not only was the baronet rather fond
of the sound of his own voice, but he also managed not to
take in anyone else's arguments. Just banged on with his
own ill-informed opinions like a discordant drum.

It was, perhaps, dislike which had prompted Cam to follow him the evening before, but he'd learned long ago to
trust his instincts about people and their motives. And something about Sir Everard made him suspicious. That he'd

been unable to catch the man in anything more nefarious than a midnight trip to the shore didn't mean Cam had given up his instinct to find out what the other man was up to.

He entered the breakfast room to find Sir Everard himself holding forth on his theories relating to the *proteosaurus*, a marine lizard that had been found just down the coast in Lyme Regis by the celebrated fossil collector Mary Anning.

Like her father before her, Mary made her living by selling the fossils and bones and oddities she found embedded in the chalk cliffs and sand near her home. It was dangerous work, and often required the help of local laborers and even tethering herself to the shore to keep from being swept out to sea by the powerful waves.

No doubt Gemma would have something to say about that despite the fact Mary had taught herself French so that she could read the work of Cuvier, and could likely more knowledgeably discuss a fossil's origins than most men, she was effectively ignored so that men like Sir Everard could pontificate about the fossils she'd discovered.

Gemma wasn't wrong, he thought as he listened to Sir Everard posit—wrongly in Cam's opinion—that the fossil in question was related far more closely to the crocodile than Cuvier had theorized. The world of geology, and fossil hunting in particular, were male-dominated. And when he saw men like Sir Everard gaining acclaim while Gemma and women like Mary Anning were denied entry into the Royal Society, it rather made Gemma's point for her.

When Cam had filled his plate from the sideboard he turned toward the table.

"Ah, Lord Cameron," said Pearson, a plate of kippers and eggs before him, as Cam took a seat on the other side of the table. "You must tell us what you think of this *proteosaurus* Sir Everard is discussing. I must say, I had thought Cuvier had the right of it, but Sir Everard makes a good argument."

Indicating to the footman behind him that he'd like coffee, Cam made himself busy with his cutlery to give himself time to avoid the question. He had no wish to insult his host, but nor did he wish to give Sir Everard the idea that Cam agreed with his assessment.

Fortunately, Lord Paley, seated on his other side, chose that moment to speak up. "I rather think Lord Cameron might be one of those fellows who is better able to articulate himself after he's had coffee or tea."

To Cam's relief, Pearson laughed. "Fair enough, old fellow. Fair enough."

When their host turned his attention back to the other men, Cam spoke to Paley in a low voice. "I appreciate the help, there. I was afraid I'd be forced to give my true opinion of Sir Everard and that would be a bad thing for all of us, I think."

"I merely thought that if I found the fellow tedious," said Paley in an equally low voice, "someone of your stature in the collecting world must find him insufferable."

Cam wasn't sure if he should be flattered or wary at the compliment. It was true he was well known in the collecting world, in part because of his role as editor of the *Annals*. But he was hardly of stature. "I rather think tedium is evident to most people whether they are well regarded or not."

"Fair enough," said the other man, raising his cup of tea. "Though our host seems to hang on his every word, doesn't he?"

Cam took a bite of his eggs before speaking. "I suspect he's just trying to be a good host. Given his usual preference for solitude I'd imagine a gathering like this would be a bit challenging."

Paley laughed. "You are determined to be kind when I am determined to be quite the opposite, Lord Cameron."

Cam laughed too. "I did sound a bit priggish, didn't I? Let's just say I am trying to be agreeable in the face of some challenges."

By the time Cam finished his breakfast, both Pearson and Templeton had left to look at something in Pearson's collection, leaving Cam and Paley with Sir Everard, who for some reason, seemed keen to speak to them.

Or rather, keen to speak to Cam.

Pushing his plate forward, the large man got up from his chair and came to sit across from the two men.

"You're related to one of the Beauchamp House heiresses by marriage, aren't you, Lord Cameron?" he asked without preamble.

"I am," said Cam, careful not to let on his interest at Sir Everard's question. He'd thought he would have to be the one to broach the topic of Beauchamp House. Clearly he'd underestimated the other man's boldness. "My brother, the vicar hereabouts, married Miss Sophia Hastings a couple of months ago."

"There's another, though, isn't there?" Sir Everard pressed. "Another Hastings sister at Beauchamp, I mean. Calls herself a geologist, I believe?"

Cam felt himself bristle on Gemma's behalf at the other man's dismissive tone. "Miss Gemma Hastings is a geologist, yes," he said in a deceptively calm tone. He was rather surprised at his reaction to the man's condescension, but there was something particularly vile about such a dullard belittling Gemma's place in their field of study.

"You are acquainted with the chit, then?" the older man

pressed. "Able to wrangle an invitation to the house, I mean?"

Cam blinked. Was this man actually attempting to garner an invitation to Beauchamp House after effectively calling one of its mistresses a pretender? He'd known the baronet was bold given his attempt to search the shore last night, but he hadn't thought him presumptuous enough to inveigle an invitation through Cam's familial connection.

"I believe I could arrange something, yes," Cam said after a minute. "You'll wish to see the Beauchamp House collection, I suppose?"

Sir Everard nodded. "Yes, of course. It would be foolish to come this close to such a renowned collection and miss out on seeing it for myself. Despite her lack of any true understanding of the science behind it, I've heard Lady Celeste had a rare knack for choosing important items to keep for herself."

"I say," Lord Paley interjected before Cam could reply, "you wouldn't mind if I were to tag along, would you? I've long wished to see Lady Celeste Beauchamp's artifacts. What a spot of luck that you're connected to the house, Lord Cameron."

Not bothering to comment on Sir Everard's dismissal of Lady Celeste's intellect, Cam nodded to both men. "I should be able to garner invitations for you both. I know Miss Gemma will be quite pleased to show us the finer points of Lady Celeste's collection."

In a fit of pique, he added, "She's quite knowledgeable about the study of fossils and their origins herself, you know. I've read some of her work and it's sound analysis."

He'd rejected it for the *Annals*, but they didn't need to know that. It wasn't because her analysis was flawed but because he'd seen a similar argument in a different publication not long before he read hers. It wasn't her fault that she'd arrived at the logical conclusion.

But if he expected Sir Everard to look chastened and apologize, he was doomed to disappointment.

Ignoring the mention of Gemma completely, the baronet grinned. "Excellent. Excellent."

And to both Cam and Paley's astonishment, his task complete, Sir Everard left the breakfast room.

"I thought you two would come to blows," Lord Paley said with a laugh once Sir Everard was gone. "You're not involved with the Hastings chit, are you?"

"What?" To his embarrassment, Cam's voice went unnaturally high. "Why would you ask that?"

"Calm yourself, man," said Paley with a laugh. "I simply noted your defense of the lady. But if you tell me it was only annoyance at Sir Everard's snide tone, I will believe you, of course."

"Of course that's all it was," Cam echoed him. "And I dislike hearing anyone I consider a friend disparaged in such a way. Lady Celeste was said to be one of the great minds of her generation, lady or no. And Miss Gemma was handpicked by Lady Celeste to oversee her collection and use it for her studies. It's infuriating to hear someone as foolish as Sir Everard demean them, that's all."

Lord Paley nodded, looking thoughtful.

"I'll just go write a note to send round to Beauchamp inquiring whether the three of us, or anyone else who might wish to join us, might come view the collection tomorrow."

He stood and gave a slight bow.

Cam wasn't sure if it was the viscount's watchful eye he was trying to escape or his own reaction to hearing Gemma's intellect dismissed. Either way, he needed a moment to himself.

* * *

The skies above Beauchamp House were gray with clouds and the wind had Gemma's hair, unruly at the best of times, flying around her face as she and Sophia stood on the drive bidding Aunt Dahlia goodbye.

"You're sure you won't just stay through the holidays?" she asked her aunt for what must have been the hundredth time. "There's no need for you to go back north. Especially in this weather. Travel will be must better in the spring."

"When the rain will make the roads impassable?" her aunt asked with a raised brow. "Don't fuss, Gemma. I wish to go back to Manchester. I have responsibilities with the Ladies' Lecture Society and I've neglected them for a month already."

"Perhaps we could help you form something similar here," Sophia, hugging her cloak more tightly around her, offered. "I could suggest any number of ladies in the neighborhood who might be interested. In fact, Benedick might also—"

Aunt Dahlia pounded her heavy walking stick into the shell drive. "Enough! I must go and that's that. I've loved this time with you girls, but my life is there."

She hugged each of the sisters, taking the sting from her words. "I can't begin to tell you how proud I am of you both. Sophia, I had hoped you would devote yourself exclusively to your painting, but if you must marry, then Lord Benedick is as fine a choice as you can have made."

Turning to Gemma, she smiled. "And Gemma, your work here, cataloging and studying the collection Celeste left for you, will be of the greatest scientific importance. If Celeste did leave you something, then you must find it and make your mark. It will be in the analysis of fossils that you distinguish yourself. Poor Mary Anning's analysis is ignored because men have taken her finds and imposed their own theories on them. Celeste has left you an opportunity to be the first to study her fossils. Do not squander it."

She didn't mention their conversation the night before about the importance of remaining unmarried, but Gemma heard the warning anyway.

"Yes, aunt," she said obediently.

And then the sisters were watching their aunt and her maid climb into the large and comfortable traveling carriage that had come with the house. Gemma had seen to it that they were supplied with a basket of food, hot bricks for their feet, and heavy carriage blankets.

To her surprise, Gemma felt tears spring to her eyes as she watched the horses take off at the signal from the coachman and begin the journey.

"Come," Sophia said, slipping her arm through hers. "Let's get inside before we both turn into icicles."

She must have sensed her sister's distress because she didn't comment when Gemma surreptitiously wiped her eyes.

Inside, after removing their coats, scarves, and gloves, they repaired to the breakfast room, where Serena was sipping a cup of tea.

"I take it Miss Hastings has departed?" she asked, no doubt taking in the sisters' glum expressions.

"She has," Gemma said as she spooned eggs onto her plate at the sideboard. Despite her mood, she was ravenous. Cold weather always left her hungry. For good measure she added two pieces of toast to her meal before taking a seat beside Serena.

"I know you'll miss her," said the widow, who, as the niece of Lady Celeste, had been chosen to act as chaperone for the four heiresses over the course of their year in the manor house. "But, I've had a letter this morning that might cheer you up."

"Do tell," Sophia said as she took a seat opposite them. "We could use a bit of good news."

"Ivy and Daphne have decided to return to Beauchamp House for the rest of the year," Serena said, handing Gemma the letter that had been folded on the table beside her teacup. "Ivy wrote that she and Daphne crossed paths at a dinner party in town and that they'd both lamented what Daphne called 'the hair-witted conversation to be had at *ton* entertainments.'"

Sophia stifled a giggle while Gemma scanned the note. "It would seem that Maitland's slang has begun to influence her."

The letter was penned in Ivy's tidy penmanship, and was dated a week previously. "They'll be here soon, according to this. She says they're leaving tomorrow."

Sophia clapped her hands. "Just the thing we needed to distract us from Aunt Dahlia's departure. I hadn't realized how much I missed them while they'd been in London, but I can't help but feel their absence every time I come to the house now."

"Gemma and I rub along together well enough," Serena said with a nod, "but we've felt the loss of all three of you since your marriages have taken you away from the house."

"Things have changed so much since we first arrived," Gemma said. "There have been so many dangers and adventures. And weddings. It's hard to believe it's been under a year."

"There's still time for more adventures," Sophia said with a grin. "And weddings for that matter. Are there any gentlemen on your dance card, sister?"

"You know me better than that," Gemma said firmly.

"I intend to remain unwed, like Aunt Dahlia and Lady Celeste."

"You won't hear any argument from me," Serena said. Her late husband had been an unpleasant, sometimes brutish man. "I fully support your decision. Though of course I am happy for Sophia and Ivy and Daphne. It simply isn't for everyone."

"I cannot afford to let anything distract me from my studies," Gemma said with a shrug. "I have a responsibility to the women who came before me. I cannot let them down."

Sophia tilted her head. "I hope you won't let Aunt's views on the matter pressure you too much. It is possible to have both a loving relationship and a fulfilling career in your chosen field of interest. Men do it often enough, certainly."

"But men are able to ignore the mundane tasks of running the household and caring for children," Gemma retorted.

"Our own Mama should show you that not all ladies are tasked with those duties either," Sophia said with a raised brow.

Their parents had been largely absent from both Gemma and Sophia's lives, so wrapped up in one another that they were uninterested in their children except insofar as they could be held up as reflections of themselves. The raising of the sisters, and much of their education, had been left to Dahlia, who had seen to it that they were educated far better than the daughters of their parents' middle class peers.

"Yes," Gemma responded, "and look how she imposed on Aunt Dahlia to afford herself that luxury."

"I won't argue with you," Sophia said after a moment. "But I do wish you wouldn't close the door on marriage before you've even had a chance to see if you might find a man who would suit you. It will sound silly to you, I fear, but I didn't know life could be so content until I met Benedick."

"It doesn't sound silly," Gemma said softly. It actually sounded wonderful. Gemma couldn't remember a time before she felt this nagging in her gut. That said she had more to do. More to see. More to learn. Thus far she'd found nothing and no one who'd managed to quiet that sense of hunger. And she wasn't sure she ever would.

Aloud, she continued. "It sounds wonderful. I'm happy for you. Truly."

That kind of fulfillment might not be intended for her, but she was happy beyond words that her sister—and Ivy and Daphne—had found it.

They'd moved on to less fraught conversation when the footman, Edward, appeared with a note. "This came for Miss Gemma from Pearson Close."

As Gemma took it from him, she felt the scrutiny of her sister and chaperone.

"Why are you receiving clandestine letters from the mysterious master of Pearson Close, I wonder?" Sophia said thoughtfully.

"It's hardly clandestine when it's delivered in full sight of the two of you," Gemma said tartly as she unfolded the missive. Scanning the words, she continued. "It's from Lord Cameron. He asks if he might bring Viscount Paley and Sir Everard Healey round tomorrow to see the collection."

"Of course," Sophia nodded. "I'd forgotten he was staying at the Close this week for Mr. Pearson's gathering of fossil collectors."

"You could have told me, you know," Gemma chided her sister. "I wouldn't have been angry. Not very angry, at any rate."

Serena, however, was focused on something else. "I

know I've supported you in your decision not to marry, but I do think you should take this opportunity to put your best foot forward among these men, your scholarly peers."

Gemma felt a prickle of unease. "I wasn't intending to put my worst foot forward."

"Of course you're intelligent and can hold a conversation with them," Serena said kindly. "But perhaps we can take this opportunity to ensure that your attire is as confident as your knowledge of geology."

Gemma looked down at her gown, a practical gray woolen that was warm and didn't show dirt when she was cleaning artifacts in the collection. "What's wrong with my attire?"

"Nothing is wrong with it, dearest," said Sophia in the tone Gemma recognized as her managing voice. "But men are shallow creatures and I fear they will take you more seriously if you take a bit of time to make yourself pleasing to the eye. And I must admit I've been longing to see you in some colors."

"That's just because you're an artist," Gemma said with a scowl. But she had to admit, though she'd never say so aloud, there was a certain appeal to the notion of making a certain fossil-hunting gentleman of her acquaintance look at her in a different way. Not that she intended to let anything come of it, but it would give her a certain satisfaction to see something in his eyes when he looked at her besides exasperation.

"Fine," she told the other ladies. "I will allow you to dress me tomorrow. But I will not allow you to have Tilly curl my hair. The last time you convinced me to try it, Sophia, I had the stench of burning hair in my nostrils for weeks."

The incident had happened when the heiresses embarked on one of their first social outings not long after their arrival at Beauchamp House. Against her better judgment, Gemma had allowed her sister to talk her into trying something new with her coiffure. It hadn't been a pleasant experience.

Her hair was fine and straight and frankly, the time and effort it took to coax curls out of it was not worth it to her.

"She's gotten much better since then," Serena said with a laugh.

"We promise," Sophia said, placing her hand over her heart. "This is going to be fun."

"I'm glad you're amused," Gemma said with a roll of her eyes. Though inside, she was looking forward to tomorrow.

And not just the discussion of geology, either.

Chapter 3

"Ouch." Gemma made a face as Serena's maid, Tilly, stuck a pin into the coil of curls she was transforming from a blowsy fright into the sort of elegant style Serena herself would be happy to wear.

"Now, Miss Gemma," the maid scolded, "You know I'm as careful as an ewe with a newborn lamb with you."

"She's always been thus, Tilly," Sophia, the traitor, said from her comfortable chair to the side of her sister's dressing table.

If she weren't attempting to convince the gentlemen from Pearson Close of her fitness for their company, Gemma would never have put this much effort into her attire. But Sophia and Serena had convinced her that perhaps her intellect alone was not enough to prove her bona fides to them. As much as it pained her to admit it, men seemed to care as much about a lady's looks—perhaps more—than they did for the sharpness of her mind.

"You are here for moral support," she reminded Sophia tartly. "Taking Tilly's side against me is not that."

"We're all on the same side, miss," said the maid reproachfully as she twisted another lock of hair into a coil. "I'm as intent on you showing those gents your smarts as anyone. It's about time someone took us females serious-like."

"Seriously, Tilly," Gemma reminded her automatically. She'd taught the girl to read soon after the heiresses arrived at Beauchamp House and now they were working on her spoken language. Tilly had ambitions beyond life in service and Gemma was as invested as she was in making her dream of becoming an educator come true.

"Seriously," the girl repeated. "Seriously."

The sisters exchanged a smile in the mirror before Sophia responded to Gemma's earlier rebuke. "I am here to ensure that you are as fine as a five pence when you go downstairs to greet your peers. It is frustrating, I know, that ladies are expected to be well turned out as well as intelligent amongst these sorts, but it is the way of things. Think of it as catching more flies with honey."

Gemma frowned. "I've never liked that expression. I do not wish to catch flies in the first place."

"Do not be so literal," Sophia said, her exasperation evident in her tone. "You take my point. Otherwise we wouldn't be here right now."

Turning her attention to Tilly, she asked, "Which of the gowns I sent over did you settle on? The blue or the green?"

"The blue brings out her eyes very well, Lady Benedick," the maid said before stepping back from the dressing table.

"There, Miss Gemma, all finished."

Gemma, who had closed her eyes to the image in the glass, now opened them and was surprised at what she saw.

She'd never been particularly careful about her looks. Indeed, she could often be found with a pencil tucked into her messily coiled braid when she was in the library scouring the latest journals from the world of natural science. It had been a trial to her mother when she and Sophia still lived in Manchester. Aunt Dahlia had thought it a foolish concern. And unlike Sophia, who as the eldest, and the most intent on pleasing her elders, and who made an effort with both her appearance and her studies, Gemma had decided to please herself. Only when Sophia had insisted she pay lip service at the very least to society's expectations, had she allowed herself to be pinned and coiffed and laced. But it had never felt comfortable. And certainly didn't give her the sort of confidence it gave her sister.

Still, staring at the tidy, even elegant hairstyle she now wore, gave her a little glow of satisfaction.

Was this why Sophia had always made such a fuss over her hair then?

"Let those boors ignore your thoughts on the *icthy*-whatever now," Sophia said with grin from behind her.

"*Ichthysaurus*," Gemma said automatically, correcting her sister just as she'd corrected Tilly earlier.

"Come on, miss, and let's get you into the blue velvet. It's nearly ten thirty and the gentlemen are arriving at eleven."

Dressing was not nearly the ordeal as the hairdressing had been, but once Gemma was buttoned into the long sleeved velvet, as beautifully made as it was practical, with a bright white fichu for warmth at the neck and finely embroidered red roses at the hem, she was once again feeling an uncustomary surge of pleasure at her appearance.

"If we aren't careful, all of this elegance will go to my head and I will never have another thought for fossils or science," she said wryly as she surveyed herself in the pier glass.

Careful not to wrinkle the gown, Sophia gave her a quick hug. "I've always tried to tell you, it's possible to care about one's coiffure and gown and whatever academic interest one has. You need not trade one for the other. Indeed, I think of my pretty gowns as armor. Maybe now you will view them in the same way?"

"That all depends on how this morning's tour of the collection goes," Gemma said with a rueful smile. "But I do admit that it's nice to be pleased with my appearance in the glass rather than feeling as if I'll disappoint you."

Sophia blinked, her eyes narrowed with concern. "Dearest, you could never disappoint me. Not in a lifetime. I might tease you about your windblown hair and dirty hands, but you must know I don't mean it."

This time the hug she gave her was unmindful of the gown and Gemma felt a wave of affection for her sister wash over her. She'd missed her in these months since she'd married and moved just down the road.

"I know it," she told Sophia, returning the hug. "I simply wish to please you. That's all. And it feels as if a great deal of the time what pleases us is at cross-purposes."

"I am on your side," Sophia said. "Always."

"And I'm on yours," Gemma said, her smile wide. "Now, let's go downstairs and show Serena how well I can look when I'm made to care about it."

They found Lady Serena in the sitting room with a bit of darning, and her gasp when Gemma entered the room was what she'd hoped for.

"Gemma," she said, beaming, "you look as fine as I've ever seen you. I hope these gentlemen are able to listen to your scientific talk without being distracted by your radiance."

This was something that hadn't occurred to Gemma and she turned to her sister with alarm. "Will they do that? I do not wish them to be inattentive because of my hair and a silly gown. I will go upstairs and change at once."

But Sophia held her fast by the arm. "She's only teasing, my dear. Do not, I pray, go destroy all of Tilly's hard work because of a jest."

Serena, her expression contrite, hastened to reassure her as well. "I know we say that gentlemen have very short spans of attention, but I feel sure they will be able to manage. Aunt Celeste was forever complaining about the way that lady scholars insisted upon being dowds to be taken seriously, too."

"You never told me that," Gemma said with a pang of distress. "I thought she was a devotee of sensible dress."

"Only when it came to practicality," Serena said with a shrug. "She was quite fond of pretty things, and I vow had more hats than any lady has a right to. But for those occasions when it was necessary to wear a less-than-fashionable gown—while digging in the sand and soil for fossils, for example—she did so."

Gemma had been here for nearly a year and she still didn't feel as if she truly knew everything there was to know about the woman who had bequeathed her estate to four strangers.

"So, if you needed it," Sophia said with a grin, "you now know that Lady Celeste would have approved of your gown."

The idea pleased Gemma, though she was not quite comfortable discussing it aloud. Instead she turned to the subject of the luncheon menu. In addition to touring Lady Celeste's collection, the gentlemen from Pearson Close would also be sitting down to a light luncheon afterward. The idea had been Serena's, who had thought it would be an opportunity for Gemma to have further conversation with them about her favorite subject rather than sending them on their way as soon as they'd seen the fossils.

Without Serena and Sophia, and even Tilly, Gemma was quite certain she'd have been able to conduct herself passably with her fellow fossil-hunters, but she would without doubt have done so without making much of an impression. At the very least, this way she had learned how much she appreciated having embroidered roses on her gown.

And that was something for which she'd be eternally grateful.

"Lady Celeste Beauchamp was rumored to have quite a collection," said Sir Everard as he, Lord Paley, and Cam rode in the Pearson Close coach over the somewhat bumpy road to Beauchamp House. "I appreciate the invitation, Lord Cameron. I had thought to make a trek there myself before I left the area, but it's much better to get in the door with a relation by my side."

Perhaps realizing how that sounded, he amended, "To ease the introductions, of course. I find that having a male relation along makes the ladies much more comfortable in social situations."

Cam rather thought the ladies of Beauchamp House would have some arguments with the assertion but decided to let the comment pass. After all, this trip had afforded him the opportunity to learn more about what Sir Everard's motives were in both his midnight visit to the beach and the more conventional but no less suspicious visit to the collection. The man was after something, and Cam wanted to know what.

His own motives for this curiosity were not clear to him either. Logic would dictate that the familial connection between his family and Gemma's made it incumbent upon him to protect her from whatever harm Sir Everard posed to her, and by extension, the Beauchamp House collection. But he could just as easily have informed his brother of the man's suspicious activity and gone on about his own business.

Honesty meant admitting that as a collector himself, he wanted to know what it was Sir Everard thought to find on the cliffside property and how he might make use of it in his own studies. Fossil hunters were a competitive lot and there was a certain sense of anticipation at the idea of snatching an important find out from under the other man's nose.

That, however, would also mean snatching whatever it was from beneath Gemma's nose. And there was the rub. If she were a man he'd have no misgivings about it. Obviously he wouldn't steal it. He wasn't that competitive. But honor dictated he give her the opportunity to reject this mysterious prize (which he still didn't know was actually a prize) before making his own claim upon it.

Life was far less complicated when one wasn't bending over backward to please a woman. His brothers might all be cozily trussed up in the bonds of matrimony, but he, thank you very much, would prefer to keep his life simple.

Or at the very least, he would choose a bride who was sweet and biddable and did as she was told. Not someone like Gemma Hastings, who was quick-tempered and didn't have a mild bone in her body.

"I have heard your brother's wife is a very refined lady," said Lord Paley, interrupting Cam's brooding. "I believe the Hastings family is from Manchester?"

Wondering where this conversational gambit was headed, Cam nodded. "I believe they are, yes. Her father is some sort of merchant, I believe? But Sophia and her sister Gemma are both well mannered and intelligent."

"I look forward to meeting them both," the viscount

said with an approving tone. "With the added inducement of the collection amassed by Lady Celeste and the estate, I should think Miss Hastings has quite a few suitors vying for her hand."

It was said with the hint of a question in the tone. As if he were asking for Cam's assessment of the situation.

Before Cam could respond, however, Sir Everard broke in. "Never say you've got your eye on the Beauchamp fortune, Paley? If the chit is pretty enough, perhaps I'll make an attempt on her as well."

Cam felt his temper rising at the words. "Do not forget, Sir Everard, that the lady in question is related to me by marriage. I won't have you speak of her with such disrespect."

The other man threw up his hands. "Of course. Of course, old man. No offense intended. I, of course, misspoke."

"Of course," Cam said with a lightness he didn't feel. Aside from his distrust of the man in general, he also added a disgust for his attitude toward ladies to the marks against him. He hoped whatever it was that brought the fellow to Beauchamp House would prove to be worth the time he'd have to spend in his company.

"Besides," Sir Everard continued, "even if Miss Hastings turns out to be a fright, it's the Beauchamp Lizard I'm really after."

Despite the fact that he'd been waiting for just such an admission from the man, Cam was still surprised by Sir Everard's bald declaration.

Trying to maintain a sense of calm he didn't feel, Cam asked casually, "What's the Beauchamp Lizard?"

"Lady Celeste was said to have found it on the cliffs below her house," Sir Everard said, his eyes bright with excitement. "If it makes up part of the collection, I mean to make an offer to Miss Hastings for it. She's the owner of the collection now, is she not?"

"But what *is* it?" Cam asked again. For a man who liked the sound of his own voice, Sir Everard could be dashed skimpy on details when he wished to be. He still couldn't figure out why, if it had already been unearthed, the other man had been trying to visit the place where it had come from. In the middle of the night.

Though it made some sort of sense to think that if one valuable fossil had been found in a place, others might also be had there. Assuming it was a fossil he spoke of.

"You don't actually believe it exists?" Paley asked, his tone dismissive.

Then, perhaps noting that Cam was still looking at them as if they had branches growing from their ears, he took pity on him.

"About a dozen years ago," Paley said, "a rumor ran through the collecting community hereabouts that Lady Celeste Beauchamp had found the skull of what had to be one of the largest of the ancient lizards to be unearthed in this part of England. But almost as quickly as the rumor spread, it was squelched by the lady herself who said it was all a misunderstanding. That it was only a horse skull that had been buried on the beach."

"It's quite easy to tell a horse skull from that of a lizard," Cam said with a frown. "Why would she make that mistake? Lady Celeste was not a novice. She traveled to Paris to see Cuvier's collections and has a quite thorough bit of scholarship in the library at Beauchamp House."

"That's just it," Sir Everard said with a gleam in his eye. "What if she wasn't mistaken? She was a canny enough sort. Perhaps she wished to protect herself from prying eyes. What if she simply hid the Lizard in her own collection, in plain sight? If I spy it among the contents I mean to purchase it without having Miss Hastings any wiser. If, of course, I don't decide to marry the girl and have the entire collection."

"Isn't it a little early to be speaking of marriage?" Paley asked with a moue of distaste. "You haven't even met the lady properly yet."

"If the collection is as fine as it's rumored to be, Paley, it doesn't matter if she's covered in scales under her petticoats," the other man retorted.

Then, perhaps recalling that Cam was a sort of relation to the lady in question, he turned a narrow eyed gaze on him. "I hope I can count on your discretion, Lord Cameron? I know you wish to purchase the spinal column I outbid you for in that London auction last month."

Cam gave a mental curse. It had been a particularly galling defeat at the auction held on behalf of Mary Anning and her family. He'd seen the fossilized spinal skeleton the year before as part of Lord Lawler's collection and hadn't had the ready cash to purchase it then. But when he was ready to do so at the auction, Sir Everard had bid almost five times the fossil's worth. Cam was a devoted collector, but even he wasn't prepared to pay a year's allowance from his father for one artifact, no matter how important it might be. When Sir Everard had indicated to him that he might be willing to part with it for a far more reasonable sum, Cam had been thrilled, though outwardly noncommittal. The other man's words now indicated that Cam's motives hadn't been as inscrutable as he'd hoped.

Now he calculated how serious Sir Everard was about his prize versus the likelihood that this Beauchamp Lizard even existed. How likely was it that Lady Celeste had found a lizard skull of such importance and chosen not to share it with the world? Thinking of what he knew of

Lady Celeste's character and how she prized scholarship, he doubted it.

"I will be silent as the grave," he said with an inclination of his head to the other man. "I do not believe you'll find the skull in her collection, but if you do, I will say nothing."

He felt a pang of conscience at promising to keep quiet about something Gemma had a right to know about. But if it wasn't in the collection, then he could speak freely to her. And, despite his impatience with her at times, he had enough faith in her abilities as a geologist to know that if there was a skull as fine as the one Sir Everard described in the collection, then she would have noticed it.

"Excellent," said Sir Everard, who actually rubbed his hands together like the villain in a melodrama Cam had once seen on the stage.

Cam was suddenly grateful he knew what it was the baronet had been looking for on the shore now so that he needn't spend more time in his company.

A few minutes later, they were welcomed into the entry hall of Beauchamp House by the newly appointed butler, George, or rather Stephens, who had been elevated from the position of first footman after the unfortunate dismissal of his predecessor.

"Lord Cameron," said the young man with gravity. "The ladies are expecting you in the drawing room."

Cam and the other men handed over their coats, hats, and gloves, then were ushered upstairs to the drawing room where the warm fire was welcome after the chill of the ground floor.

As they were announced he saw Sophia, Lady Serena and another, unfamiliar lady rise to welcome them.

"Gentlemen," said Lady Serena, the portrait of elegance

and grace, "we are so pleased you were able to come today." Cam had long thought her to be one of the loveliest women he'd ever met. Though he had no particular attraction to her, it was someone with that sort of grace and charm that he wished for in a bride. She had also proven herself to be quite practical as a chaperone to the four heiresses, a quality he also found impressive. Not all ladies could claim that for themselves.

Of course, three of her charges had been married rather hastily, but nobody was perfect.

But who was the third lady? And where the devil was Gemma?

"Lady Serena," said Lord Paley into the lull left by Cam's silence, executing a perfect bow. "What a pleasure to see you again. I believe we've met in London once or twice."

"Indeed we have, Lord Paley," said Serena, offering the man her hand.

Turning she gestured to Sophia and the stranger. "May I present my friends Lady Benedick Lisle, and her sister, Miss Hastings?"

Cam felt his breath catch.

This lovely creature was Gemma?

He'd known she wasn't a hideous monster, of course. Any man with a pair of eyes could see that she was attractive enough. But in that blue velvet gown that accentuated her small bosom and hinted at curves he'd never noticed before, coupled with an elegant chignon and a healthy glow in her cheeks, she was extraordinarily beautiful.

Something his two companions didn't fail to note.

Beside him, he felt Sir Everard's elbow in his rib. "Well, well, well. The Hastings chit cleaned up into a beauty, didn't she? Perhaps I won't need to purchase the Lizard after all, eh?"

Paley was bowing over Gemma's hand and Cam noted that he lingered longer than was strictly appropriate.

It wasn't that he was jealous, Cam assured himself. He simply didn't wish for Gemma to be overly bothered by the blandishments of the two men. After all, she had pronounced her desire to remain unwed any number of times.

Bringing the men here had been a mistake. He would be sure to apologize to her later.

"I must admit," Sir Everard said smoothly, "I was quite pleased at Lord Cameron's invitation. I have long heard about the extraordinary collection dear Lady Celeste amassed before her untimely death. But I hadn't realized her most impressive find was you, Miss Hastings."

To Cam's annoyance, Gemma actually blushed at the baronet's flattery. What on earth was wrong with her? Where was the Gemma who would normally send this fool packing for being so presumptuous?

Perhaps recognizing the danger Sir Everard posed, Sophia stepped forward and slipped her arm through his, "I quite agree with you about my sister, Sir Everard. But I hope you won't mind escorting me as we tour the collection? Precedence, you know. Lord Paley will escort Lady Serena, and dear Gemma will be with Lord Cameron. I do hope you'll explain it to me. I've never had a head for such things, as Gemma will tell you."

Despite his disappointment, Sir Everard couldn't resist a captive audience and with a show of gallantry allowed Sophia to slide her arm through his and lead him away.

Paley, meanwhile, looked delighted to be paired off with Lady Serena. "I hope you'll tell me more about your aunt, Lady Serena," he said with an easy smile. "I've heard so many intriguing tales, but I can only imagine yours are far more interesting."

They followed the other pair, leaving Cam and Gemma standing some three feet from one another.

She did not look pleased. He, on the other hand, was relieved. At least he needn't strain himself to make sure the other two men didn't say something untoward. That he had no fears for Sophia or Serena didn't occur to him.

"Shall we?" he asked, offering Gemma his arm with a flourish.

Chapter 4

What on earth had Serena and Sophia been playing at?

Gemma took Cam's arm with what she knew was a lack of grace, but she was too annoyed for niceties.

Hadn't the whole point of having him bring some of the gentlemen from Pearson Close been to ensure she'd be able to speak with them? She was treated to Lord Cameron's company on an all too frequent basis. If they were going to discuss the latest news in the fossil-hunting world, it would have happened by now.

(It had not.)

"A penny for them," said her companion as they climbed the stairs toward the gallery where Lady Celeste had displayed her most prized finds. "If I didn't know better, I'd say you were not best pleased with my company."

Leave it to Cameron to state the obvious. A true gentleman would have ignored her pique.

Still, she hadn't missed the appreciation in his eyes when he first entered the drawing room. And it was hardly his fault that Sophia and Serena had schemed to place them together.

Her innate sense of fairness made her relax a bit and the smile she gave him was genuine.

"Of course not. I am merely trying to recall which of Lady Celeste's treasures will be the most intriguing to Lord Paley and Sir Everard."

"I've never seen the collection either," he reminded her. "What might I want to see?"

And just like that she was annoyed again.

"It's not from want of opportunity," she reminded him tartly. "You've been to visit your brother any number of times since his marriage and have never once come to Beauchamp House to see it."

"Perhaps you've forgotten the occasion of our first meeting," he reminded her, "but I have not. I know we seemed to make up the quarrel once my brother and Sophia arrived that day, but I left with the impression you were not fond of me. I thought it would be . . . unwelcome for me to ask you to show me."

That assertion made Gemma stop in her tracks, in the center of the carpeted hall.

So much for keeping her temper.

Removing her arm from his, she turned to face him.

"You are a gentleman who has traveled the world in search of natural artifacts," she said in a low voice so they wouldn't be overheard. "You have dined with royalty and no doubt wooed ladies on three continents. Am I really to believe that you were afraid to ask me to show you a few fossils that, despite my appreciation for them, are hardly the sort of groundbreaking discoveries you've seen before? Because I was intemperate enough to argue with you at our first meeting when you mistook me for a not very bright gentleman? Truly?"

As she spoke, his cheekbones reddened. As did his ears.

His voice was equally low when he responded, stepping

closer so that she could hear him. "I've met seasoned diplomats who would have difficulty knowing how to handle you in a mood, Miss Hastings. And I do not know from whom you have got your information, but I'm hardly a penny dreadful explorer who digs fossils with one hand and woos ladies with the other. I have traveled, yes. I have seen some of the important specimens, but that doesn't mean I have no interest in others. As you well know, there are bones and fossils that have been in collections for decades that are only now revealing their place in the history of our world. So please do not paint me as some sort of snobbish Lothario with more hair than wit."

Gemma swallowed at his words, and tried to maintain her composure.

There was some truth in what he said. Though she was hardly going to admit that now. Not when he was standing so close and she could see the dark ring of blue that circled his pupils.

And definitely not when her eyes were drawn to the lines that framed his mouth as he spoke.

When had Lord Cameron Lisle become so handsome? The thought made her frown, which he took as a response to his words and so continued.

"As for our first meeting, I explained myself already, but I will repeat, I thought the article was written by a man. But that doesn't mean I ever mistook you for one. And far from thinking the author of the piece not bright, I thought it was well reasoned but unsuitable for the journal at that time. The very fact that you are still holding a grudge after so many months should be reason enough to show why I have not importuned you to show me the collection. You are the sister of my brother's new wife. I cannot insult you without sowing discord in my family. And as you know, I value my family above all things."

They stood close enough that anyone who came upon them might suspect a different conversation altogether.

"There you two are."

At the sound of Sophia's voice, they both stepped back with almost comical haste.

Sophia looked between them for a moment, as if trying to determine what sort of confrontation she'd just missed.

Knowing how easily her sister could read her, Gemma didn't dare meet her eyes.

"Sir Everard and Lord Paley are eager to hear your descriptions of the collection, dearest."

The glance Sophia gave Cam was speculative. Gemma knew well enough what sort of quizzing she'd face after the men were gone and resigned herself to it. At least she'd have the morning to devise some sort of explanation.

Because right now, she wasn't quite sure what had just happened.

That went well.

The ironic thought reverberated in Cam's head as he trailed the sisters into what looked to be a workroom, judging by the wide table and neatly arranged tools along the wall behind it.

It was a familiar sort of room for anyone who had spent time cleaning and examining bones and stones.

But he couldn't help but notice the feminine touches. A floral chintz covered pair of chairs with a tea table between them in one corner. A small bookshelf with frequently consulted resources on the history of the Sussex coast and its soil, the proceedings of the Royal Society, and if he wasn't mistaken, a couple of Cuvier's works. Sir Everard must have missed that, or they'd have been treated to his stubbornly incorrect opinions on the Frenchman and his theories.

Lady Celeste, Cam knew from what Sophia had told him, had been a highly intelligent lady with many interests. He'd been reluctant to think she could possibly have been as well read and knowledgeable as reputed. In part because he was a believer in the old adage that a jack of all trades was master of none.

And yet, the workroom did more to convince him of the lady's genuine interest and knowledge in geology than the most ardent defender could.

"The bookshelf is my doing," Gemma was saying to Sir Everard, who had taken her arm, Cam noted grimly.

So much for the order of precedence.

"Lady Celeste's library is quite impressive," Gemma continued. "But I wished to have my own books here so that I might use them to help understand and authenticate my finds."

Sir Everard's eyes narrowed as he tried to make out the titles on the shelf, but fortunately he was forestalled from comment by Paley.

"I see you are mindful of creature comforts as well, Miss Hastings," he said with an approving nod to the chairs. Despite his earlier declaration of interest in Gemma, Cam noted, Paley's arm was still threaded through Lady Serena's.

Interesting.

"I'm afraid those were here when I arrived at Beauchamp House," Gemma admitted with a laugh. "I would never have been bold enough to remove such lovely furniture from one of the other rooms. Especially to a room like this where they might become soiled. But I believe Lady Celeste had these made for this room particularly. I readily admit, I do retreat to them sometimes when long hours standing over the worktable have my back in knots. She thought of everything, you see."

"My aunt was nothing if not practical," Serena noted with a smile. "And as she got older, she had no reservations about providing for her own ease. And I do believe many of the improvements here in Beauchamp House were undertaken with the heiresses in mind."

"What a pity you weren't here long enough to take advantage, Lady Benedick," said Sir Everard with a laugh. "Though I suppose what you've missed, your sister gains."

Gemma stiffened. "I may be the only one of the four to be in residence at the moment, Sir Everard, but that doesn't mean that I would keep my sister or the others from enjoying the House now that they're married. On the contrary. They are free to come and go as they please. And after a few days together none of us was prepared to hold the others to the strict terms of the bequest."

"But as the last heiress it will become yours, will it not?" Sir Everard pressed her.

"If I remain unwed until the first of February, yes," Gemma said coolly. "But as I said, it is not something about which any of us is overly concerned. And I have no intention of marrying anytime soon."

Or at all. Cam could almost hear her add.

Certainly she had no interest in marrying a man of Sir Everard's ilk.

At least he thought not.

If he'd learned anything at all from today's events it was that he didn't know nearly as much about Miss Gemma Hastings as he'd thought.

"Now, is there anything else in this room you wish to see?"

Sir Everard might be pompous, but even he recognized a maneuver to change the subject in Gemma's words.

"Tell us about this specimen here, Miss Hastings," Sir

Everard said, with a gesture to a long fossil lying in the center of a dark blue cloth.

"A particularly fine spinal column from a sea lizard," Gemma said, removing her arm from his and carefully taking up the fossilized bones in her hands. "I found it on the shore just below the bluffs here. I keep returning—especially after storms and particularly strong tides—to see if the rest will reveal itself, but so far I've had no luck. As you know, there can be years between discoveries in the same location. So I try to be patient."

"Might there be a skull in the collection that could be paired with it?"

Sir Everard's tone was casual but Cam knew exactly what the other man was digging for.

Oblivious to the subtext of the baronet's question, Gemma shook her head. "Alas, no. That was my first thought, too. But there is nothing of this size in the main collection. But there are several boxes of Lady Celeste's finds in the attic that I haven't yet had a chance to search through. Perhaps I might find some other part there."

At the mention of boxes, Cam saw Sir Everard's eyes light up. Of course he'd find that interesting given his interest in the no-doubt apocryphal Beauchamp Lizard. He could see the other man working up the nerve to ask for a look in the attics, but before he could do so Gemma made it unnecessary.

"Lady Celeste put her most impressive finds in her collection here, in the gallery, so I have no doubt that the boxes contain little more than ammonites and some smaller bits. But it will be amusing to see what she found interesting enough to keep nonetheless."

But Cam had underestimated the baronet's determination to leave no fossil unturned.

"If you would like," Sir Everard said with a patronizing

smile, "I will have one of my servants itemize the contents of the boxes for you. I cannot think you should wish to worry yourself over such trivial matters when there are finds like this to be had."

Paley, who had been watching the exchange with interest, spoke up. "I'm sure it would be far more convenient for Miss Hastings to have the boxes out of her way altogether. I'm always looking to expand my own collection. What if I were to purchase the boxes from you, Miss Hastings?" He then named a sum that had Cam's eyebrows rising into his hairline. Gemma herself looked a little shocked as well.

Before she could respond, Serena spoke. "Until the year is completed, the sale of any part of Lady Celeste's estate is strictly forbidden, Lord Paley. And I will let Gemma speak for herself, Sir Everard, but I think you would have better luck convincing the Avon River to flow in the opposite direction, Sir Everard."

"I'm afraid she's right," Gemma said with a smile. "I wouldn't part with any of Lady Celeste's findings for the world. Even if it were legally possible. I've been looking forward to examining each and every item in the boxes myself for months now, but there's been so much excitement. I hope now that the weather has turned cold I will be able to lock myself indoors to do the job properly."

"They understand, of course," Cam said for his companions. Though it was plain from the expression on Sir Everard's face that he did not, in fact, understand.

It was more difficult to read Paley, since he was by far the more polite of the two.

Either way, they would not be leaving here today with any lizard, Beauchamp or otherwise.

For Gemma's sake, Cam was pleased.

Chapter 5

The tour of Lady Celeste's gallery was far less exciting that Gemma had imagined it would be.

First of all, she got the feeling that Sir Everard was looking for some item in particular. Over and over again he asked her whether these were all of Lady Celeste's most important finds. And if perhaps they shouldn't go up to the attics to retrieve the boxes she'd mentioned so that they might see if there might be some hidden treasures among them.

Then, Lord Paley had been so overly solicitous that she'd got the impression he didn't take her seriously as a scientist, or even a collector. And more than once she caught him speaking to her bosom. She had to admit that the blue velvet gown did show it to advantage, but perhaps it had been a mistake to believe Serena and Sophia's insistence that looking her best was the way to have these gentlemen give her the respect that was her due as a fossil-hunter.

And finally, Cam, who had been so heated in his defense when they'd been alone in the hallway earlier, spoke very little as she removed item after item from the stands upon which Lady Celeste had placed them. He'd asked questions, of course. He'd wondered aloud if a femur, which Celeste had noted to be that of a large mammal found close to Lyme, might be similar to one Cuvier had described. His questions and remarks were always insightful and despite her earlier pique, she found herself grateful for his presence. If she'd had only Sir Everard and Lord Paley to show round it might have felt like an entirely wasted morning.

Thus it was with some relief when Lady Serena announced that it was time for luncheon.

"I owe you an apology, Miss Hastings," Cam said as they followed the others downstairs toward the dining room. "Though I'd read your work and knew you were not unintelligent, I must admit I thought you were not quite equipped to understand the collection you'd inherited."

Before she could complain, he held up a staying hand. "I was wrong, Miss Hastings," he said, his voice tinged with the ring of sincerity. "I should have known better."

Gemma blinked. Of all the things she might have expected of this day, an apology from Cam was not one of them.

She paused in her descent of the stairs and faced him. "I must admit it gives me some sense of validation to hear you admit to your earlier prejudice," she said with a nod. "I only wish we could have had this conversation earlier so that for our siblings' sake we could have got on better."

He nodded in agreement, a single dark curl glancing over his brow. To her surprise, she had to fight the urge to brush it back.

What on earth was the matter with her?

"The blame for that can fall on me," Cam said, obviously unaware of Gemma's tender impulse. "But I hope that we can now be friends."

"I would like that," Gemma said and was surprised to find she meant it. Would wonders never cease?

Their newfound amity was something she was eager to explore, but to her disappointment, however, she was seated beside Sir Everard for the meal, and as he wished to discuss the boxes yet again it was not the most scintillating of conversations.

"You must tell us what you intend to do once your year of residence at Beauchamp House is at an end," Lord Paley, who was seated on her right, said. "I cannot think a young lady as lively as you will be content to remain buried in the country, no matter how its proximity to the shore might tempt you to dig for fossils. I hope you will come to town for the season."

If he had asked her to save the first waltz at Daphne's ball, Gemma thought wryly, Lord Paley could not have announced his interest more plainly. He was not an unattractive man. He was perhaps a bit older than she would have considered in a husband. But with his tall athletic frame, and silvering dark hair, he was handsome in his way. But she felt not an ounce of attraction to him, though his interest in the collection had been genuine. And he clearly knew nothing of her at all if he thought she'd dislike being here in Sussex for any duration.

She contemplated for a moment how best to respond.

But Cam spoke before she could.

"I do not believe Miss Hastings considers an extended stay in a house with a fine library, and proximity to the shore to be as much of a hardship as most ladies of your acquaintance, Paley," Cam said with a raised brow. "Lively though she may be."

This last made Gemma's eyes widen. Perhaps he did understand her better now.

Realizing his mistake, Lord Paley backtracked a little.

"I didn't mean to imply that Miss Hastings was anything but an original," Lord Paley said hastily, his concern evident in his drawn brows. "And she's not like any other young lady I've met. But that is why I believe London would benefit from your presence, Miss Hastings. A lady with your gift for conversation and intellect must need stimulation." He laughed wryly. "Even I am not content to spend all my days amongst my collection."

It was prettily said, and Gemma unbent a little. He was a well-meaning man. Just not the one who could make her give up her vow to remain unwed.

"I am often in my sister's company," she said aloud. "And I find that she and her husband, Reverend Lord Benedick, are quite intelligent enough to keep me from withering into a husk from boredom. Not to mention Lady Serena," she gestured to their hostess, who had watched the interplay avidly but didn't intervene, perhaps knowing Gemma could take care of herself.

Lord Paley turned to Lady Serena with an abashed look. "Lady Serena, pray forgive me. I didn't mean to give offense. Of course Miss Hastings has you to keep her in good conversation."

If Gemma didn't know her chaperone could fend for herself, she might have leapt to her rescue. But it was entirely unnecessary. Serena could very likely conduct witty repartee in her sleep.

"Think nothing of it," the widow said, her blue-gray eyes lit with laughter. "I will readily admit I am the last person Gemma would come to for conversation about her work. I know nothing of fossils and what's more, I have little interest in them. It's not that I don't appreciate them and what they tell us of the past, but I do not enjoy interacting with the small lizards my son likes to smuggle into the nursery when his nanny isn't looking. I most certainly do not wish to entertain the notion of an enormous one with large teeth."

Everyone laughed, as she'd intended, and the brief tension was broken.

This allowed Serena to steer the conversation toward less uncomfortable topics and when the meal was at an end, the gentlemen declined to take tea and were soon in the entrance hall preparing to leave.

Only when the door had closed behind them and the ladies were safely back in Serena's sitting room did Gemma let out the breath she'd been holding in.

"If I ever agree to welcoming more than one unwed gentleman to luncheon again," she told her sister and chaperone, "I pray you will dose me with laudanum and send me to bed for a week."

The drive back to Pearson Close was far less congenial than the drive there had been. For one thing, Sir Everard was fuming at the fact there had been no sign of the Beauchamp Lizard in the collection, and Gemma, perhaps guessing that he had been the one out on the shore the other night, had been less than encouraging at the idea of opening the attics of the house to the man.

Cam had been relieved, of course, because as he'd suspected, the Lizard was just a myth. He had no need of lying to Gemma because of his promise to Sir Everard. For some reason that mattered more to him now than it had when he'd actually made the promise.

It had nothing, he assured himself, to do with the way she'd looked in the blue velvet gown she'd worn for their tour. He was just feeling companionable because of the time they'd spent in conversation that morning.

Thus it was that they arrived at Pearson Close far less convivial than they'd been when they set out and the three men split up to find their own entertainment as soon as they stepped inside.

Curious about the typography of the land hereabouts, Cam retired to the library, where he searched out whatever he could find about this part of the Sussex coast, and the geographical composition of the area.

He was poring over a study of the local soil composition in a large chair near the fire, when he heard a door behind him open with a thud.

"I've several studies and essays on all sorts of important finds that would be perfect for *The Natural Scientist*," he heard Sir Everard say in that boastful way he had of making his every accomplishment sound like the most consequential thing anyone had done in the history of the planet.

The other man, who was no doubt Roderick Templeton, the editor of the aforementioned journal, made an interested but noncommittal sound before he undoubtedly made his escape.

Unable to do the same, Cam prepared himself for conversation as Sir Everard approached the fire and lowered himself into the chair beside his.

"Lord Cameron," said the baronet with a nod before leaning over to see what Cam was reading. "I see you're investigating the local soil. I piqued your interest in the Beauchamp Lizard, didn't I?"

Rather than respond to the question, Cam asked instead, "You really thought it would be in the collection, didn't you?"

"I hoped," said Sir Everard. "But I won't give up. I am confident it's there somewhere. Though I have another notion of where I might find it."

"And where is that?" Cam asked, curious despite himself.

Sir Everard leaned forward, as if fearful of being overheard. "I think it's on the shore."

Cam frowned. "What do you mean?"

"I think she reburied it."

So that's why he'd attempted to go down to the bottom of the cliff the other night. He thought Lady Celeste had put the skull back into the ground where she'd found it.

"What makes you think that?" he asked, careful not to show his interest. The least hint of competition from him and Sir Everard would stop talking altogether. He was that sort of man.

"It's just a theory," Sir Everard said, "but what better place to hide it but in plain sight? There were the rumors that it was just a horse skull. Well, what if Celeste really believed that? I think her reputation was probably exaggerated and she really did think she'd made a mistake. And what better way to hide a mistake than to put it right back where you found it?"

"So you think that she found an important lizard skull, then convinced herself it was a horse skull and hid it to save herself from embarrassment?" Cam wasn't sure if he thought the notion was more condescending or fantastical.

"Ladies are very proud when it comes to their intellectual prowess," Sir Everard assured him with the air of a man who had encountered legions of bluestockings in his time. Cam was far more convinced he'd had several discussions *about* bluestockings that he'd mistaken for actual social intercourse with the species.

"They can't bear the slightest bit of scrutiny, y'see," Sir Everard continued. "It turns their minds when they're questioned. So, of course if someone suggested what Lady

Celeste found was a horse skull, she'd turn right around and put it back. Stands to reason. Much better to hide it than to expose herself to the examinations of actual geologists and collectors, who have educated themselves about the subject for decades. I think she got scared and hid it away."

It was amazing to Cam that this man could walk about with the weight of the self-importance he bore on his shoulders.

From everything he'd heard about Lady Celeste, she was not only Sir Everard's intellectual superior, she was the last person in the world who would fear public scrutiny of her work or her finds. She'd made a point of building her home and its collections into a one-of-a-kind place where her hand-chosen heiresses could make names for themselves in the intellectual world.

That woman would not, at least not in Cam's estimation, mistake a horse skull for a lizard skull, or the other way round.

"I mean to visit the shore below the Beauchamp House cliffs," Sir Everard continued.

Cam was about to protest, but realized that it would be better to be with him when he made his trip than not.

"I might have a way for you to get there without going onto Beauchamp House land," he said aloud. He knew there was access to the little beach from a path leading from the vicarage. They could pay a call on Benedick and go down to the shore afterwards. It wouldn't hurt to have Ben along with them just in case Sir Everard did find something.

Cam wasn't sure of many things, but he knew he'd be damned before he let this buffoon steal a fossil that was meant to belong to Gemma.

Or, he reminded himself, Beauchamp House.

Sir Everard's round face split into a grin. "I knew making your acquaintance would come in handy, old man."

The next morning, after a good night's sleep, Gemma viewed the visit from the gentlemen the day before in a somewhat more philosophical way than she had last night. At the very least, she reasoned, she'd come to a sort of cessation of conflict with Cam. And if she'd not received the sort of acceptance of her place in the community of fossil-hunters from Sir Everard and Lord Paley, at least she had been able to hold her own in conversation with them. Which was no small thing.

After a quick breakfast, she went back upstairs and donned one of the gowns Sophia had been so disparaging of before. Because honestly, digging in the earth was not the time to worry about fashion, Gemma thought as she tied her thick boots. Adding a wide-brimmed bonnet, to shelter her from the wind, she retrieved her bag of hand trowels and other tools for unearthing stones and bones and the like, and made her way downstairs.

Despite the bonnet, she found the wind was strong enough to need the added protection of her cloak hood. And as she neared the sea stairs, she wondered if she shouldn't tear a page out of Mary Anning's book and lash herself to the railing of the stone steps.

But now that she was out here in the brisk air, the salt and spray foam in her nostrils, she couldn't bear to go back now.

Carefully, she made her way down the stairs in the cliff-side and saw at once that, as she'd hoped, the storm had brought forth debris from the sea, but had also eaten away some of the chalk from the cliff. She'd need to get closer, of course, but there were some promising protrusions from the sloping of the chalk into the sea.

Using her broad walking stick to steady her against the wind, and as a means of propelling her forward, she made her way across the narrow strip of pebbled beach toward the far edge of the crescent-shaped piece of land. There, the pebbles jutted against the chalk where the cliff came out to meet the sea.

She saw her target as soon as she got a closer look up at the upper slope. There, emerging from the chalk in a manner eerily like a headstone from this angle, she saw what was likely just a stone. But something in her gut told her that it needed to be looked at more closely.

Though she had felt eerily as if she were being observed in the past week or so, today there was no sense of it. So without a backward glance, she began the slow, steady climb up to where the jagged object—stone or bone—awaited her.

By the time she reached it, she was breathing heavily from the exertion of moving against the wind against the steep incline. But finally, she was there, and ignoring the hazards of dirt to her cloak, she stabbed her walking stick into the chalk like a spear and collapsed onto the ground beside her find.

Despite the cold, she had to remove her gloves to touch it with her bare hands. And the more she felt, the more she saw, the more she knew in her heart that this was a truly important find.

It was a fossil, not a bone. And she wouldn't be able to tell for sure until it was unearthed completely, but it was a skull. If she didn't miss her guess, a rather large one.

Pulling her gloves back on, she retrieved a hand trowel from her tool bag and carefully removed as much chalk from around the base as she could. But she'd worked for no more than ten minutes or so before she knew she'd need help with it. It would take a great deal of time to dig it out. And it would be too large for her to carry up the sea stairs.

It went against her every instinct to leave it here, but given that this bit of shore was on Beauchamp House property, it would be all right for the time it took her to fetch Stephens and Edward from the house.

She rested her hand atop the fossil, which had likely been here for hundreds of thousands of years, bid it a silent adieu and made her careful way back down the cliff.

As soon as she stepped through the French doors on the terrace, she sensed the change in the house. A laugh from the drawing room—definitely male, and belonging to the Duke of Maitland if she weren't mistaken—had her discarding her cloak, bag and stick and setting off at a pace far too unladylike for someone of her age.

When she burst into the drawing room she found that—as she'd hoped—the Marquess of Kerr and his Marchioness, the former Ivy Wareham, and the Duke of Maitland and his Duchess, the former Lady Daphne Forsyth, were seated around the tea tray with Lady Serena—who was the duke's sister—and her seven-year-old son Jeremy, making up the rest of the party.

"Gemma!" cried Ivy from the table before rising to greet her with a hug. "It's so good to see you. I take it you were out digging, you madwoman. Are you aware of what the temperature is?"

Daphne had risen and Gemma was astonished when the normally standoffish mathematician hugged her as well. "It's been too long. You have no idea what sort of nonsense the people in town talk about. I'd forgotten during my time here with you all. But it's nothing but rot and gammon all the day long."

Gemma grinned at her use of slang. At her look, Daphne raised her brows. "Maitland has been teaching me cant. I find it allows one to speak with the necessary vehemence some situations call for."

"Hullo, Gemma," the duke said, waving from his seat at the tea table. "You must wait until she's really in a temper. The slang becomes almost as incomprehensible as in the crowd outside a Bermondsey boxing match. It's truly impressive."

"I acquired the most fascinating dictionary by Francis Grose," Daphne said with enthusiasm. "Were you aware that *boxing the Jesuit* is way to describe male—"

"I'm sure you can educate your friends on that very colorful definition when poor Kerr isn't here to expire from embarrassment, my dear," the duke said with a glance at the marquess, his cousin and Ivy's husband, who did indeed appear as if his neckcloth had suddenly shrunk three sizes.

"I'm sure he knows what it is," Daphne said patiently. "It's something all men do, you told me yourself that—"

And now it was the duke's turn to redden. "Perhaps, Kerr we'd best take young Jeremy to the nursery to see if he can beat us at soldiers."

Jeremy frowned, certain he was being removed from the most interesting conversation. But the prospect of soldiers with his favorite uncle and cousin was distraction enough.

"It's good to see you, Gemma," said Lord Kerr, clasping her shoulder as he passed on his way out the door.

Maitland, Jeremy on his shoulders, leaned in to kiss the top of Daphne's head. "I'd say be good, but I know what kind of mischief you get up to away from one another. Together, you're a menace."

When they were gone, Serena rose as well. "I'll go send a note round to Sophia. She'll be furious if I don't let her know you're here."

Alone, the three ladies moved to the tea table. Fortunately, there was still some in the pot, so Gemma found an empty cup and poured.

"It's good to be back," Ivy said, sitting back in her chair with satisfaction. "I'd used different words but Daphne is right about the level of discourse in town. And everyone is so bent on showing up everyone else. It's competition, but for silly things like who has the most invitations, or who throws the most lavish party. None of it is at all meaningful. And it's all so—"

"False," Daphne finished for her. "I disliked it before I came to Beauchamp House, of course. When I was gambling for my father, to keep him in waistcoats and brandy, I was able to ignore it, but now that I've known friendship, the interactions with people in town seem that much more tiresome. Especially since I had the great misfortune to marry one of the most eligible peers in the country. I ask Maitland every day why he couldn't have been a common laborer, but he hasn't given me a satisfactory answer yet. It's all very trying."

Gemma bit back a grin. It was such a relief to see them. She still had Sophia and Serena here, of course, but Ivy and Daphne were the only ones who had no guardianship role over her. Sophia would always feel like her elder because she was, well, her elder sister. And Serena was her chaperone. But these two had never been anything but her friends. And something in her relaxed at knowing they were here.

"So, you were out digging," Ivy asked before biting into one of cook's lemon cakes. "Did you find anything?"

At her word's Gemma's eyes widened. "Oh my goodness, I almost forgot!"

Quickly she told them about the fossil she'd found in the chalk. She didn't mention her hope that it was important.

She didn't want to bring bad luck on herself before she had more information about it. It never did one any good to count one's chickens, after all.

"Well, what are you here with us for?" Daphne asked her with a frown. "We will be here for the foreseeable future. Go gather the footmen and collect your fish head, or whatever it is."

Laughing, Gemma left them to do just that. Perhaps by the time she finished, Sophia would be there too and they could have a proper heiress reunion.

Since Paley was the only other member of the Pearson Close guests who knew about the Beauchamp Lizard, and Cam didn't relish spending more time than he had to with Sir Everard, Cam invited the viscount to join them on their ostensible visit to the vicarage.

He'd been afraid Lord Paley would have found something else to do but to his relief, the viscount agreed to the jaunt with some alacrity.

"I should like to see the cliffs from another angle," he said with a smile. "Topography, you know, the second favorite interest of the fossil hunter."

The three men set off in the late morning in the hopes that the sun might have warmed things up, but to no avail.

Benedick's welcome was warm, however, and he ushered the three men into his study with the promise of brandy, which he dispensed with the efficiency of a churchman used to handing out beverages, albeit tamer ones.

"I hope you found the ladies at Beauchamp House well yesterday," Ben said once the visitors had settled into his study. "I don't mind telling you—though my wife would not like it—she was quite happy to know that a few of the collectors and scholars from the Pearson Close party had come to call on Gemma. The sisters are quite close, and Sophia felt the slight of her sister's lack of invitation as sharply as Gemma did."

Sir Everard looked nonplussed. "I cannot imagine it was ever a possibility. Especially given Pearson's abhorrence for female company."

Before Cam could step into the breach, Lord Paley spoke up. "I found Miss Hastings to be quite knowledgeable about natural science and especially the history of the soil and fossils recovered from this area. Your wife must be very proud of her."

He then went on to extol the virtues of Gemma's beauty and fashion sense, the latter description causing a line to appear between Ben's brow.

"I believe she had a new gown for the occasion," Cam responded to his brother's questioning look. He didn't add that the way she'd dressed her hair had drawn every male eye to the soft skin at the nape of her neck, or that despite its modest long sleeves and high neck, the gown had shown her bosom to advantage.

"Ah, that must be it," Ben said, ever the diplomat. "Well, I am pleased you were able to tour Lady Celeste's collection in any event."

"Speaking of Lady Celeste," said Sir Everard, "I wonder if you can recall her ever mentioning a particularly fine fossil she found on the beach below Beauchamp House?"

Cam fought the urge to roll his eyes. This fellow had a one-track mind.

Ben shook his head. "I'm afraid I didn't come to Little Seaford until after her death. And the vicar who was here before me left rather hastily after some bad business earlier in the year.

"Speaking of the shore," he continued, "As part of that

investigation into Lady Celeste's death, a door was discovered in the cellar of this house leading out to the shore. I've not had much call to use it, certainly not at this time of year, but it's a unique feature for a vicarage, don't you think?"

"You've never told me about a secret door," Cam complained.

"This is the most I've seen you since I came to this village," Ben responded with a raised brow. "And that includes the month you spent in Lyme this summer."

But Sir Everard wasn't interested in the brothers' conflict. "Is the door still accessible, Lord Benedick?"

Cam and Ben both glanced at the window, which showed the skies were darker and the wind was whipping the boughs of the bare elm on the other side.

"It is," Benedick said with a nod, "though I don't know that I would recommend a walk on the shore at the moment. There was a storm last evening too so there may be obstructions to an easy jaunt. Perhaps you can come back next summer when . . ."

"What is a bit of weather when there may be fossils dredged up from the storm there on the shore as we speak?" Sir Everard said, getting to his feet. "I will go even if you three will not. A true collector does not allow a triviality like that stand between him and the possibility of the perfect specimen,"

"These are new boots," Paley said with a sigh even as he too rose from his chair.

Clearly fashionable garments should be added to the list of items that would not hold back a true collector, Cam thought wryly.

And since there was no way he would allow the other two men to comb the shore for finds while he lingered behind, he too got to his feet.

Ben looked at the trio with a sigh of resignation. "Let

me get my coat. And I'll have my man make sure there is hot tea and coffee waiting for us when we return. One moment."

He hurried downstairs, leaving the three collectors alone.

"You know where the cellar is, do you not?" Sir Everard's tone indicated that he expected to be led there. Immediately.

It would be rude for them to set off without Ben, but on the other hand, the sooner Sir Everard saw the shore, the sooner he could be rid of the fellow.

"Follow me."

By the time they stepped through the cellar door leading into a short stone passageway, Ben had joined them, as had his butler and footman, who carried hot bricks and a flask of brandy. It was an odd parade, but Cam supposed they'd all seen odder ones. Collectors often found themselves going out in inclement weather and strange circumstances. The hope of a rare find was greater than self-preservation at times.

As soon as the men emerged from the door onto the shore, which was bordered on one side by an angry-looking sea and on the other by steep chalk cliffs, it was evident that last night's storm had done more than simply dredge things up.

The far end of the cliffs, where the beach first began to bow inward from the water's edge, had begun to erode away from the overhang above. And in one spot in particular there appeared to be a large stone sticking out of the chalk, like a hand waving for help.

"There," shouted Sir Everard before he all but sprinted over the pebble beach toward the mudslide.

It was a good way to twist an ankle, but even so, Cam jogged after him, followed by Lord Paley and Benedick.

By the time Cam reached the base of the cliff from which the stone protruded, Sir Everard had already begun to climb against the wind and through the sucking mud toward what would likely turn out to be a piece of wood. Not willing to risk his own safety by stepping into what might be unstable ground, Cam examined the trail that the other man's boots had left as he'd climbed.

Was that the mark of a walking stick, he wondered, leaning down to take a closer look at what looked to be a hole in the mud.

"He is particularly eager," Ben said as he and Paley reached Cam's side. "I should think he'd wait until better weather if he wanted to search this bit of cliff."

This would be the time to tell his brother about the Beauchamp Lizard, but with Lord Paley there to listen in, and perhaps tell what he'd overheard to Sir Everard, he dared not. And there was the added issue that anything he told Ben would most assuredly make it back to Sophia and therefore Gemma.

"It is a skull, I believe," shouted Sir Everard from his higher vantage point. "I do not have my tools. We'll need to dig with our hands."

It was clear from his "we" that he meant the three other men should come up and assist him. An idea which Cam didn't think particularly sound given the fact that the mud might give out from beneath them without warning. But Lord Paley and even Ben began to make the careful climb upwards, so not wishing to be the odd man out, he went after them.

Soon they were all sunk boot-deep into the mud around the piece and having decided to ruin their gloves rather than lose fingers in the cold, began to dig.

They were almost to the point where they might be able

to shift the piece to loosen the mud's hold on it, when a shout came floating on the wind.

Cam thought he might have imagined it, but then he heard it again, this time more incensed and sounding very much like Miss Gemma Hastings.

"What are you doing?" she shouted. And when he dared to look over his shoulder, he saw her, bundled up in a large coat, her scarf wound tightly round her neck, and a walking stick in one hand, a case of tools in the other. "Step away from there at once!"

Whether she shouted from anger or because they would not have been able to hear her otherwise, he didn't know. But from her expression, he suspected it was the former.

Behind her, he saw George, the footman-turned-butler, with a pry bar in his hand.

And suddenly he realized that the mark he'd seen in the mud had been from a walking stick.

Gemma's walking stick.

"This is Miss Hastings' find," he told Sir Everard. "I saw the mark of her walking stick but didn't make the connection until now."

Sir Everard, who was elbow deep in mud and struggling to loosen the earth around the fossil, grunted. Then, as if realizing what Cam had said, he shook his head. "That's impossible. There's no way a lady can have got this far up the slope. I found this myself. You saw me do it."

"I demand you come down here at once." Her voice was closer now, and yes, it was definitely anger he'd first heard there. She was livid if he didn't miss his guess.

And at the moment he couldn't blame her.

"Sir Everard," he said, trying to sound reasonable, though he was feeling anything but. "This is Beauchamp

House land. Surely you can recognize that even if you were the first to discover this piece, by rights it should go to the owner of the house."

"You know that won't hold up in court, Lord Cameron," the big man said with a huff of exertion. "Besides, I came here to find the Beauchamp Lizard. If this is something similar I won't let it out of my grasp. You know how important something like this can be for a collector's reputation."

He did know, which was why he wanted Gemma to have it. She'd obviously been here while they were at the vicarage.

"This is wrong," he said firmly. "I beg you will reconsider."

"Sir Everard," said Lord Paley, who had risen from his crouch beside the hole the men had managed to dig around the fossil. "If Lord Cameron is right, then the fossil belongs to the lady. I cannot think you would abandon your honor simply to enrich your own collection."

But Sir Everard's expression was mulish. "I mean to have it. And none of you will stop me from getting it."

Chapter 6

Gemma stood her booted feet braced against the wind that threatened to knock her over with its force as she waited for some response from the men on the slope. It would be difficult to hold a conversation, it was true, given the sound of the wind, but at least one of them had heard her. She'd seen clearly enough the look of understanding on Cam's face as he'd turned to her.

"George," she said to the butler, "come with me. We must get my skull away from them."

"But Miss Hastings," he argued, "I can't just take it away. They're gentlemen. And Lord Benedick is there. He's a vicar. It ain't—isn't—right."

He'd been trying to correct his grammar since rising from footman to butler, and if she weren't fuming, Gemma would have smiled at the correction. It had taken a month of lessons, but his speech was improving by the minute.

But she *was* fuming. All because of the gentlemen assembled.

Perhaps excepting Ben, who cared as much for fossils as his wife did.

"George, that is my fossilized skull." She turned to look him in the eye as she spoke. "I would not mind if Lord

Benedick were to take it, because he would most likely give it to me. But the rest are not to be trusted." She didn't even bother to mention Lord Cameron because her disappointment in him was keen. She'd thought they'd come to some kind of understanding today. That he'd at long last recognized her as a fellow scientist. But his attitude had been as ephemeral as the waves washing onto the shore beside her.

She almost jumped out of her skin when the man himself appeared beside George.

His approach had been hushed by the wind, she realized.

A glance at him revealed that he'd been just as immersed in the mud on the cliff as the others had been. Even his neckcloth was spattered with the stuff.

"I have tried to convince Sir Everard to give up his claim on the fossil," he told her without preamble, "but he refuses."

Ben, looking equally bedraggled, came up beside his brother. "The man is a little unhinged, I'm afraid," he said in a low voice. "He keeps going on about lizards and Lady Celeste."

"It is the skull of a marine lizard," Gemma said with a frown. "Others have been found hereabouts but this one is much larger than any I've seen or heard of. Which is why it is so important that I'm able to claim it for my own collection. It is *my* find."

"I know how important it is," Lord Cameron said with more sympathy than Gemma thought he'd offer her. "But, for what it's worth, I don't think he'll be able to shift it out of that mud today. The weather is too damp to get a grip on it and without the proper tools, it will be impossible."

"Which is why I brought these," Gemma said raising her case of digging tools.

They turned to look at the slope, and saw Lord Paley throw his hands into the air and began the slow descent down to the rock-covered shore. When he reached their huddle, he too was exasperated. "I tried to convince him that he should leave it to you, Miss Hastings," he said, frowning as he tightened his muddy scarf around his neck. "But he is like a dog with a . . . well, a bone, I suppose."

The play on words made them all laugh, defusing the situation a bit.

They were silent for a few moments as they tried to figure out what to do.

"What if we allow him to think you've capitulated?" Cam asked thoughtfully. "He obviously has no intention of leaving the field to you at the moment. But he cannot stay here all night, and he'll need help to remove it. You can tell him you've decided to let him have it. Then once he's gone, we'll come back and remove it."

"I do not like to advocate telling falsehoods," Ben said his brows drawn, "but in this instance, I think it may be the only way you will get your fossil, Gemma. For it is quite plain that Sir Everard will not give up the field until he's convinced you won't take it from him."

Gemma didn't like the idea of lying to get what rightfully belonged to her. "How can I be sure he won't send someone to get it in the meantime?"

"We'll be going back to Pearson Close with him," said Lord Paley. "I will ensure that he doesn't send anyone back. I give you my word."

"You and I will come at first light to retrieve it," he said, turning back to her. "Long before Sir Everard has a chance to dispatch anyone or to come here again himself. But you'll have to leave it for now, if only to prove to Sir Everard now that you've given up the fight."

She looked through the dimming light toward where the baronet still tried to shift the fossil. As if he felt her gaze on him, he looked up then and gave her a defiant stare.

She'd known she disliked him during his visit, but she'd not guessed just how much contempt he felt for her. Clearly his flattery and interest had been a ruse to get close to the collection.

"All right," she said, finally, turning back to the others. "I'll do it. Tell him I have no intention of claiming it, and that he may come back tomorrow to get it. But I hope you will be prepared to protect me tomorrow when he discovers it's gone."

"The prior claim is yours, Miss Hastings," Lord Paley assured her. "And besides. Are not ladies allowed the prerogative of changing their minds?"

She didn't bother to tell him the myriad of ways in which such an assumption made life in male-dominated fields more difficult for ladies.

At this point, she'd fought for her scholarly sisters enough for one day.

"I think it would probably be better if you were not here when we convince him to leave with us." Cam's expression was that of a man who knows he will be contradicted.

But Gemma was tired of conflict. "I'll go back to the house. But I'm trusting you to ensure he doesn't stay, or find some way to remove the skull before I have a chance to come back."

"I give you my word," Cam said, echoing Lord Paley. Despite their previous arguments, Gemma believed him.

"Come, my dear." Lord Benedick gestured to her. "I'll escort you back to the house while these two deal with the tantrum Sir Everard is likely to have when they make him depart."

With one last look over her shoulder to where the baronet stood hunched over the skull, Gemma allowed her brother-in-law to lead her away.

Behind her she heard Lord Cameron say in a low voice, "This might get ugly."

She didn't linger to hear how the other man responded.

For the first time in a long while, she let someone else handle things.

If possible, the carriage ride back to Pearson Close was more uncomfortable than the scene at the cliff had been.

Cam and Paley were silent as Sir Everard raged about their failure to intervene on his behalf. "You may as well have been stone statues," he said with disgust. "If the skull is gone when I arrive tomorrow, you mark my words, I will sue."

Mentally, Cam ran through the list of solicitors who might defend Gemma against the baronet's baseless claims. Because now, more than ever, he intended to remove the fossil and get it into her hands as quickly as possible. Sir Everard was not only a bully, but his determination to effectively rob Gemma of what—whether it was the Beauchamp Lizard or not—by rights belonged to her, or to the Beauchamp House estate, had solidified Cam's determination to thwart him. Not only was he the worst possible representative of the fossil-collecting community as a whole—and Cam had little doubt he'd use the fossil to puff himself up as far more influential than he actually was—but he was simply a small-minded boor.

Fortunately for Cam and Paley, when they returned to Pearson Close, the baronet chose not to tell all and sundry about his having been thwarted by a scheming harpy (his term) because his fear that someone else would swoop in and take the fossil was greater than his need for consolation. Or maybe, Cam thought cynically, he wasn't sure which side his fellow collectors would take. Lady Celeste's reputation had been impeccable among the fossil-collecting community, and there were many among Pearson's guests who had admired her.

Acquaintance with Sir Everard, however, did much to reveal the illusory nature of his accomplishments.

Mindful that servants' gossip could ruin the plan to save the fossil from Sir Everard, Cam made his way to the Pearson stables after dinner to request his mount be ready before sunup, and swore the man to secrecy.

Later, as he lay in bed staring up at the damask canopy, he considered the idea of using this time spent with Gemma to assess her as a potential bride.

There was something attractive about the idea of marrying someone who would be able to understand his passion for collecting as well as trying to place the things he found within the scientific history of the earth.

And she was lovely. It would not be a hardship to bed her, of that he was certain.

But it was these things that also made him wary of her.

He'd long ago come to the conclusion that he needed the sort of wife who was affectionate but not particularly dependent on him for her happiness.

When he was a youth he'd seen just how destructive it could be when a husband was distant—or in his father's case—was unfaithful. He had seen the light go out of his mother's eyes in the space of a few months. And though she'd seemed to recover later, Cam couldn't help but feel that it would have been better if the Duke and Duchess of Pemberton had maintained some distance from another from the start. That way his mother would never have had to be hurt at all.

Cam had no intention to commit infidelity, but thought it better, since he was his father's son, not to put himself in a situation where it would even matter. Unbidden the memory of Gemma's animation yesterday when she was talking about the collection came to his mind. She was lit from within. So passionate. He simply could not be responsible for snuffing that light.

No matter how much he was drawn to her.

His decision made, he turned on his side and tried to sleep.

"It simply doesn't make sense to risk your neck on the cliff stairs when there is a perfectly functional corridor through the wine cellar," Serena said as she and Gemma breakfasted the next morning at a far earlier hour than was their custom.

Both the chaperone and Sophia had been incensed on Gemma's behalf the day before when they learned of Sir Everard's attempt to steal the lizard fossil. Sophia had even offered to come along with her when she returned to retrieve it, but Gemma, knowing just how much her sister detested getting up early, had assured her it would not be necessary.

Serena, however, had at the very least insisted on being there when Gemma set out with Cam, Stephens and the footman Edward.

And true to her word, she had been at the breakfast table when Gemma came down.

Her suggestion that the excavation party should use the secret passageway had been a surprise, however.

Gemma was not particularly fond of enclosed spaces and had not been through the tunnel more than once or twice because of it. "I will give Stephens and Edward, and even Lord Cameron, leave to use the passageway. But I will be using the cliff stairs."

At Serena's scowl of frustration, she continued,

"Despite the harshness of the wind, the view of the sea as one descends the stairs is one of my favorite things about Beauchamp House's location. I won't deny myself unless I absolutely must."

The chaperone looked as if she'd like to argue further, but perhaps seeing Gemma's expression, she sighed. "I won't press the point," Serena said. "But, I do think it might be easier to remove your bone without being seen by having George and William carry it up through the passageway."

It was something Gemma hadn't considered. "That is sensible. Especially considering that Sir Everard may very well arrive while we are there. Cam's note said that he and Lord Paley were able to convince him to leave it until some of the others from Pearson Close could accompany him and witness his triumph."

That bit of persuasion had made Gemma laugh aloud since it was perfectly calculated to appeal to the man's self-regard.

"But," she continued, "he may very well decide when he awakens this morning that he simply cannot wait."

Too nervous to eat any more of her eggs, she pushed the plate away and took a last gulp of tea just as Cam entered the breakfast room.

"I thought I'd find you dressed and waiting on the front step for me," he teased, and Gemma was charmed despite herself.

Once again, he was dressed for warmth as well as style, and his many caped greatcoat, which he hadn't bothered to remove given they'd be departing soon, had somehow been scrubbed clean of yesterday's mud. Gemma felt a pang for his poor valet—her own maid had upbraided her roundly last evening when she came in.

"I'll be only a few moments," she said rising from the table. "I have to get my gloves but I'll be right down."

Cam watched as she hurried from the room.

He'd only been half-joking.

He really had expected to find her tapping her foot while she waited for him at the door. He supposed he should be relieved that she'd relaxed enough to sit down to breakfast given just how nervous she'd been last evening about leaving her precious skull behind overnight.

Having been forced to wait for help to retrieve his own discoveries before, he could sympathize. It was one of the reasons he'd volunteered to point Sir Everard in the other direction, and to come back and assist her today.

And there was something about Sir Everard that he didn't trust. It would be just like the fellow to agree to wait until later today, then double back before anyone was the wiser.

Of course, that's what he and Gemma were doing, but since Gemma was the rightful owner of the skull, theirs was the lesser sin.

"I appreciate the way you're helping her," Lady Serena said as she poured him a cup of tea and gestured for him to have a seat.

She was really a stunningly beautiful lady, he thought not for the first time.

It was unfortunate he didn't feel the same kind of attraction for her as he did for her wholly unsuitable charge.

"I know Gemma appreciates your assistance as well," Lady Serena continued, breaking him out of his reverie.

He turned his attention to the widow. "Given that Sir Everard wouldn't have known about the little beach here without my having brought it to his notice," he said aloud, "it's the least I could do."

She nodded, her blue eyes shining with approval. "She will never say it aloud, but your acceptance of her into the scholarly fold, as it were, means the world to her. Gemma is quite proud, but I know she craves what we all want—to be taken seriously."

He was silent for a moment, trying to figure out whether he should confess that his attitude toward her work had changed.

"I'm ready," the subject of their discussion said from the doorway.

Cam looked to see if she had overheard any of their conversation but Gemma seemed unaware.

"You'd best be off, then," Serena said with a smile. "Gemma, dear, be sure to bring Lord Cameron back when you're finished. We owe him a hot drink and a seat by the fire at the very least."

"Of course," the heiress said with a roll of her eyes. "Though I'm quite sure he's endured far more uncomfortable weather than a Sussex seaside winter."

After a quick bow to his hostess, Cam offered Gemma his arm and escorted her to where George waited in the entry hall with her coat.

"William and I will be along shortly, Miss Hastings," said the butler as he allowed Cam to take her fur-lined pelisse from him.

He held it for her as she slid her arms in first one sleeve then the other, resisting the temptation to run his hands over the shoulders to smooth out the fabric. At least, that's what he told himself was the origin of the impulse.

Her gown today was far less tempting than the blue velvet from the other day—a dark gray wool that had been chosen for warmth and not fashion—but it was becoming and reminded him once again that there was a rather tempting body to go with the sharp mind.

Unaware of her escort's thoughts, Gemma pulled away as soon as her coat was on and donned her bonnet, speaking to the butler as she did so.

"Now, George, do not forget to bring a litter to assist you with carrying the skull through the tunnel. It's quite large, and though I do not doubt you'd be able to carry it in your arms, I do not wish you to risk dropping it. It is quite precious and we dare not risk it sustaining any blemishes."

"Yes, Miss Gemma," the butler said with a nod. "William has already found the one we used when Miss Ivy was stricken and it will do the trick."

With one last glance behind her, as if she were afraid of forgetting something, Gemma finally turned to Cam. "Let's be off then."

And rather than go out the front door—or the passageway he knew led directly to the shore—she led him toward the first floor and the drawing room with French doors leading into the gardens behind the house.

Chapter 7

As she led Cam through the gardens, which, with the exception of the evergreens, were as plain as a lady of the previous century without powder and patch, she waited for him to comment on their route. Surely he knew about the cellar passageway and wondered why they were taking the stairs, precarious in the best of weather.

But he surprised her.

"I am sorry for the way our first meeting went," he said, and Gemma had to shake her head a little to see if she'd heard him right.

"In the autumn," he clarified as if there were more than one first meeting to choose from. "I should have been more diplomatic about the rejection of your findings. Less dismissive."

Aside from the fact that her nose was in danger of falling off from cold, Gemma was also feeling some trepidation about seeing her marine lizard fossil again. What if it were not, in fact, as spectacular as she'd thought it was. What if it were simply the skull of a horse, killed in a shipwreck hundreds of years ago?

She was not concerned about her companion's bad behavior from months ago.

Still . . .

"I accept your apology.. I can assure you I've not thought of it since." A lie, but she was hardly going to spill out her heart to him now. It wasn't the time for it, and besides that, she didn't wish to show vulnerability at the moment when he finally seemed to take her seriously.

"Well, I have," he said, halting in his tracks and putting a hand on her arm. "It was foolish of me. You've shown yourself to be a serious scholar and I didn't take you seriously. It was badly done of me. I simply wish you to know that I have changed my opinion."

She chafed to get down to the shore, but sensed that he needed to say his piece.

Then a troubling thought occurred to her.

"This has nothing to do with the way I was dressed yesterday, has it? Because I can assure you, I was just as knowledgeable the day before as I was with my hair dressed and my bosom on display."

She'd expected perhaps he would respond with stuttering outrage, but she ought to have known better.

He laughed. "No, Miss Hastings, it has nothing to do with your gown. Or your very agreeable bosom."

She felt her cheeks redden with heat. "Agreeable bosom indeed."

"You're the one who brought it up," he said, then snickered for some reason she didn't quite understand.

"What's so funny?" She didn't like not being in on the joke.

"Oh no," he said, taking her arm in his and beginning their trek again. "I've already said 'bosom' in a lady's hearing. I won't compound the issue by explaining what is a highly inappropriate jest."

"You're the most frustrating man," she said in a harassed

tone. "How am I to know anything if everything is kept from me?"

But he would not relent no matter how she pressed him.

"If we're to be discussing bosoms and the like," she said finally, in a grudging tone, "then I suppose we might be excused for using one another's Christian names."

"In for a penny, in for a pound?" he asked wryly. "I suppose it makes sense."

"Then, Cameron," she said regally, "let us proceed. I am freezing and I wish to ensure that my fossil has endured no damage in this wind."

"It would be my pleasure, Gemma." His voice sent a frisson of something up her spine. A feeling that intensified when he said her name.

What had she got herself into?

Trying to ignore her new awareness of him, she returned her focus to the ground beneath her feet.

When they reached the sea stairs, the wind was such that further conversation was impossible. And she wasn't too disappointed in that. Such moments as they'd just shared were dangerous. Especially for a woman who had no intention of ever entangling herself with a man, as she was. Yes, it was possible for lady scholars to marry without sacrificing their studies, but such things were rare. And rather than risk having her goals subsumed by those of her husband, she'd rather not jeopardize them in the first place. Remaining unwed had been the best course for her Aunt Dahlia, after all. And Lady Celeste. Though, to be sure, Lady Celeste's solitude had not been her choice.

Still, it was better to nip whatever it was she felt in Cam's presence in the bud.

Anything else would risk danger.

Further thoughts on the matter, however, were impossible, as the climb down the stairs was far more treacherous than it had been the day before. At this hour, a thin sheet of ice had formed along the treads, and she was grateful for the railing and Cameron's grip on the back of her coat. By unspoken agreement, they made their way slowly, one step at a time.

They were but halfway, however, when she glanced over at the area where the fossil had been and gasped, stopping.

Lord Cameron had to pull up short to keep from running her over.

"What is—" He broke off when he looked over and saw what had alarmed her.

Cursing the ice that slowed their progress, she and Cam went as fast as they could without endangering their own necks. When they finally reached the beach below, Cam began to run, his caped greatcoat flapping behind him.

Hurrying as fast as her skirts would allow, Gemma thought at first that the red near the victim's head was a kerchief of some sort. But as she got closer, she realized it was something far worse.

"Don't come too close," Cam said over his shoulder. "You don't need to see this."

"But perhaps I can—"

"Gemma," his voice was sharp, and something about it told her he was feeling some intense emotion. "Please don't argue with me. I would like to unsee it if I could."

She blinked at that. And stopped where she stood, several yards from the fallen man.

"But who is it?" she pressed, turning to face the other direction.

"It's Sir Everard," Cam said tensely. "He's quite cold so he's likely been out here for hours."

Unspoken was the realization that the baronet must have doubted Gemma's word just as much as she'd doubted his.

And the fool had risked his life by coming to get the fossil on his own.

"The magistrate is away for the holidays," she said suddenly, thinking back to how they'd handled things when Daphne and Maitland discovered a dead body in the library.

The hysterical thought arose that they should write some sort of process guidelines for such occurrences to keep on hand in Beauchamp House. Especially given the number of accidents and mysterious deaths that had happened here in the past year.

"He may have left someone in charge in his absence," Cam said, bringing her attention back to the present matter. "Perhaps we can send one of the footmen to check at Northman's house. I'm sure he has a secretary at the least."

A shout from the other side of the beach alerted them to the arrival of George and William.

"I'll go back to the house with William and see to it," she said. "And I know it's not important since a man has lost his life, but is the fossil there? I didn't see it when I first looked because of all the—"

"No," he responded before she could finish. "It's not here. The marine lizard skull has been removed. It's gone. And it's very likely the reason why Sir Everard was killed."

As it happened, the Northmans had not yet left for their holiday travel and so it was the squire himself who entered the drawing room some two hours later.

"I thought it must be a mistake when I got your message, Miss Hastings," he said without preamble, "for I thought the likelihood of there being another murder at Beauchamp House was nigh impossible. But clearly, I was wrong."

"You might have a bit of courtesy, Northman," Cam

said with a scowl from where he sat beside Gemma on the settee. "A man lost his life."

Given that Sir Everard was dead, he'd decided to leave the guarding of the body to William and had gone indoors not long after Gemma left him. He'd found her in the drawing room with Serena, her eyes suspiciously red as if she'd been weeping. Without waiting to be asked, he'd told George to send for Ben and Sophia. He might not know Gemma all that well, but at a time like this, she'd want to have her family around her.

Now, with Northman barreling in like a bull in a china shop, he was doubly glad he'd called them. Ben's diplomacy would clearly be needed if they were to get through this interview without Cam throttling the squire with his own neckcloth.

"We're obviously quite disturbed, Squire," Ben said, rising from his seat beside Sophia. "It's a dreadful business and we'd like to get it settled as quickly as possible."

"I can speak for myself," Gemma interjected with a frown. "I realize it's another odd occurrence at Beauchamp House, Squire Northman," she said, "but as none of the other deaths could be blamed on the inhabitants of this house, I don't see the point of your criticism. It's hardly our fault that we've been targets for such goings-on. And I can assure you I had nothing to do with Sir Everard's death. Which you will learn as soon as you look into the matter. I could hardly know that Sir Everard planned to return to the shore in the night."

The magistrate made a begrudging noise. Then, he frowned.

"You said 'return', Miss Hastings," he pointed out. "Was he here before? What was your relationship to this Sir Everard. Your footman told me only that he'd been staying at Pearson Close."

Serena who had been sitting at the tea tray, brought him a steaming cup and he took it from her. At her insistence, he lowered himself into a chair near the fire. But the hospitality didn't dim his curiosity.

"Well, Miss Hastings?" he prompted. "You'd best tell me what you know or I'll find out some other way."

Cam stiffened at the man's tone. He had all but accused her of intending to lie.

He opened his mouth to object, but stopped when he felt a hand on his arm. He glanced up and saw that Gemma was frowning. She shook her head in a silent plea for him to stand down. Reluctantly he gave her a small nod and waited for her to speak.

"Sir Everard was one of three gentlemen from the party at Pearson Close," she began with an admirable degree of calm, "to pay a visit to view Lady Celeste's collection of fossils and bones two days ago. Lord Cameron, Lord Paley and Sir Everard."

She was perched on the edge of the settee and the vibrations from a tapping foot beat a tattoo beneath them.

At the mention of Cam, the man's brows drew together. The magistrate's gaze settled on him speculatively.

"What's the nature of this party at Pearson's place, then?" he asked, addressing Cam. "I'd heard he had a group of gentlemen there but not much more. I wouldn't have thought a visit to see a bunch of old stones would prove a temptation away from card games and cigars."

Clearly, Northman couldn't imagine a reason for men to gather that didn't bear some resemblance to White's or Brooks'.

"It is a symposium of sorts," he explained. "Where collectors and scholars of geology might discuss important developments in the discipline, recent finds, that sort of thing."

"So, you sit around and talk about bones and soil and whatnot?" Northman didn't bother hiding his skepticism. "Seems a dull way to spend a house party, if you ask me. But then, I didn't much care for that sort of thing at university either."

Ignoring the man's dismissal of geology, Cam continued, "When I learned of Miss Hastings' interest in fossils, I offered to bring some of the other gentlemen to see Lady Celeste's collection. I thought it would give her an opportunity to share in some of the same sorts of conversation on offer at Pearson Close."

As soon as he finished he realized his mistake.

If Gemma's slight intake of breath wasn't enough to alert him, of course.

"Why would a lady wish to attend a party like that at Pearson Close?" Northman clearly had a guess. And it wasn't one that reflected well on Gemma. "I shouldn't think that sort of gathering would interest a lady no matter how much of a bluestocking she might be. Though all those gentlemen gathered together in one place without any other ladies to offer competition might be just the thing for a spinster who had already seen her three closest allies wed before her."

"Now see here," Gemma said with a scowl. "I had no interest in—"

Cam cut her off before she could finish that thought. It was one thing for Northman to speculate, but quite another for her to put his thoughts into words.

"It is precisely *because* she was not able to attend the symposium that I brought these gentlemen to visit her," Cam said. "To talk," he emphasized. "About fossils."

The words hung in the air.

"It was all perfectly proper," Serena assured the magistrate after a minute. "Sophia and I were here to chaperone and Gemma was able to show the gentlemen all of Lady Celeste's collection and discuss fossils and collecting without fear for her reputation. And if you think she welcomed them here with an eye toward securing one of them for a betrothal, well, you don't know Gemma very well. That was the farthest thing from her mind."

Cam would vow it hadn't been the farthest thing from Serena and Sophia's minds, however. But they were discussing Gemma at the moment. And though she might have been flattered by Sir Everard's and Paley's compliments, he doubted sincerely she'd considered either of them as potential matches.

"So, we know why this Sir Everard was here in the first place," Northman said thoughtfully, "but why did he come back? And why the dev—er, deuce, would he wish to go out onto the shore in this weather?"

This time, Gemma gave him a brief summary of their contretemps yesterday, complete with her plans to come back this morning with Cam to retrieve her skull.

"You went back to Pearson Close with him?" Northman asked Cam. "And you didn't tell him about Miss Hastings and her plans to go back?"

"Of course not. I gave her my word," Cam said with a frown. "As did Paley."

"She gave Sir Everard her word but she didn't mean to keep it, did she?" Northman had turned his gaze on Gemma, who sat up straighter. Cam could practically feel the indignation oozing from her pores.

"He tried to steal my discovery," she said with ill-disguised hauteur. "And I didn't give my word, I didn't have to. He dismissed my claims as if I didn't even exist. As far as he was concerned, my prior claim didn't matter. My leaving was enough to convince him he'd won. He was horrid."

"Seems to me, Miss Hastings, that you had a very good reason to wish Sir Everard dead."

The room fell silent as everyone stared at the magistrate.

"I don't think you understand my sister very well, Mr. Northman," said Sophia coming to stand behind the sofa at Gemma's back. "She has difficulty killing flies. It would be impossible for her to inflict physical harm on another person. Even one as odious as Sir Everard."

"And how would she have known he would return in the middle of the night?" Serena said calmly. "He wasn't supposed to return until later today."

"I think you've got the wrong end of the stick, Squire," Ben said, coming to stand beside his wife. "Gemma didn't do this."

Beside him, Cam felt Gemma relax a little at the defense. He wanted to offer a consoling touch but now was hardly the time. Not when all eyes were on her.

Northman, however, had turned his gaze on *him* and Cam couldn't help but feel the weight of the man's speculation.

"You could have killed him, though, couldn't you, Lord Cameron?" Northman asked thoughtfully. "Mayhap you didn't care for the way the man insulted your lady. And since you were also in attendance at Pearson's house party, you might very well have heard him leaving in the middle of the night to return to Beauchamp House's bit of shore. It would have been easy enough to follow him here and beat him with his own pry bar."

"That's ridiculous," Cam said sharply. "I had no reason to wish Sir Everard dead. I thought he was out of order to refuse Miss Hastings' claim but that was hardly enough reason for me to murder the fellow. We had a plan to come back this morning and I had no reason to think it wouldn't work."

"We don't even like each other," Gemma assured the magistrate, focusing on the man's designation of her as Cam's "lady."

When he turned and widened his eyes at her, she shrugged. "It's true. We've done nothing but bicker since we met. I'd sooner expect you to murder *me* than murder on my behalf."

She turned back to the magistrate. "Neither of us killed Sir Everard, Mr. Northman," Gemma said firmly. "Not me, and certainly not Lord Cameron."

Northman didn't look particularly convinced, but rose from his chair. "I will have my men remove the body to the doctor's in town so that he may examine it. Perhaps that will give us more information about the circumstances of the fellow's demise."

There was one detail about the body that Cam hadn't shared with Gemma, and despite knowing she would resent the omission, he said aloud, "There is one more thing about the body, Mr. Northman." Reaching into his coat pocket, he retrieved the note he'd managed to secrete there while Gemma's back was turned. "This was beside the corpse. A warning, I believe."

He felt Gemma stiffen beside him. "Let me see that!" she said sharply. "Why didn't you show me?"

But Northman had already taken the page—torn from a diary or journal it would appear based on the jagged edge. The magistrate stared down at it and frowned. "You should have told me about this first thing," he said to Cam.

"I'm telling you now."

Gemma made a noise of impatience and Northman

turned a cryptic gaze toward her. He proffered the page and she all but snatched it from his hand.

Cam knew what it said, but seeing the color drain from Gemma's face made him realize that whatever his response had been, hers was compounded by the fact that she was its target.

"*Stop looking for it or you'll be next,*" she read aloud in a voice that was uncharacteristically shaken.

"Who else knows about this fossil?" Northman asked pointedly. "Besides you lot? And Lord Paley?"

"I have no notion of who Sir Everard might have told," Cam said with a shake of his head. "He seemed reluctant to speak about it last evening for fear of someone attempting to take it, but to be honest, I have little trust in his discretion. He was a boastful man and I would think it next to impossible for him to keep such a discovery to himself."

The magistrate nodded. To Gemma and Cam he said, "Don't either of you leave the county. And since I know the other ladies in this house have fancied themselves to be amateur Bow Street Runners, I will warn you, especially Miss Hastings, not to interfere in my investigation. Leave this business to men who know what they're about. It ain't seemly for a lady to get mixed up in this sort of thing."

Before Gemma could argue, Serena stepped forward and put her arm around Gemma's waist. "I promise you, Mr. Northman, I will see to it that Gemma stays out of trouble."

Northman made a sound that sounded suspiciously like a snort.

To Cam, he said, "I'll be round to Pearson Close later this afternoon to interview the rest of the guests. I'll thank you not to warn them ahead of time so that they all agree on the same story."

It was far more canny than Cam would have given the man credit for. He nodded.

And with that, the Squire left, shutting the door behind him.

"I cannot believe we're being forced to deal with that horrible man yet again," Serena said, rubbing her forehead. "I love you girls dearly, but could you not have avoided getting involved in murder for this one year?"

Gemma, who seemed to have recovered from her shock over the threat, gave the chaperone an impulsive hug. "I promise none of us did it on purpose. And hopefully this particular misdeed will be solved with little discomfort for you."

"I'm more concerned about your safety, Gemma," Sophia said, lines of worry between her brows. "Whoever killed Sir Everard seems intent on warning you against searching for the fossil. I know it's a waste of breath, but I do hope you'll heed that warning."

"But if I simply step away and allow this—this murderer—to steal without any sort of a fight, then what's to stop him from killing the next time he wants something?" Something about the determination in Gemma's tone made Cam's chest tighten. An image of her body in place of Sir Everard's rose in his mind's eye and he clenched his jaw.

"Northman will find the culprit," he told her with a surety he didn't feel. "You must at least let the man do his job." Seeing her skeptical response, he continued, "Or, if you are not content to wait for Northman, let me look into the matter. I'm sure I can find out whoever he told about the fossil."

But instead of gratitude he saw impatience in her eyes.

"I am not a child to be placated with promises of sweets. I'm perfectly capable of finding the fossil on my own and when I do—"

She stopped at Sophia's hand on her arm. "Dearest, you've obviously had a trying morning. Perhaps it would be better to discuss this later, when you're feeling less distressed."

At her sister's words, Gemma's mulish expression deflated a bit. "I'm sorry. It's just that I'm so frustrated. That awful man tried to take what I am convinced is the bequest Lady Celeste left for me, and now some other terrible person has killed him and in the process stolen my fossil."

She sighed. "And I sound like a monster for speaking so of a dead man. What a wretched person I am."

"We needn't attribute saintly characteristics to the dead," Ben said quietly, laying a hand on her arm. "There's no shame in recalling them as they were. Nor is there glory in praising them undeservedly."

Cam was struck, as he always was, by his brother's ability to say the right thing at the right time.

It was a skill he had never mastered and he was grateful for Ben's presence here today.

"I'll go down and sit with William for a bit, I think," the vicar continued. "It can't be an easy task to watch over a body in this weather."

Ben was also a master of understatement, Cam thought on a smothered laugh.

Before the vicar left, however, he gave Gemma a hug. Then laid his hand on Cam's shoulder.

"I'm here if you need to talk," he said quietly. "Both of you."

Sophia took her husband's arm. "I'm coming with you."

With a sigh, Serena rose and said, "I'll go see if cook will send some tea out to them."

She was careful to leave the door open, however, something Cam noted with a mixture of amusement and resignation.

He was hardly going to attempt a seduction so soon after finding a corpse.

Or at any time with this particular lady, for that matter.

But Gemma's first words once they were alone told him she was thinking of anything but seduction.

"Where the devil is my fossil?"

Chapter 8

Gemma felt Cam's eyes on her as she paced from the window to the fireplace and back again.

But she couldn't help herself. It was impossible to sit still while the most important fossil she'd ever come across was missing. A fossil that had very likely been the cause of a man's murder.

"Where is it?" she asked again. "Did the killer take it? Or did someone else happen upon it before Sir Everard even returned to the cliff?"

She stopped, some of her frenetic energy dissipating at the memory of the dead man. He'd not endeared himself to her, but he hadn't deserved to have his life cut short for being boorish. What if he had family?

At that thought, she collapsed into the chair Serena had so recently vacated.

She couldn't imagine what she'd do if something happened to Sophia. Or anyone she'd come to know and love since her arrival in Sussex, for that matter.

"It seems unlikely that anyone would stumble upon that stretch of shore in the middle of the night by chance." Cam leaned forward in the chair opposite hers, his elbows on his knees. "We must assume that the killer, very likely someone Sir Everard brought with him, took it."

She nodded. It did seem the most logical explanation.

"If he brought an accomplice," she said, "it must have been someone from Pearson Close. One of the other collectors."

"Or his valet," Cam said thoughtfully. "He did say that Chambers often assisted him in his excavations."

"Then we must speak to this man," Gemma said, her spirits rising at the thought of some occupation to help her find the skull. "I have no intention of allowing a murderer to make off with my skull."

But Cam was already shaking his head.

"You heard what Northman said. He expressly warned you against looking into the matter yourself."

Gemma waved that objection away. "He warned me against investigating the murder. Not the missing skull."

"If you won't listen to Northman's caution, then listen to the killer's," Cam argued, his expression turning forbidding. "If you need reminding, Sir Everard was bludgeoned to death with his own digging tools. I cannot allow you to put yourself at risk for a similar fate. I won't."

"You aren't the one who decides what I may and may not do," she said with a glare.

"Now is not the time for stubbornness, Gemma," Cam said, thrusting his hands through his hair, as if to keep from gripping her by the arms. "Just let me search for it. I promise to report on it to you as soon as I learn anything."

But she shook her head. "Either you assist me, or I search alone," she said firmly.

She watched as he slid his hands down his face in exasperation.

"I know you think it's sheer bullheadedness on my part," she said, taking pity on him, "but you have to understand that I've spent the better part of a year at Beauchamp House with little hope of finding out where Lady Celeste hid my inheritance."

At his questioning look, she continued. "All of the others had detailed instructions and quests outlined for them. Puzzles and mysteries to solve. But Lady Celeste left my letter unfinished." Gemma felt her eyes well. "She died before she could complete it. That's what the note from the solicitor said that accompanied it. So, if she did indeed leave this skull for me—and I am convinced now that she did—then l must be the one to find it."

Cam's expression softened and he took her hand. "I know it must be incredibly frustrating for you, but I cannot believe Lady Celeste would wish you to risk your life to find this fossil."

"No," Gemma said quietly, "But nor would she expect me to simply cede the field to someone else.

"I must be the one to conduct the search, Cam," she said. "And if you insist, then you may help me."

"Help you?" Cam shook his head. "I most certainly will not. You don't need to be mixed up in this business. A man was murdered, Gemma. It's not a jaunt to the shore to dig for stones."

"That's why you'll be there." Really, who would have guessed Lord Cameron Lisle was such a prig?

"To protect me," she clarified, just in case he hadn't figured it out. "It's really quite brilliant. You'll assist me, and I'll find the stone."

"It's not brilliant at all," he countered. "If something were to happen to you, Sophia would be livid. And when Sophia is unhappy, Benedick is unhappy. I do not relish a thrashing from my brother the vicar, Gemma."

"Oh come now. You can't tell me you're afraid of your own brother, can you?"

That was a bridge too far, apparently.

"I'm not afraid of Ben," Cam said in the voice of a man who needed very much to assert his bravery. "I am simply not willing to risk jeopardizing my relationship with him by helping you put yourself in the path of a killer."

"But I'm sure it would be perfectly rational if you had been the one to discover the skull first." Gemma rolled her eyes. "Why is it when a man wishes to pursue something, it's a noble cause that everyone should rejoice over, but if a woman wants to embark on a search for her own property, it's far too dangerous and she should stay at home and . . . and . . ." she searched for the perfect womanly activity to illustrate her point.

"Knit? Cook? Sew? Polish her fossil collection?" Cam asked.

If anything, his attempt at levity made her even angrier. "Any of those things," she said heatedly, stomping her foot for good measure. "And I will not sit still this time. I will not let my discovery be taken from me."

To her shame, tears sprang into her eyes. She'd worked so hard to gain recognition in the world of geology, and the excitement she'd felt when she caught sight of the skull protruding from the mud had been like nothing she'd ever felt before. She'd felt in her bones the importance of it. How dare that . . . that man . . . attempt to steal it from her.

She gulped back a sob and before she knew what was happening, Cam was on his knees before her, pulling her into his arms and flipping them so that he was in the chair and she was in his lap.

It was utterly improper, but at the moment she didn't care for such niceties. Not when he was so warm and strong and it felt so good to be held close.

"Hush now," he whispered, his breath tickling her ear. "Hush. I'll help you. I'll help you find your skull."

She pulled away a little to look him in the eyes and found something there that made her stomach give a flip. "You will?" she asked, her voice hoarse with tears.

"I will," he said, and his eyes glanced down at her mouth.

Without conscious thought, she closed her eyes and whispered, "Thank you."

Then, in what at the time she'd doubtless considered a gesture of gratitude, she kissed him.

What the devil was he about?

Cam tried to form a coherent thought, but Gemma Hastings in his arms with her mouth pressed against his was far too overwhelming to allow anything to cross his mind but disbelief followed by sheer exhilaration.

It was clear from the tentative nature of the caress that she wasn't practiced in the art of seduction, but her mouth was sweet and he let her explore a bit before leaning into her, opening his mouth a little, to tease her.

That surprised a soft "oh" from her as she opened her own mouth and he nipped her lower lip before tasting her with his tongue.

She clung tighter, and he felt her hands slip up and around his neck. He smiled against her as she tilted her head and took to the art of kissing as she did everything else.

With unabashed enthusiasm.

Soon they were exchanging bits of dialogue in a conversation only they could understand.

When she made a noise of satisfaction as he caressed her breast, it sent a lick of fire through his veins.

"Gemma, do you know where my . . . ?"

No two people could have leapt away from a kiss faster than they did.

Though her eyes were still hazy with passion, Gemma had jumped to her feet and turned her back to him.

Cam, meanwhile rose, grateful for the length of his coat.

But they hadn't been hasty enough to hide what they'd been up to.

Lady Serena had seen far more than she should have, if her expression was anything to go by.

Damn it.

He'd even made note of the open door.

"Lord Cameron," Serena said coolly. "I would like to have a word with Gemma alone, please."

He bowed. "Of course, Lady Serena. Miss Hastings, I will speak to you later, if I may?"

Having turned back to face him, Gemma nodded. Her lips were a little swollen from his kisses and he felt a mix of protectiveness and anxiety at the sight.

He'd been afraid of angering Ben by putting her in danger.

Little had he realized he was far more dangerous to her than Sir Everard's murderer was.

"Of all my charges, Gemma," Serena said in an exasperated tone as she shut the door, "you are the last one I'd expect to find in such a scandalous position. What were you thinking?"

Gemma could hardly argue with her. She was just as surprised as her chaperone was by what had just happened. She'd never have guessed she'd be caught in anyone's arms. Much less Lord Cameron Lisle's.

"I was upset," she explained, and to her own ears it sounded like a weak excuse. "He was comforting me."

"With his tongue?" Serena asked with a disbelieving laugh.

"I know what you saw wasn't precisely proper," Gemma said, "but it's hardly the worst behavior you've seen from the Beauchamp House heiresses."

"And why should the others' behavior matter?" Serena countered. "You are responsible for your own actions. And I'm afraid that I cannot simply forget what I saw and let this slip by. I am assuredly the most lax chaperone in all of England, if not Europe. But never let it be said that I do not hold my charges accountable."

"It isn't your fault," Gemma protested. "As you say, I'm responsible for myself and so was Ivy. She's the only one really who ignored the proprieties."

"Do not try to tell me that Daphne and Sophia didn't anticipate their vows," Serena said with a shake of her head, "for I will not believe you. But they are beside the point. We are speaking of you."

Gemma swallowed. She'd never thought to be on the receiving end of Serena's look of disappointment. It didn't feel good at all.

"Do you love him?" Serena asked, her expression grave.

It was a simple question, but had no simple answer.

Gemma hadn't even liked Cam until this week. Could she grow to love him? Perhaps. But that was not part of her plan. And she'd certainly never thought to kiss him.

"I don't know," she answered. "Not yet."

Serena sighed and took Gemma's hands in hers. "I must write to your parents about this. There's no other option. I am acting as your parent while you are here."

"But what about Sophia?" Gemma asked. Though the idea of Sophia learning what had happened was more alarming than having her parents find out, if she were being honest. "She's a married woman now. Why cannot she be the one to decide?"

Serena thought about it. "I suppose that will be acceptable. Though you must agree to abide by her decision."

"Of course," Gemma said with a nod. She trusted Sophia. And though she'd married a vicar, she hadn't changed her opinions on the strictures that society placed on women. She would understand that Gemma shouldn't be forced into marriage because of a few kisses.

No matter how toe curling and wonderful those kisses had been.

She wondered what Cam was thinking right now.

Was he just as alarmed as she was at the prospect of a betrothal?

Surely he was, she reasoned. He had no more wish to marry her than she had to marry him.

Why did that bother her so much?

Just then a knock sounded at the door and Sophia stepped in and shut it behind her.

"Cam told me I was needed in here." Her eyes were troubled as she glanced from Serena to Gemma. "What's amiss?"

Serena gave Gemma an encouraging smile and said, "I'll leave you two to discuss this alone."

To Gemma she said, "I trust you to make the right decision."

Then she was gone and Sophia looked alarmed. "What's going on? Has something happened?"

Deciding that plain speaking was best, Gemma said, "Serena caught me kissing Cam."

It was clear from her sister's expression that Gemma confessing she'd been in on the Gunpowder plot with Guy Fawkes would have come as less of a surprise.

"What?" Sophia blinked. "I have to sit down."

She collapsed onto the settee.

Gemma sat down beside her. "I know it's unexpected.

But the important thing is that it was only the one time. Really just a slight indiscretion. Nothing to concern ourselves about."

There, she thought. That should convince Sophia to let this whole matter pass without any sort of betrothal nonsense.

"A slight indiscretion is treading on someone's toes on the ballroom floor," her sister said with a frown. "A slight indiscretion is bumping into someone accidentally. Being found kissing one's brother-in-law is not a slight indiscretion."

"Oh please, Soph," Gemma argued. "We all know how silly and hypocritical the rules about how ladies should behave are. And only Serena knows. There's no reason for it to go any farther."

"I know," Sophia returned. "And I'm sure Ben knows too because Cameron is very likely telling him at this very moment."

Gemma blinked. "What? Why would he do that?"

"Because he's an honorable man, Gemma," Sophia said with a look of disbelief. "I know you have had your disagreements with him, but Cam is not the sort of man who would shirk his duty. You are an unmarried lady. He is an unmarried man. There is every reason for him to do the right thing."

"Marry me, you mean?" Gemma could hardly believe her sister was uttering these platitudes. "What happened to the Sophia who was ready to storm the patriarchy and show her art no matter what the cost to her reputation?"

"She is still here, my dear," her sister assured her. "But there is a time and a place for resisting society's strictures, and since I've married Benedick I've seen far too many examples of what can happen when a lady is ruined. It isn't a happy existence."

"Oh come. I will hardly be ruined because of a few kisses," Gemma chided.

"All it takes is the whisper of scandal and you will not be received anywhere."

"I've always planned to pursue my studies and remain unwed," Gemma said defiantly. "I will be independent like Aunt Dahlia and Lady Celeste."

"My dear," Sophia's voice was sympathetic. "Aunt Dahlia lives on the kindness of our parents. And Lady Celeste, despite this magnificent house and library she built, was dreadfully lonely."

It was Gemma's turn to blink.

"You would be financially secure, of course, thanks to the inheritance from Lady Celeste," Sophia said. "But you wouldn't be able to be received by Ivy or Daphne without damaging their reputations. And I would have to see you in secret lest word get back to the church hierarchy and endanger Benedick's position."

Gemma stared at her.

"All because of a few kisses." This time it was a statement rather than a question.

"Is it really such a dismal prospect?" Sophia asked softly, taking her sister's hand.

Gemma reflected on the matter.

Cameron was, at the very least, a gifted fossil-hunter.

He was also an honorable man, who clearly bore a great deal of affection for his family.

In agreeing to help her find the lizard skull, he'd also proved himself to be a loyal friend.

And there was no question about his kissing skills, which were, so far as Gemma could tell, exceptional.

"Perhaps not dismal," she admitted aloud.

"Maybe instead of a hasty wedding," Sophia said slipping an arm around her, "we can arrange a betrothal.

If at the end of a few weeks you are still against the match, you can agree to go your separate ways. That will silence any rumors of overfamiliarity between you, and will give you a bit of time to get to know one another better."

"Won't that be odd? If we choose to break things off, I mean?" Gemma asked, frowning. "We will still have to see one another from time to time because of our family connection."

"More odd than being married to someone you do not wish to be married to?" Sophia asked wryly.

"I see your point," Gemma said with a nod.

The sisters sat in silence for a moment. Then, Sophia turned to her. "So, tell me all about it. Was it a good kiss?"

Gemma grinned. "Very good."

Very good, indeed.

Chapter 9

"You did what?"

Cam had expected his brother to be angry, but he had perhaps underestimated the degree to which Ben would express this anger.

"Now, Ben," he said, raising his hands in a surrendering motion. "You needn't lose your temper. It's not seemly for a vicar to engage in fisticuffs."

Though Cam knew it took a great deal to raise his brother's ire, it would appear that this was one of those occasions.

"There is every reason for me to lose my temper, you lout," Ben said through clenched teeth. "There are millions of women in the world for you to seduce. But who do you decide to lay hands on at the first opportunity? My sister-in-law. I knew you were a rake, Cam, but I thought even you would draw the line at my wife's sister."

They were in the empty library, where Cam had pulled him so that they wouldn't be overheard. Which was a good thing, considering that Benedick was shouting the dashed roof off.

"It was badly done of me," he said, attempting to cool things down with a preemptive admission of guilt.

Which he then ruined by giving excuses. "But you weren't there. She was crying, dammit, and I only meant to comfort her a bit. And then she kissed me, if you want to know the—"

He was stopped in mid-sentence by the very strong punch of Ben's fist against his jaw.

It was unexpected, and knocked him to the carpet.

For a minute, he had no thoughts beyond the pain in his face.

Followed closely by satisfaction. If he could have punched himself in the jaw he'd have done it as soon as he stepped out of the drawing room.

He moved his lower jaw from side to side. Though it hurt like the devil, it wasn't broken.

Looking up he saw his brother looking down at him with exasperation. "I shouldn't have done that," he said. "It isn't vicarly."

"Feel better?"

"Not as much as I'd hoped," Ben admitted. He reached down and offered him a hand. "I think there's some brandy hidden in here."

On his feet again, Cam walked over to one of the large overstuffed chairs that faced the fire. The rest of the furniture was more suited to ladies but she must have had some gentlemen guests—or anticipated them—to have furnished her library with chairs obviously built for the comfort of large bodies.

He sat, then leaned his head back and lifted his forearm to cover his eyes and sighed. He'd awakened this morning feeling like the veriest saint. He was going to help Gemma, who only days ago had been a thorn in his side. It was self-less of him. Yes, he'd be double crossing Sir Everard, whom he'd come to loathe, in the process, but that was beside the point.

And now Sir Everard was dead, Gemma's fossil was missing, and he was facing the prospect of a hasty wedding.

Because there was no way his brother was going to let him off the hook for this.

What a difference a few hours could make.

"Here," he opened his eyes to see his brother offering a generously filled glass of brandy.

He put his arm down and took it. "It's not poisoned, is it?"

"Not my style," said Ben, taking the chair opposite. He extended and flexed the fingers of his right hand as he sipped from the glass in his left.

Cam took a swig of the brandy and was pleased to find it was quality. No cheap liquor for Lady Celeste either. The more he learned of her the more he respected her. She'd been clever enough to choose Gemma after all.

At the thought of her, he couldn't help but remember her mouth on his. Her sweet curves pressed against him as if she couldn't get enough. He couldn't either. But he didn't mention it, of course. He had no wish for a black eye to go with his bruised jaw.

He would have liked to avoid the subject altogether, but that was not going to happen while Ben was drawing breath.

"I barely know the girl, Ben," he said aloud. And even as he said the words he felt their inadequacy. Couples who knew one another far less than they did were married every day.

"You should have thought about that before you kissed her, idiot," his brother said without any of his usual carefully worded tact. "What were you thinking?"

Then, recalling perhaps why he'd punched Cam in the first place, he held up his hand. "In general terms, please. I don't want to break my hand."

Cam shook his head. "It was the heat of the moment," he said wryly. "It wasn't planned. I wasn't trying to seduce her. Hell, I didn't even mean to kiss her."

"You must be attracted to her," Ben pressed. "I mean, if you weren't—and I am going to believe that she kissed you, just for the sake of argument—then you wouldn't have kissed her back."

"Of course, I'm attracted to her," Cam said. Really, his brother was such a simpleton at times. "She's lovely. Maddening as hell, but lovely."

"So, why is the idea of marriage such a problem?"

Cam leaned back in his chair and sighed. "I have been thinking about settling down, but hadn't made up my mind yet. And I'd certainly not thought to choose someone like Gemma. For all that she's beautiful she's the opposite of what a wife should be."

"What should a wife be, then?" Ben asked, tilting his head with puzzlement.

"Don't be an ass," Cam said, feeling his ears go a little red. "You know what I mean. We all have an idea of what we'd like in a bride. I'm simply saying that Gemma is not what I envisioned."

"And I'm asking what you envisioned," Ben said patiently.

"Someone more . . ." Cam struggled to put the idea into words. "Someone more like Lady Serena. Beautiful, calm, sweet. She would make the perfect wife."

"Oh!"

He glanced at the door and saw Gemma there her mouth agape. But she quickly regained her composure.

"I'm sorry, I didn't mean to interrupt. I'll leave you to your conversation."

With that she was gone.

"Now who's an ass?" Ben asked.

Cam, already on his feet, didn't argue.

For once, he was in full agreement with his brother.

Cam passed Sophia in the hallway but when she tried to stop him, he waved her off. "I have to find Gemma," he said as he brushed past her.

"She's in the fossil workroom," she called after him.

He cursed himself for a fool, though to be honest, he wasn't sure why he was so worried about what Gemma had overheard. Didn't she deserve to know the truth? She wanted a marriage between them no more than he did. She didn't even like him. She'd made that perfectly clear in their every interaction since that disastrous first introduction.

True, they had reached a detente of sorts since then, but it was hardly a complete change of opinions.

As he neared the double doors of the fossil gallery, he felt an unusual flutter of nerves. Which he immediately repressed.

He had likely hurt her feelings. That was all. Once he explained his reasons for saying what he had, they would have a good laugh about it. She was a woman of sense. She would understand.

He'd approached the gallery from the far side of the house, so the workroom was on the other side from where they'd entered only yesterday.

And though there was no sign of Gemma in the gallery itself, he could hear a scrubbing sound from the workroom.

When he reached the door to that chamber, it was to see her wearing an apron over her gown and standing at the worktable, using fine brushes to clean the dirt from what looked to be a stack of ammonites.

"What are you doing?" he asked, though it would have

been obvious even to young Jeremy, Lady Serena's lad, what she was doing.

"I'd like for you to go, please," she said firmly, not raising her eyes from the task at hand. "I'll figure out what to do about my fossil on my own. Think no more about what happened earlier. My sister won't force me into a marriage neither of us wants. And . . ." she paused. He saw her jaw clench before she went on. "Lady Serena will not force me either. So, you'll be free to court her if that's what you wish."

That was quite a speech.

It was the utter lack of intonation that told him just how hurt she was by what she'd overheard.

He really was an ass.

"Gemma," he said, "let me explain."

She didn't look up, but kept on brushing, occasionally changing to a firmer one when the softer was inadequate. "There's nothing to explain. I am quite aware of my own shortcomings. I walk like a man, I sometimes talk like one. I'm not nearly as pretty as my sister or Serena. And you're right. She would make a far better wife than I would. Nothing you said was untrue. It's just been a long day. I've never seen a dead body."

Seeing that she would not be rising to speak to him face-to-face, he bent so that he could see her face. "Gemma," he said softly, "I have no intention of wooing Lady Serena. Or anyone really. At least I hadn't. Until what happened between us."

She stopped scrubbing and glanced over at him. "You needn't be kind to me. We've always spoken honestly with one another. Do not, I pray, start wrapping things up in cotton wool now. What happened was a mistake. Neither of us should be forced to pay for it with our freedom."

He'd been thinking much the same, but hearing it from her lips made him want to dig in his heels. "Unexpected, perhaps, but not a mistake, surely."

"Cam," she said, a little desperately. "Stop. I understand you feel guilty about hurting me, but there's really no need for it. I know the truth now, and that's far better than muddling along with some farce of a betrothal that would fall apart later. It was only a kiss."

"Only a very good kiss," he said, reaching out to touch her cheek. "Do you think it's like that with everyone?"

"Since I've never kissed anyone else, I'm sure I don't know," she said primly. She didn't look up at him.

Then, with a sigh, she looked up at him. Her cheeks were pink, and her eyes were red. Whether from her tears earlier or more recently, he couldn't know. But he felt a stab of guilt over it just the same.

She'd never looked more appealing.

Cam closed his eyes at the thought. Dammit, he was only here to apologize. Not notice her appeal.

"Well?" she asked, her tone impatient.

He said the first thing that came to him. "What made you come here? To the workroom, I mean?"

She looked surprised at the question, but shrugged. "It's where I'm most comfortable. And cleaning fossils helps me think."

"Think?" He really was the most imbecilic man in the nation, he thought with an inward sigh.

But she seemed to find this amusing. Or something . . .

"Yes, Cam, think. I know you've heard of it, though I feel sure you are of the opinion that ladies don't engage in the practice very often."

"That's not fair," he said scowling. "I never said anything of the sort. And I thought we were friends."

"Perhaps not in so many words," she admitted. "But it's quite clear to me now that what I'd thought was a friendship between us was only some foolish misunderstanding on my part."

She shook her head a little. "I don't blame you. Serena is lovely. And the perfect sort of proper lady a man would wish for in a wife. If I were a man, I'd marry her myself."

He didn't laugh at her joke. This was far worse than he'd thought.

He took her hand. "Gemma, I think you are just as lovely as your sister or Serena. What's more, you're intelligent and brave. But even you must admit that we would likely kill one another before the bridal trip was over."

He said the words and meant them, but a small part of him protested the notion. They might be at loggerheads frequently, but there would certainly be passion. And as he'd told her, that wasn't something that happened every day.

Gemma smiled at that. "I think I could restrain myself. Annoying though you may be."

He smiled too. It would be much easier to come to some sort of solution if he didn't want to kiss that dimple that appeared only when she smiled.

"What will we do, then?" she asked. "It's plain as a pikestaff that we cannot simply go on as before. Serena and Sophia, while not ready to force us into marrying, at the very least expect a betrothal to protect my reputation."

It was what he'd come to realize too. He had no wish to ruin her reputation, or to see her cut off from her family and friends because of his mistake. He might not have kissed her first, but he'd not pulled away. And for all that she considered herself a full participant, he was a gentleman and had more experience in these matters. He should have stopped it before it got out of hand.

"I think we should, at the very least, enter into a betrothal," he said. "You may cry off in a month or so. Once we've had a chance to squelch any rumors. For we both know that even if Serena told no one about what she saw, servants talk and they might have overheard something. I wouldn't be surprised if they were remarking upon the fact that we've been in this room together alone for an extended period of time."

At that, Gemma muttered a curse and scrambled to her feet, pulling her hand away from his in the process.

He felt strangely bereft at the loss. But he, too, got to his feet.

"We really will have to do this, then?" she asked with a moue of distaste. "I am not very good at pretense. My face is far too quick to reveal my thoughts."

"Will it be so distasteful, then?" Good lord, he was turning into some sort of mooning schoolboy. If he didn't stop himself he'd be writing her poetry and composing ballads to sing up at her window.

She narrowed her eyes, and looked at him for a moment. And he felt as if she were trying to see into his soul.

"Perhaps not so distasteful," she admitted. "Mayhap we can use this as an opportunity for my education."

He nodded. "I would be happy to teach you more about geology. I've brought some of the latest journals from France with me and . . ."

When she moved closer and slipped her hands over his shoulders, he felt a frisson of alarm. And desire, if he were being entirely honest.

"I do not need you to teach me about fossils, Cam," she said with a raised brow. "But as I mentioned, you were the first person I'd kissed. And as I mean to remain unwed, I would hate to miss out on the opportunity to experience all the pleasures to be had from life."

His eyes went wide with alarm. "Oh no. Gemma, this is not a good idea." He tried to remove her hands from his shoulders, but his traitorous brain slipped his arms about her waist instead.

"I think it's a very good idea," she said, leaning forward to touch his nose with hers. "If we're to be betrothed, why not behave as other betrothed couples do?"

"I . . . Gemma, we can't . . ." If Ben found out about this he was going to do more than plant him a facer.

But when her lips met his, Cam couldn't think about what-ifs and consequences. His only thoughts were for the warm woman in his arms and just how much he wanted her.

When he began to kiss her back, Gemma felt as if she'd scaled the chalk cliffs in one leap. Her heart beat faster, her breath caught in her throat and she felt a pulse deep in her belly. Whatever their reasons for this betrothal, she knew one thing with every sinew of her body: they were very good together.

She'd been upset at what she'd overheard. What woman with any sort of self-respect wouldn't? He'd practically come right out and said Serena was his preferred choice. And though she'd understood it—Serena was by far the most beautiful and accomplished lady of her acquaintance—the comparison had hurt. Because she knew she wasn't nearly as sensible a choice as Serena was.

His explanation had stung, but it would have hurt more if he'd lied. And though she wasn't quite sure whether his compliments of her were genuine, it had been kind of him to say so.

But whether he thought she was the perfect choice for a bride, he most certainly agreed that there was something else between them. His confession that it wasn't as combustible with everyone had been very flattering.

And as he licked into her mouth and pulled her closer to his hard body, she couldn't deny that she was pleased that she made him feel this way. Even if their betrothal ended in a few months, she would use this time to learn everything she could about what went on between men and women. And if she ended up with a broken heart—because she knew she could very easily fall in love with him no matter how much of a dolt he could be—then she would have at least known the pleasure of holding him in her arms.

"Again?"

This time the interruption came from Sophia, who was looking exasperated as she stood in the door to the workroom.

"If you're going to be behaving this scandalously, it's obvious that we should get the two of you married sooner rather than later."

Pulling away from Cam far more slowly than she'd done earlier when Serena found them, Gemma slipped her arm through his. "First things first, Sophia," she said with a grin. "You must wish us happy on our betrothal."

And in the flurry of congratulations, Gemma sent up a silent prayer that she'd made the right decision. Because she knew in her heart of hearts that this might be her undoing.

Chapter 10

Gemma and Cam celebrated their betrothal over luncheon with Lady Serena, Sophia and Ben.

And for a temporary measure meant only to protect Gemma's reputation, it felt damned real to Cam.

So real, in fact, that when, instead of discussing wedding details with her sister and chaperone, Gemma announced that she was ready to go to Pearson Close, he laughed. He couldn't help it.

They'd both been up since before dawn, had seen a dead body, been interrogated by the local magistrate, and been compromised into a false betrothal.

Any other lady would have taken to her bedchamber with smelling salts.

But, as he'd realized months ago, Gemma was not like any other lady.

"I'm serious," Gemma said frowning even as she slipped her arm through his as they left the dining room. "We must go examine Sir Everard's belongings before Mr. Northman does. I fear he may have already got there ahead of us, but it's worth a try, at the very least. There may be some clue to who killed him, and therefore who has my fossil."

Cam stopped to look at her, not unaware of his brother smirking behind them. Ben was likely pleased to see another man having to contend with the mad starts of a Hastings sister.

He'd always been happier when he had company.

To Gemma he said, "I know I agreed to help you find your fossil, but—"

"Yes," Gemma interrupted, "and the best way to do that is to see if there's anything in Sir Everard's things that will give us a clue. It might not go amiss if we interview his valet. Did you not say he often helped his master in his endeavors? He will likely object to our examining Sir Everard's papers. You will have to distract him, somehow." She beamed at him as if he were a prized pupil. "I have faith in you, though, Cam. You can be quite persuasive when you want to be."

Before he could reply, she said, "I'll just go fetch my coat and hat. I'll only be a moment."

With that, she hurried up the stairs.

Cam felt as if he'd just been knocked over by a gale force wind.

"So, I see you've been given your orders," Ben said wryly, clapping him on the shoulder. "Welcome to my world."

"Thanks so much for your help," Cam said with a glare.

"Come now," Ben said cheerfully. "The Hastings sisters may know their own minds, but they make up for it in other ways. Sophia hardly ever orders me around like that anymore. At least, not when I've been doing my best to keep her happy."

"So you just do her bidding?" Cam asked aghast. He'd be dashed if he would allow himself to be led around by the nose.

"I wouldn't quite put it like that," Ben said with a shrug.

"I try to do what will make her happy. And she does the same for me. But sometimes we both fail. In which case, we argue, then make up. To be honest, the making up is the best part sometimes."

"You're a very strange fellow," Cam told his brother.

"You should hear Archer," Ben said with a shake of his head. "He's been married longer than any of us. He knows far more about dealing with a wife. Though of course, every lady is different."

This was a whole world that Cam hadn't even known existed, he realized. He was almost sad he'd not be welcomed into this husbands' club.

But only almost.

Tillie was buttoning her into a long-sleeved persimmon-colored velvet when a knock heralded the arrival of Ivy, followed close behind by Daphne.

Seeing that they were wide-eyed and obviously wished to discuss the morning's events, she said to the maid, "I can manage the rest, Tillie. Thank you."

With a nod, the girl slipped from the room.

"It would appear that we chose the wrong morning to sleep in," Ivy said with a shake of her head and she came forward and gave Gemma a fierce hug. "What an awful thing for you to see. And then to be imposed upon by Lord Cameron like that. Do you wish me to tell Kerr to have a word with him? Or perhaps both he and Maitland. I know he is Lord Benedick's brother, but that can be no excuse for his behavior."

"No matter how many facers Lord Benedick plants on him with his fives," Daphne added staunchly.

Despite herself, Gemma laughed. "There's no need to send your husbands to talk sense into Cam," she told her friends. "Though I am grateful for the offer. And contrary to what you must think, Ben and Sophia aren't forcing me into anything. It's to be a temporary betrothal until some time has passed. For propriety's sake. I would have dispensed with the whole thing, but Sophia, rightly pointed out to me that a ruined reputation might mean that I would be cut off from my friends and family."

She took them each by the hand. "I couldn't bear it if you were unable to receive me because of my own foolishness."

"We would never do that to you," said Ivy fiercely, her eyes stern behind her spectacles. "Not even if Kerr ordered it of me."

"And I wouldn't wish to put you in that position," Gemma said. "Though I do appreciate the loyalty."

"And what of Lord Cameron?" Daphne asked, her blue eyes searching. "Was the thrashing the vicar delivered sufficient or should we have it followed up on by Maitland and Kerr?"

"He didn't deserve a thrashing at all," Gemma said with a shake of her head. "I was a willing participant in the kiss, and if Serena hadn't walked in on us, no one would have been any the wiser."

"Oh poor Serena," said Ivy with a shake of her head. "I believe she hoped you, at least, would manage to finish out the year without compromising yourself."

"One cannot compromise oneself, Ivy," said Daphne with a shake of her head. "Unless one were to do the female equivalent of boxing the Jesuit in public, I suppose, but really that's simply outside the realm of anything Gemma would be likely to—"

Deciding she'd best get back downstairs before Cam left without her, Gemma cut Daphne off mid-thought. "I'm sorry to go before we have time to speak more candidly about this, but I'm afraid Lord Cameron is waiting for me downstairs and we must be off."

Ivy's eyes narrowed. "That's a new gown, isn't it?"

"Where are you going?" Daphne demanded.

Gemma picked up the hat Tillie had left out for her and busied herself pinning it to her hair. "We are going to question Sir Everard's valet at Pearson Close."

"You're investigating the murder, aren't you?" Ivy asked, wide-eyed. "Poor Serena."

Before they could begin questioning her further, Gemma kissed them each on the cheek and fled.

But not before she heard Daphne call out, "Good luck."

She wasn't sure whether her friend referred to Cam, or the search for the murderer. She'd take the luck for either.

When Gemma finally reappeared, she'd changed into another formfitting velvet. This one was a dull red color and was partially covered by a pelisse of the same shade. The color accentuated the peaches and cream of her complexion and was set off by a jaunty hat adorned with a cluster of flowers he couldn't identify. None of it seems particularly practical for the current weather but as they would be indoors most of the time, it didn't seem to be an issue.

And he had to admit, she was in fine looks.

"I took the liberty of having your curricle brought round," Gemma told him as she stepped forward. "I hope you don't mind."

He looked up to see what Ben thought of this but he was gone.

The coward.

"Certainly not," he said aloud. "I suppose we should go if we're to get there before Northman."

He gathered his coat and hat and gloves from George and soon he was lifting Gemma into his curricle. It wasn't the most practical of vehicles in this weather, but with the bonnet up and the hot bricks and carriage blankets William brought them, it would be bearable.

Once they were on the road, Gemma turned to him and asked, "How shall we get me into the house?"

"Dash it," Cam said, "I forgot about Pearson's ridiculous no females rule. Perhaps I should go alone. I'll turn back."

He made as if to direct the horses to do just that but Gemma put a hand on his arm. "Don't do that. We can figure something out. Just give me a minute."

Reluctantly he did as she asked, though he wasn't particularly hopeful of their prospects. It wasn't as if they could dress her in men's clothing and sneak her in that way.

"What were Mr. Pearson's plans for today?" Gemma asked. "Did anyone plan on going out for some reason? Perhaps a trip to the pub?"

But he shook his head. One of the most disappointing aspects of the house party had been Pearson's reluctance to introduce his guests to the local attractions. Which was a shame given the proximity to Lyme and other well-known fossil grounds. And there had been no question of a large group traveling to see the collection at Beauchamp House. Pearson, of course, disapproved of Lady Celeste and her decision to leave her estate to four ladies.

"As far as I know, everyone was intending to remain at the house," he said aloud. "Though I suppose with the news of what happened to Sir Everard, there will be some who wish to go into town to get more details. Or perhaps leave altogether."

"Perhaps that will be our cover story, then," Gemma said with a nod. "We're coming to bring the sad news. It did happen at my home. And you're my betrothed so there's no surprise in our coming together."

"Northman warned us not to tell them before he could," Cam reminded her. "And Pearson doesn't even allow female servants in his house. How do you expect to get past the butler?"

"It isn't our fault that Northman is taking so long," Gemma said innocently. "And the butler can hardly toss me out on my ear with my handsome fiancé—who is a guest of his master—at my side, can he?"

"Handsome, eh?" He gave her a sideways look and she blushed and refused to meet his eyes.

"You know perfectly well you're handsome, you devil." The single dimple he liked so well made an appearance.

"But I didn't know you thought so," he said softly, holding the reins in his other hand so that he could slip his arm through hers. "I'm quite flattered."

"Don't let it go to your head," she said tartly, though there was a hint of breathlessness in her voice. "I still think you're stubborn as a mule."

He barked out a laugh.

"That sentiment is mutual, Miss Hastings," he said grinning.

He was still smiling like a fool when the curricle approached Pearson Close.

A groom stepped forward to take the reins and when Cam asked if he'd seen Northman that morning the man shook his head.

"No visitors at all today, my lord."

Relieved that one obstacle had been avoided, he leapt down and moved to assist Gemma from the vehicle. He'd halfheartedly decided to keep things platonic between them while they were here so as not to antagonize Pearson, but that went the way of the marine lizards when she slid down the front of his body as he lifted her to the ground. He clenched his jaw at the teasing contact, and frowned at her. But Gemma's only response was an innocent lift of her brows.

She wasn't going to give an inch, he realized.

But really, had he expected anything less?

Of course not.

Laughing softly at his own foolishness, he took her arm and they walked together up the front steps.

When they reached the door, it opened before Cam could lift the gargoyle knocker.

Fanshawe blinked when he saw Gemma at his side.

"Lord Cameron," he said solemnly. Then, looking down his nose at Gemma, he intoned, "I hope you know your companion will not be allowed inside. Mr. Pearson has very strict rules about females.."

"Oh, I only wish to remain in the entry hall," Gemma assured him. "I'm Miss Gemma Hastings, by the way. And we've come to speak with Sir Everard's valet."

At the mention of Sir Everard, the butler's face turned, if possible, even more dour. "Why would you wish to do that?"

"We have some news to give him," Gemma said solemnly. "It's about his master. Something very unfortunate has happened. I'm afraid he won't be returning to Pearson Close."

Fanshawe's mouth dropped open, his usual impassive expression erased in his shock. "Do you mean to say that Sir Everard is dead, Miss?"

"I'm afraid he is," Gemma said.. "And I discovered his body, I wanted to be the one to tell his valet. What's his name? Chambers, is it?"

The butler was still taking in the news that one of the

houseguests was deceased. "I don't know, Miss. This seems most irregular. And there's been no news of it from—"

"It's a most irregular matter, Mr. Fanshawe," she said, cutting him off, and Cam watched as the older man struggled to decide whether he should allow her in or not.

"I assure you, Fanshawe," Cam said, "it's all above board. I can confirm the dreadful news about Sir Everard. And while my betrothed speaks to Chambers I'll just go gather my things. I'm removing to my brother's house for the duration."

It was the perfect solution. He would let Gemma speak to Chambers downstairs—with Fanshawe in attendance so that she wouldn't be endangered on the off chance Chambers was the one who'd killed his master—while he nipped up to search Sir Everard's rooms.

Fanshawe, however, was focused on the other news now. "Miss Hastings," he said, looking mortified. "If I'd known you were the betrothed of Lord Cameron I would not have been so . . ."

"Think nothing of it, Mr. Fanshawe," she said with a wave of her hand. "We only just got engaged this morning. You did nothing wrong." She clung to Cam's arm like a limpet and looked up at him with such adoration he felt like a puppy in the hands of a toddler.

"Indeed," was his only response. "Now, Fanshawe, if you'll just take Gemma to see Chambers now?"

They watched as the man struggled to decide what he should do. Finally, with the utmost reluctance, he gestured them inside.

Once they were in the entry hall, he frowned at them. "I'll just go see if he is available. I'm afraid Mr. Chambers likes a tipple and with Sir Everard's absence he's been indulging himself." His bushy brows drew together as he frowned at Gemma. "Wait here."

Before they could respond, he had disappeared through the door leading to the kitchens and servants quarters.

Just as Cam was about to remark on Chambers' intoxication, Gemma was sprinting toward the staircase.

"What are you doing?" Cam hissed, hurrying after her. "Get back here."

"You get up here," she said in a low voice, over her shoulder, as she hurried up the carpeted stairs. "If we don't get to Sir Everard's bedchamber before Fanshawe emerges with Chambers we'll lose our chance."

She meant, of course that she'd lose *her* chance to search the baronet's rooms. But by now he'd realized it was impossible to change Gemma's mind once she had decided a course of action. So, mindful that they didn't want to be caught out by the butler, Cam hurried to catch up with her.

Chapter 11

Though she would very much have liked to take a detour into Mr. Pearson's collections room, mindful of the reason for their presence in the house, Gemma let Cam lead her toward what had been Sir Everard's room during his stay at Pearson Close.

"I can't believe you've got me into this," he said under his breath as they hurried down the hall.

"You really are far more circumspect than your swash-buckling reputation had led me to believe," Gemma said, careful to keep her voice just above a whisper. "I would have thought a little housebreaking was child's play for an adventurer like yourself."

Cam snorted. Or was that a growl? It was so hard to tell when he was dragging her alongside him.

"Contrary to what you may have heard," he said, his harassed tone all too clear, "I am not a common thief, nor am I accustomed to circumventing the authorities."

She almost tripped when he stopped short before a door near the end of the corridor.

"This is Sir Everard's room?" she asked in a low voice.

When he didn't immediately respond, she realized how unnecessary her question had been.

"Sorry," she muttered. "Nervous."

Cam turned to look at her, and she was surprised when he gave her a rueful smile. "Me too," he said.

Then placing his ear against the door, to see if there was any movement within, he listened for a moment. Seemingly satisfied, he depressed the thumb latch and in one swift move, hustled them both through the open door.

The room was dim thanks to the gray skies outside and the lack of any indoor illumination. Cam found a candle near the door, lit it and gave it to Gemma. Then he moved with admirable stealth to the lamp on the writing desk and lit it as well.

With light it was easy to see that Sir Everard's valet was perhaps not the most adept at his chosen occupation. The floor was strewn with clothing and papers and all sorts of items that a gentleman of a certain social status would bring along on a week's long stay.

"Someone has been here before us," Cam said with a frown.

"Or Sir Everard was a very untidy person," Gemma offered, scanning the disarray. "Though I believe yours is the more accurate assessment. Even a valet with a penchant for drink would not dare leave his master's rooms like this."

"He might if he knew his master wasn't coming back," Cam said.

"We can discuss it later," she said. "Fanshawe has likely found him by now. I'll take the desk, you look through the papers on the floor."

Cam didn't argue, but knelt amongst the papers nearest the bed. Gemma moved to the desk and began scanning the documents strewn across the surface.

Most of what she found were scientific papers that had been disordered to such a point that it was impossible to tell which page went with which study without the kind of careful examination for which they had no time. So she just began stacking them in a tidy pile.

"Any luck?" Cam asked from the floor, not looking up from his own task.

"They're geological studies and scientific papers," she said as she worked, "but they're so disorganized it's impossible to tell which page goes with which study."

"We might have time to—"

The sound of voices in the hallway stopped him mid-sentence.

"Fiddlesticks," Gemma said crossly. "I hoped we'd have more time than this."

She finished pulling pages into a stack and clutched it to her chest.

Cam, likewise, got to his feet holding a similar sheaf.

"What do we do?" Gemma asked, looking with alarm at the door as the voices got closer.

It had been her idea to brazen their way into Sir Everard's bedchamber but her scheme hadn't got much farther than that.

Cam, however, was already at her side, pushing her into the adjoining dressing room.

They had just managed to shut the door when she heard the bedchamber door open and hit the wall.

"I might have known she was up to no good," she heard Fanshawe say in an aggrieved tone as she and Cam huddled together on the other side of the dressing room door. "But I hadn't thought Lord Cameron would be in on her scheme."

"All the ladies up at Beauchamp House are trouble," Squire Northman muttered in response.

Gemma let out a little huff of anger at that unfair bit of criticism, and Cam clapped a hand over her mouth. When she glared at him, he widened his eyes and put a finger to his lips. She got the message and indicated that he could remove his hand. Which he did, but not without another gesture for her to keep quiet.

Really it was too unfair that she had to remain quiet while her character was being unfairly maligned.

Unfortunately, this interchange was too late to keep the men on the other side of the door from hearing her initial outburst.

"Who's that?" Fanshawe demanded, causing Cam to swear silently.

Then, before she even knew what was happening, Gemma was propelled backward against the window and being thoroughly kissed. But though the kiss was breathtaking, she wasn't too overcome to notice Cam removing the stack of pages from her hands. Nor did she miss the way he fiddled with the window behind her. She felt a burst of freezing air on her back, then almost as quickly as it happened, it was gone.

Her attention was diverted again, however when Cam pressed the full length of his body against hers, and she was lost in the heat and strength of him. She slipped her arms up around his neck and slid her fingers through the silky hair at his nape.

For several moments she forgot where she was and was lost to the sensations his every touch sent coursing through her.

She was opening her mouth wider to welcome him in when the door to the dressing room burst open.

"Lord Cameron!"

Fanshawe's pronunciation of the name drew out every syllable in a very good impersonation of a scolding nanny.

Though she'd known their intrusion was coming, it still managed to make Gemma jump in surprise.

Cam, however, was unfazed. Not hurrying to move away from her, he pulled back and rubbed his nose against hers, before kissing her softly one last time.

Then he put his mouth at her ear and whispered, "Follow my lead."

Gemma was too bleary-eyed to argue and allowed him to pull away then bring her against his side.

"What is the meaning of this, Lord Cameron?" Fanshawe demanded. "I did you a courtesy by fetching Chambers, but I didn't intend to allow the lady above stairs. You know that Mr. Pearson does not hold with females of any sort in this house."

"Fanshawe, don't be such a prig," Cam said with a laconic drawl. "The lady is my betrothed and . . . well . . ."

Northman, who had been watching them through eyes narrowed with suspicion raised his brows. "She wasn't your betrothed when I visited Beauchamp House earlier this morning, Lord Cameron."

Cam's laugh was so utterly knowing and just-between-us-lads that Gemma wanted to pinch him. It was only thanks to their audience that she did not.

"You know how it is, old man," he said with a shrug. "A bit of danger goes a long way toward changing a lady's mind."

"That's all well and good, Lord Cameron," said the magistrate, "but what has that to do with your presence in Sir Everard's dressing room? Which just so happens to be connected to a dead man's disarrayed bedchamber?"

Gemma was having a very difficult time not answering the man's questions. Subterfuge was not her forte. But Cam was not a stupid man. He had some sort of endgame in mind for this and she had to let him follow his plan.

"They wished to speak with Sir Everard's valet," Fanshawe told him before Cam could answer. "But the fact that he's nowhere to be found, coupled with the untimely death of Sir Everard leads me to believe they knew all along he wasn't here and merely wished to divert my attention so they could pilfer through Sir Everard's things."

Cam laughed softly. "Do you hear that, dearest?" he asked Gemma. "They think we came here to steal from Sir Everard."

Gemma laughed, but it sounded hollow to her own ears.

Before she could say anything, however, Cam continued. "I hope you won't think too badly of me," he said to the other two men. "But I'm afraid, we came here for a far less nefarious reason."

"Well, we haven't got all day, man," said Northman with a scowl. "Spit it out."

Gemma felt Cam squeeze her hip, and she read it as a warning. What on earth was he going to say?

"Well, you know how it is, lads," he said sheepishly. "Beauchamp House is thick with chaperones. And it's dashed cold outside at the moment. So we thought of Sir Everard's rooms, which are unoccupied at the moment and . . ."

Gemma felt her face turn scarlet. Cameron was going to pay for this. She wasn't sure how yet. But she would make it something truly painful for him. And preferably involving bees. There would be no bees about until summer, of course, but didn't they say revenge was best served cold?

"And why, might I ask were your own rooms not adequate to your needs, Lord Cameron?" asked Northman, his mouth tight.

Not wanting to be seen as some passive party to this charade, Gemma jumped in before Cam could. If she were going to be painted as the sort of hussy who would accompany her betrothed to another house so that they could be amorous, she would dashed well make herself a participant with agency.

"It was my idea, Squire Northman," she said, snuggling closer to Cam. In a low voice, as if she were afraid of being overheard, she said, "I thought it might be more exciting."

To her satisfaction, Squire Northman, who was perhaps the most imperturbable man of her acquaintance, blushed to the roots of his sparse hair.

Beside her, Gemma felt Cam shake with laughter. Take that, she thought smugly.

"That is . . ." Northman, began, then fell into a coughing fit. When he had regained his voice, he continued, "I'll just ask you two to leave Pearson Close for the time being. Though I must ask you, for investigative purposes, was this room ransacked when you arrived?"

"Oh yes," Gemma said in a mournful tone. "I suspect poor Sir Everard's valet is to blame. If he's really run off as Mr. Fanshawe said."

They stood in an uncomfortable silence for a moment before Northman regained his composure and pulled himself up to his full height.

"Be off with you, then," he said sourly. "And do not speak of what you found here in this room to anyone else."

"And of course I must ask that you and Mr. Fanshawe keep our little secret, too, Squire," Gemma said with a bat of her eyelashes. "We are betrothed, but I shouldn't like my sister or her husband the vicar to learn of our little . . . adventure."

"Go, Miss Hastings," Northman said in a tone of desperation. "And Lord Cameron, I advise you to be more sensible when it comes to following the whims of your lady. She's going to get you both into a great deal of trouble."

Without pausing to reply, Cam slipped an arm around

Gemma's waist and escorted her to the door as quickly as they could go without running.

Before they reached the hall, Gemma thought she heard the Squire say, "Dear God, I do not envy Lord Cameron the chase she's likely to give him."

They were downstairs and bundled up in their outerwear in minutes.

It wasn't until they were settled back in the curricle that Cam finally spoke.

"More exciting?" he almost shouted. "Are you mad?"

Chapter 12

Cam wasn't sure whether he wanted to kiss Gemma or spank her.

"I'm not a child, Cam," she said with a roll of her eyes, which alerted him to the fact he'd spoken the thought aloud. "I do know what happens between men and women."

"But that isn't . . ." he searched for the right words. "That is to say, that sort of . . ."

Gemma sighed, and patted him on the hand. "I know this has upset your sense of propriety," she told him kindly, "but we had best not sit here in the drive of Pearson Close or Mr. Northman will suspect our reasons for being here weren't quite as carnal as I made them out to be."

Cam blinked. Then realized she was right.

But rather than turning toward the main road that led to Beauchamp House, he directed the horses in the other direction.

"Where are we going?" Gemma asked, looking far more suspicious than a woman who had just admitted to taking her betrothed to someone else's rooms because it stimulated her had a right to be.

"So now you don't trust me?" Cam asked with a raised brow.

"That was pretend and you know it," she said haughtily.

"It wasn't pretend when you put your tongue in my m—"

"Lord Cameron," she said in a not unconvincing impersonation of Fanshawe, "I was playing a part. Nothing more. Pray do not refer to it again."

He had a very good idea of just how much—or little—of a part she'd been playing, but they would save that argument for another time.

"I dropped the papers out the window," he said smugly. "When we were . . . you know."

She didn't remark on his inability to name what it was they'd been engaged in, for which he was thankful.

"Oh! I wondered what you were doing," she said with what sounded like awe. "That was a brilliant idea. I'm sorry for doubting you."

"Do not praise me yet," he said ruefully. "I dropped two sheaves of papers out of a third story window. The odds of them not having scattered all over the garden are very low."

"Do not be such a pessimist," Gemma chided him. "At least we have them."

"I am a realist," he responded as he brought the curricle to a halt on the path he'd seen tradesmen take to the kitchens at Pearson Close.

Cam tied the horses to a tree branch, then stepped around to grasp Gemma by the waist and lift her down from the vehicle.

He was grateful he'd instructed the grooms yesterday to give his matched pair a rest. He had no doubt that this pair of carriage horses they kept in Beauchamp House stables would be far more amenable to remaining tied up outdoors in this weather. The grays would have broken the reins or injured themselves at such an indignity.

Just as temperamental as the grays, but equally as valuable he'd come to realize, was the lady in his arms at the moment.

When she got her feet beneath her, he saw a spark of desire in her eyes, but then she'd shaken it off and pushed him away.

"Come on," she ordered, stomping forward over the shell-covered path.

"Yes, ma'am," he said in an undertone as he followed her.

It was just as well that she was keeping the focus, he reflected as he caught up to her.

He'd forgot for a time that their betrothal and everything that went with it was only temporary. It wouldn't do to mistake lust and friendship for anything more permanent.

Once he was walking beside her, he was careful to keep them to the edge of the wood so that they would be less visible from the house. But it was slow going thanks to the mud and ice. The hems of Gemma's garments were soon filthy, but she didn't complain once.

"Which window?" Gemma asked as they neared the path alongside the house.

Cam had calculated the location based on his view out his own window, and its proximity to Sir Everard's rooms. But it had been the papers contrasting with the dark green of the holly bushes growing beneath the windows that gave him the precise location. Fortunately the wind had been blowing toward the side of the house rather than crossways, so the pages were in a relatively tidy pile.

Unfortunately, aforementioned holly bushes were well over seven feet tall. A height neither of them could boast even on their toes.

"You'll have to boost me up," Gemma said frowning up at the top of the hedge. "Make a step with your hands. Like so."

She threaded her fingers together and proffered them in the way she wanted him to do it.

Cam shook his head. "That won't work."

"Why not?" she demanded. "I'll get the height I need."

"But you've got nothing to hold on to," he argued. "You'll have to climb onto my shoulders."

He said it with an air of apology.

"I certainly will not," Gemma said emphatically. "Not in this gown."

She glanced around them, as if looking for some alternative means of getting the papers.

"Gemma," Cam said in a soothing tone, "It's the only way. You need enough time to be able to gather them all and I certainly can't climb onto your back."

"But it's . . . it's . . . it's unseemly," she finally finished.

"Where is the lady who confessed to enjoying love-making more in the bedchambers of other people?" he asked wryly.

"That was different," she hissed. "That didn't entail you putting your head up my skirt."

"If you're doing it right it does," he said with a shrug.

"I hate you," she said hotly.

"I know you do," he said. "But it's the only way."

Even as he spoke, he knelt and held out his hand to help her climb up.

Gemma scowled. Then when he didn't relent, she gave a very unladylike curse.

"Do not look," she ordered. He did his best to obey, but it was impossible not to peek just a little.

From the corner of his eye he watched as she gathered

her skirts between her legs, then lifted them so high her garters were showing.

Her legs were long and slender, and he was forced to think about the mineral composition of his latest soil samples in order to suppress the image of those legs over his shoulders in a very different circumstance than the present one.

The frigid temperature did the rest.

"If you ever tell anyone about this I will murder you," Gemma said tightly as she climbed onto his shoulders. "With a rusty knife."

"You have my word," he said, reaching up to grasp her by first one stockinged leg, then the other.

Despite his attempts at distraction, it was impossible to ignore the fact that if he were to turn his head just a fraction he'd be able to kiss the soft skin of her inner thigh. He closed his eyes and counted to ten.

"Stand up," Gemma ordered, pulling on his hair. "It's cold."

He felt a shiver run through her and cursed himself.

Without reply, he stood to his full height and walked slowly so that she was close enough to the top of the neatly trimmed holly bushes.

"A little to the right," she instructed him, and Cam did as she asked.

"Here."

It took much less time than he'd have expected, probably because she was cold and when he offered to rub her legs to make them warmer she'd told him to go to the devil.

Finally, when she had them all, she handed the sheaf of papers down to him and ordered him to kneel so she could climb off. He wasn't even completely on his knee when she hopped off and dropped her skirts down and began smoothing them.

With an imperious hand she indicated that he should hand her the papers.

He did so, deciding that she had earned the right to order him about for a little while.

Without a word to him, she set off back toward where they'd tied up the curricle and horses.

"We will not speak of this again," she said firmly as he came up beside her.

"Was it so bad?" he asked. "It only took a quarter hour at most."

"You take off your breeches and climb up on someone else's shoulders in the freezing cold where anyone might happen upon you at any minute, and tell me how much it matters that it only lasted a quarter hour."

"You have a point," he said.

Then, he heard her sniff. And had that been a wobble in her voice?

She tried to hurry forward, but he stopped her with a hand on her arm.

"Gemma," he said gently, "are you all right?"

She didn't turn but he could see that her shoulders, normally proud and strong, were sagging.

"Cameron, my day has consisted of finding a dead body, discovering that the fossil I hoped would help me establish myself as a legitimate scholar missing, kissing my brother-in-law, being hurried into a betrothal with said brother-in-law, breaking into a dead man's bedchamber, pretending I enjoy lovemaking in other people's homes, and exposing my lower limbs in the outdoors in the freezing cold where anyone might see them. I am most assuredly not all right."

Her voice broke on that last, and Cam muttered a curse and lifted her into his arms.

She clutched the papers to her chest, but didn't protest

him carrying her because she was shivering too badly to speak.

"I'm an idiot," he said to himself. If she caught her death of a cold from this he'd never forgive himself.

The walk to the curricle was brief, thankfully, and when he climbed in after untethering the horses, he shrugged out of his greatcoat.

"What are you doing?" she demanded through chattering teeth. "It's freezing."

"For once in your life, do not argue." He wrapped the coat, still warm from his body, around her, and turned to rouse the horses.

"There's room enough for a family of four beneath this coat," she said after they'd gone a few hundred feet. "You must be cold too."

Realizing that she would very likely argue until he succumbed, he allowed her to drape the coat over his upper body, too. Before they were halfway back to Beauchamp House, she'd snuggled up against his side and fallen fast asleep.

Cam shook his head ruefully.

If he didn't watch it he was going to find himself married to her.

He was no longer entirely sure that would be a bad thing.

Chapter 13

Gemma came awake with an abrupt jolt when the curricle stopped.

She realized with a start that she was cuddled up against Cam's side like an ivy vine twining around an arbor. She pulled away, trying to be casual about it, but given that he was about two inches away it was doubtful he'd failed to notice.

"We're here," he said unnecessarily.

Fortunately William appeared at the side of the vehicle then, and she hastily scrambled to climb down with his assistance instead of Cam's.

But to her dismay he was there just as she gained her footing and offered her his arm.

When she hesitated, his lifted brow was all it took to spur her into accepting his escort.

"I've got the papers here," he said as they walked. "I thought perhaps we should wait until tomorrow to go over them. You need to get warmed up after . . ."

"After exposing my legs like a common strumpet?" she asked bitterly. She truly wanted to recover her fossil, but this afternoon's escapade had perhaps been too bold even for her.

"I didn't see anything," he said with a haste that told her he had in fact seen everything.

When they reached the door, it swung inward and George ushered them inside with a tutting noise. She must have looked more bedraggled than she realized, Gemma thought with an inward sigh.

"This mud will be the death of us, Miss Gemma," said the butler with a shake of his head. "I'll see to it that Tillie takes good care of this."

She looked down and realized that, indeed, her lovely persimmon velvet was thoroughly spattered. Which reminded her of something else.

"I know I've resisted it, but I suppose you'd best choose a ladies maid for me from among the staff, George," she said. "Or perhaps Serena won't mind sharing Tillie with me for a few days until one can be hired on? Either way, one of them should be able to salvage it."

To his credit, the butler's eyes only widened for a half-second before he nodded and said he would do so at once.

"Look at me nattering on about household business while you wait," she said, realizing that Cam had been standing silently behind her. "Let George take your things. I'm sure Maitland or Kerr have something you can change into while yours are cleaned."

But to her surprise—and disappointment, she realized—he shook his head.

"I won't be staying. You need some rest, and if I'm to reach the vicarage in time for supper, I should leave now."

Gemma frowned and turned to look at him. She'd been embarrassed by her behavior in the curricle, but somehow she'd thought he'd take his evening meal here.

"I wish to discuss the best course of action in our search for your fossil with Benedick," he said. "He's a bit of a nuisance as brothers go, but he's not entirely useless."

"You're frozen to the bone, he added. "Get warm and get some rest. I'll see you tomorrow."

This last he said with such gentleness she felt her chest squeeze.

Perhaps it was better if he left now. If she wasn't careful, she'd become so attached to him she wouldn't be able to break their engagement when the time came.

"Then I'll see you tomorrow," she said with what she hoped sounded like lofty unconcern. "We can go over Sir Everard's papers."

"Yes," he said with a nod.

They stood awkwardly for a moment. How did one take leave of the man who'd had a close up view of one's naked thighs, she wondered. That wasn't even accounting for the kissing.

To her shock, when she offered him her hand, Cam pulled her closer and kissed her on the mouth.

"You didn't see that, Stephens," he said to the butler.

"See what, my lord?"

"Until tomorrow," Cam said to Gemma.

And then he was gone.

She stood dumbfounded for a moment. When Stephens coughed slightly, she realized it had been longer than she'd realized.

"Send up a bath please, Stephens," she said over her shoulder as she hurried up the stairs. At least one reason for her shivers could be taken care of.

An hour later, Cam was seated in Benedick's study. Fortunately, they were of a size, so he'd been able to borrow a mud-free, dry set of clothes. He'd need to send for his things tomorrow. Any pretense of normalcy at Pearson Close had been lost with Sir Everard's murder and Cam would rather be here, close to Beauchamp House in case Gemma had need of him.

Good lord, he was a fool.

"Already regretting your actions of the day?" Benedick asked with one of his omniscient vicar looks. Cam knew there was no actual all-knowingness behind them, but it was an effective tool in his brother's repertoire of expressions that annoyed Cam.

"Not at all," he replied blithely, despite his very real misgivings. "We'll dissolve the betrothal a few months from now and all will be well. Gemma wishes to marry me as little as I wish to marry her."

"I can't imagine she's eager to give up ownership of Beauchamp House so soon after inheriting it," Benedick agreed. "Especially after she's been the one heiress to escape the parson's mousetrap over the course of the year. I can't say I blame her for being reluctant."

That was one aspect of the situation Cam hadn't considered.

"I know it's the law that her property would become mine, but I'm not a monster. I'm sure I could have my solicitor draw something up if it came to that," he said with a frown. "She knows I wouldn't do anything with her property without consulting her first."

"Does she?" Benedick wondered thoughtfully.

"Of course she does," Cam said with a vehemence he immediately regretted. So much for appearing calm and collected.

"Does she?" Ben asked again. "It's not difficult to believe she might not know that. You don't know one another that well, do you?"

Rather than protest that they knew one another quite well, in fact, Cam instead tried for nonchalance. He set one booted ankle on his knee and leaned back in his chair.

The picture of calm.

"It isn't important," he said. "We've agreed not to go through with it."

Why did the room, which earlier had seemed a comfortable temperature, despite the cold outdoors, seem blisteringly hot?

He resisted the urge to run a finger beneath his cravat.

"Hmmm." Benedick got up to stoke the fire and Cam had a tiny fantasy of leaping to his feet and throwing all the windows open. But he remained where he was.

"I thought the two of you were better suited than we'd realized," Ben said once he'd stood upright again. "But you know best, of course. I don't know where you'll find another woman who would be content with your collection of dead things and stones."

That surprised a laugh out of Cam. "But I know very well where I can find a wife who will not put up a fuss about anything. Much less my fossil collection. Gemma would no doubt object to everything but the fossils."

"Oh, and where is this magical place where uncomplaining wives are so readily available?" Ben asked, sitting on the edge of his desk. "For I must save up the name and tell everyone at Brooks' when next I'm in town."

"Come now, Ben," Cam said to his brother with a roll of his eyes. "You know as well as I do that young ladies willing to marry into a ducal family are thick on the ground in London during the season. I could likely find a half dozen willing to wed me in the course of one trip to Almack's."

"You seem to assume that these ladies have no minds

of their own," Ben said with a shake of his head. "I think you may be mistaken in that."

"And you seem to have become accustomed to having the sort of wife who doesn't know her place," Cam said. Even as he said the words he knew he was being rude.

But Ben had never been quick to anger. "If I were a different sort of man," he said dryly, "I'd call you out for that. Fortunately for you, I only inflict physical harm on one person per day. And it's too damned cold out to duel."

It was his brother's sangfroid that made Cam feel the worst. He deserved a thrashing.

"That was badly done of me," he admitted, dropping the pose of calm and leaning forward to set his brandy glass down. "I don't know what I want, Ben, and that's the honest truth."

"I know you're uneasy in your mind," his brother replied. He'd also never been the sort to say 'I told you so'. "But perhaps this time you spend together searching for Gemma's missing fossil will give you the answers you seek."

"It's proximity that I'm afraid of," Cam said, thrusting a hand through his hair. "I fear the more time we're together, the more opportunities I'll have to compromise her beyond the point where either of us can call off the match."

Perhaps not the best thing to tell the brother who was also a sort of guardian for the lady in question. But Cam had no one else to confide in. And as Ben knew Gemma better than he did, maybe he'd have some notion of what to do.

"What does your heart say?" Benedick asked.

Cam laughed bitterly. "I don't know that I have a heart. I've spent most of my adult life pleasing only myself and seeking to fulfill only my ambitions in the quest for the next discovery. I'd always thought finding a wife would be another extension of that."

"What do you feel when you're with her?"

Cam sighed. "Did you hear what I said? I don't feel anything."

"You must feel something or you'd not be so miserable."

He hated it when Ben was right.

"I feel something," Cam amended grudgingly. "Lust, affection, protectiveness perhaps." He thought back to that moment in the curricle when she'd slept, curled up next to him like an exhausted kitten. He'd wanted to carry her up to her bedchamber at Beauchamp House and tuck her in. Then climb in and sleep next to her.

On top of the counterpane.

He was clearly losing his mind.

"And you don't think you would feel any of those things for a wife?" Ben asked, unaware of the thoughts racing through his brother's mind.

"I don't want that sort of marriage, Ben," he said, his frustration at the situation and his happily married brother overtaking him. "I'm not cut out for that sort of thing. The rest of you can be blissful with your willful wives. But I don't want the sort of thing our parents have. It's nothing but a sham."

He hadn't meant to say that.

That day he'd seen his father leaving the house of a local widow had shattered his understanding of the Duke and Duchess of Pemberton's marriage. Of what a happy marriage looked like. They might seem happy on the surface, but the rot that lay beneath had spoiled all such facades for Cam. Ben might think his union with Sophia was destined to remain blissful, but Cam knew that it was an illusion at best.

Far from protesting Cam's confession, however, Benedick instead said, "You aren't seriously telling me you won't allow yourself to be happy because Papa had a mistress when we were young? Are you?"

Cam looked up at his brother and saw that he was indeed serious.

"You knew?"

Chapter 14

Gemma luxuriated in her deliciously hot bath for far longer than was sensible, and her fingers and toes were wrinkled by the time she climbed out and was bundled into a thick towel.

She was wearing a flannel nightdress and seated at the dressing table brushing out her hair, having sent Tillie away with instructions to bring her a tray in her room for dinner, when Serena knocked on the door.

"Is something amiss?" Gemma asked, turning away from the glass to better see her.

"I was about to ask you the same thing," Serena said with a tilt of her head. "I don't think you've asked for a tray in your room in all the time you've lived here."

Gemma let out the breath she'd been holding. She'd been afraid someone had sent word of what she and Cam had got up to at Pearson Close that afternoon.

"If you must know," she admitted, "I'm exhausted. What with finding Sir Everard's body, then questioning the others at the house party, and of course the cold on top of it all, I simply want to climb into my bed and sleep for days."

"It's funny you should say you were questioning people at Pearson Close," Serena said as she sat down on the bench at the foot of Gemma's canopied bed, "because I shouldn't think that would be a particularly muddy activity."

Gemma bit back a curse. Of course Tillie would tell Serena about the state of Gemma's gown. Though in her defense, it also could have been George.

Thinking to evade more questions, Gemma decided to confess to part of what had happened. "We liberated some of Sir Everard's papers from his bedchamber and we . . . may have dropped them out the window to avoid being caught taking them out the front door." This last she said in a rush, as if saying it faster would make it sound less scandalous.

Of course that wasn't possible with Serena, who was above all things proper, and would never expose her legs to a gentleman in the course of theft.

"Oh Gemma." The disappointment and exasperation in her chaperone's voice was enough to make Gemma want to scream.

"We needed the papers, Serena," she said with more vehemence than she'd intended. In a more moderate tone, she said, "I need them to find out where my fossil is. And to find out who killed Sir Everard."

"I was hoping you would listen to Mr. Northman's warnings to stay out of the investigation into Sir Everard's murder," Serena said with a sigh. "I do not know why my aunt was so intent upon giving you all quests that led you into danger. It was most inconsiderate of her."

"But she didn't arrange to have Sir Everard murdered," Gemma protested. "Indeed, I'm the only one of the four who hasn't been left some sort of puzzle to solve by Lady Celeste." This was something she'd only admitted to Cam before now. Somehow telling him made it easier to reveal her conclusions to Serena now.

"Of course she didn't," Serena said, her neatly coiffed reddish blond hair glowing like a penny in the candlelight.

Really, it was no wonder Cam thought of her as the perfect wife. She truly was.

"I fear, however, that the other ladies' adventures have made you take Sir Everard's death as some sort of puzzle for you to solve. Even though it's obvious my aunt died before she could concoct some kind of scheme for you."

It was the same conclusion Gemma had come to regarding herself and Lady Celeste. But it smarted to hear Serena say it.

"I don't think I'm trying to make something out of Sir Everard's death." She might agree that Lady Celeste hadn't left her something besides the house, but she was certainly not making more of Sir Everard's death than it deserved. "Whoever killed him stole my fossil. I cannot simply sit by and allow that thief to get away with my discovery."

Serena rubbed her temples. "Gemma, dear Gemma," she sighed. "Please, just let Mr. Northman do his job. He is the local magistrate. He is tasked with finding Sir Everard's killer. Not you."

"Why are you so against me searching for my fossil?" Gemma asked. It was unlike Serena to be so disagreeable. She'd not objected to Ivy and Daphne getting into dangerous situations. Nor Sophia, if it came to that.

Then, something dreadful crossed her mind.

"You're trying to keep me away from Cam," she said with burgeoning horror. "Are you . . . jealous?"

Of course. She was an idiot not to see it sooner. Serena had been far more upset that morning on finding them in the drawing room than Gemma had ever seen her in her capacity as a chaperone.

"What?" Serena looked gratifyingly shocked at the

idea. "No, you may rest easy on that point. I have no designs on Lord Cameron or any gentleman, for that matter. I do not intend to marry ever again."

That response was far more of a relief than Gemma was comfortable with, but she set that aside to pore over later.

"Then what is it?" she asked, trying and failing to come up with an alternative explanation. "Why are you trying to hold me back?"

"Have you looked at your neck in the glass?" Serena asked pointedly.

Alarmed, Gemma reached up to touch her neck. "No, why?"

"Perhaps you should, then we'll talk," her chaperone said with a frown.

Turning back around to examine herself in the glass, Gemma was all set to tell Serena she must be mad, when she saw it. A purple mark just below her left ear.

Unbidden, the memory of Cam's mouth on that precise spot while they'd "pretended" in Sir Everard's dressing room.

She turned back around and knew her cheeks were scarlet. "So?" She was trying for nonchalance, but knew her blushing ruined it.

Sighing, Serena stepped forward and knelt before her. "My dear girl, you are playing a dangerous game, and I fear that you're going to find yourself in a difficult situation when the time comes for you to end this betrothal."

"I'm not a child," Gemma protested. She did feel a bit out of her depth with Cam, but since they had agreed their—whatever it was they had together—would end soon, she wasn't overly worried about it. "I know what I'm about."

"Gemma," the widow said with an intensity that made

Gemma uncomfortable, "I know what it can be like to be married in haste to man with a temper."

She blinked. Was that what so bothered her?

"I know Cam can be passionate about things," she said with a frown, "but he's not really as angry as he seems."

"What about the day you met?" Serena asked, her blue eyes dark with concern. "He was shouting."

"So was I," Gemma said patiently. "In fact, I was shouting the loudest. Because he was being a dismissive lout."

"Precisely," Serena said. "Dismissive. He had to be pressed into asking for your hand. And then he did so only after he said something that made you rush away in tears."

It seemed like a million years since that morning when she'd run away to the workroom to scrub the floors. But suddenly she realized how that scene would look to someone from the outside. Someone who had endured the heartache of being married to a man with little kindness and a great deal of cruelty.

She hugged her chaperone, who had become like another sister over the course of the year. "I can assure you that what happened this morning was as much about me listening in on a conversation that wasn't meant for me as it was about Cam." She didn't tell her that it had been about her. That was a confession for another time—perhaps never.

"But he has such a temper, Gemma," said Serena as she pulled away. "I don't want you to find yourself in the same kind of situation I was in. I won't let you. I won't see you forced into a marriage, even if your sister and the vicar try to make you do it."

The notion of Sophia and Ben forcing her to do anything was laughable, but Gemma didn't let out the giggle that hovered at the back of her throat.

"I know you mean well, Serena," she said with a

smile, "but please trust me when I say that no one will force me to do anything I don't wish to do. And despite what you might think about Cam and me, we are no more likely to marry now than we were this morning when you discovered us kissing."

"You didn't get mud all over your gown simply by retrieving papers, Gemma."

Thinking of the trek through the back garden of Pearson Close, Gemma contradicted her. "I actually did. And you must know that one can get a mark on one's neck just as easily in a warm drawing room as rolling about in the mud."

At that Serena deflated a little. "I suppose that's right."

Taking pity on her, Gemma patted her on the shoulder. "I promise you that if worst comes to worst and I'm forced to marry Lord Cameron . . ." Even as she said it, she felt disloyal in some way. As if Cam would care that she'd described matrimony with him thus. He very likely thought of it in the same way. "If I'm forced to marry Lord Cameron," she continued, "I will not be in the same situation you found yourself in. I know you think he's a hotheaded rogue, but he's not nearly as much of a bear as he seems."

But the furrow between Serena's brows didn't disappear as Gemma had hoped.

"I'll trust you in this," she said with a worried nod. "But please know that you only need to say the word and I will see to it that you're taken away from him for as long as needed to keep you safe."

Knowing that the words were heartfelt, Gemma thanked her sincerely. "You've been a good friend to all of us," she told her and was surprised to feel the sting of tears in her eyes.

"I've enjoyed this year with you girls far more than I could have imagined," Serena said with a smile. "I'm so proud of all of you. Your bravery and boldness have given me hope that one day I will be able to carve out a place for Jem and me."

"I think you already have," Gemma said, somewhat puzzled by the other lady's words. To her mind, Serena was far more settled than she was.

"Not yet," the other lady said, rising from the floor. "But soon. Very soon, I think."

Benedick leaned back in his chair. "I suppose it makes some sort of sense. You always did put Papa on a pedestal. At least more than the rest of us did. Even Rhys, and he practically worshipped him when were children." He referred to their elder brother, the heir to the Pemberton dukedom.

"I thought I was the only one," Cam shook his head in amazement. "All this time and we never talked about it. Not once."

"We knew it would hurt you," Benedick said. "For all your bluster, you were always the one who fell hardest when you lost one of your heroes."

Cam considered it. He supposed he had been easy to disappoint in those days. Not like now, when he'd built up a protective armor around himself. "You said 'we'. Who else knew?"

"It was Freddie and Archer who first figured it out," Benedick said. "They were in the village to buy Christmas presents one year and saw Papa leaving Mrs. Gill's little cottage. It wasn't hard to put two and two together. They told me, of course." Ben had been the one the other boys had confided in, even in those days. "And Rhys overheard us. You were off gathering stones, if I recall correctly. And we all agreed we wouldn't spoil the holidays for you."

"This was the year Mama was ill. wasn't it?"

Part of what had so pained Cam about his father's betrayal was that his mother had spent much of the year suffering from some mysterious ailment that he'd never really understood.

"You mean the year she miscarried," Benedick said. "They were always very careful not to tell us what was actually wrong. But I'd seen her increasing enough times at that point to know what it looked like."

Cam took in this news. "Miscarriage. Of course."

"It was one of those unspoken things that men, especially sons, didn't discuss," Benedick said. "Certainly Papa didn't tell us about it. He made some vague noises about lady problems. And then he never mentioned it again."

"Knowing this makes Papa's actions all that much worse," Cam said darkly. "That he was straying while she was ill."

He knew that it was common among members of the ton, both husbands and wives, to take lovers. But his parents' devotion to one another had been something he saw as a mark of their goodness. He'd been sixteen that year and his time at school had by that time exposed him to the unhappy home lives of his peers. Learning that his own parents were just as unfaithful as the rest of them had torn away his last veil of innocence. About his own family and the world in general.

"You're still thinking about it as your sixteen-year-old self," Benedick said gently. "Perhaps you should consider something else."

"I don't follow." Cam pinched the bridge of his nose. Maybe he should have saved this discussion for another day. This one had already been filled with more than enough excitement.

"Mama was ill from a miscarriage," Benedick said patiently. "Papa wanted to save her from illness."

The last stone in the wall fell into place. "Oh."

"One doesn't really wish to consider the fact that one's parents have ever . . ."

To Cam's relief his brother didn't name the activity that he never ever wished to have associated with his parents.

But the explanation made sense. One of the things that had so crushed him about his father's infidelity was the fact that he had—hypocritically, Cam thought—seemed as devoted a husband as ever.

"There are not very many alternatives when a lady's health can be endangered by another babe," his brother said. "There are ways to prevent it, of course, but I doubt either one of them knew much about—"

The idea of his parents discussing French letters or vinegar-soaked sponges was too much for Cam to take.

"No need to go into detail," he said raising a hand against Benedick's words. "I understand your meaning."

"So, you also understand that the situation was far more complicated than any of us could have guessed at the time." It wasn't a question.

Cam nodded. "I suppose so."

"Marriage is complicated," Benedick said with the air of a man who had learned so the hard way. "There are negotiations and intimacies that a few hours of pleasure with a mistress can't prepare you for."

"So you would take a mistress if for some reason Sophia was unable to endure your attentions?"

"We aren't speaking of Sophia and me," his brother said with a frown. "But we are speaking of Mama and Papa. And they did what they thought best in their own marriage. It's not for us to judge what decisions they made. Especially given that they took pains to ensure that we didn't know anything was amiss."

If their father had been seen by three of his sons leaving his mistress's house the pains hadn't been all that great, Cam thought. But he took his brother's point.

"I suppose I was too quick to judge," he admitted. He tried to imagine himself in his father's position—and of course it was Gemma he thought of as his wife. Would he be able to go to another woman when he was married to another? If it meant keeping Gemma alive, he knew he would do whatever it took. Though a part of him wondered why his father simply hadn't been abstinent altogether.

"I don't mean to say that Papa was a saint," Benedick said. "But nor was he a monster."

Suddenly Cam was exhausted.

"I hope you don't mind if I stay here tonight," he said. He hadn't yet bothered to ask, and he wanted nothing more than to sleep now.

"I would have insisted if you didn't ask," Benedick said with a smile. "You're always welcome in my home, brother. Even when you're behaving like a fool."

Rising to his feet, Cam stretched his shoulders and remembered the weight of Gemma on them. If Ben only knew what foolish things he'd got up to today.

But he only said, "I fear that's the only way I behave these days."

Rising from his own chair, Benedick clapped him on the shoulder. "Welcome to the club, old man."

Thus it was, that for the second time in the space of as many days, Cam found himself—though the surroundings were different—unable to sleep thanks to one Miss Gemma Hastings.

And not, to his great disappointment, for reasons having to do with the kind of pleasurable activity to which he would rather attribute his insomnia.

Benedick's revelations about the actual reason for the rift he'd seen in his parents' marriage had made him reevaluate everything he thought he knew about the nature of marriage itself and his own ability to embark upon the sort of relationship he saw between his brothers and their wives.

It was undeniable now that the connection he felt for Gemma, however unexpected, was more than simple lust—though there was an element of that, as well. But he felt an impulse where she was concerned, one he'd never had with any woman before, to protect her. Not just from the blackguard who'd threatened her. But from any number of things—small and large.

He'd found himself more worried than was reasonable at how chilled she'd become during their clandestine document-gathering outside Pearson Close. It had taken every bit of self-control he had to stop from taking George aside to ensure that her bath was hot enough and was sent up to her sooner rather than later. Not out of a need to control her, but simply because he wanted to ensure that she didn't take ill.

Cam could count on the fingers of one hand when he'd felt more than a superficial concern for the health of anyone outside his immediate family.

Was that love? He regretted that he'd not thought to ask Benedick when they'd spoken earlier. But he hadn't failed to notice that his brother seemed to pay attention to his wife's comfort—from ensuring he brought her fresh flowers on occasion, to building up the fire when she entered a room because he knew she was cold-natured. Cam hadn't been around Gemma enough to learn her preferences for such things. But he had little trouble believing that a bit more time in her company would have him performing similar tasks.

Ben didn't know it, but his revelation that their father

had strayed not because he didn't love their mother, but because he did, had changed everything.

There was no way to know the exact circumstances, but he had little trouble at all imagining the duke taking a mistress at the duchess's behest. Indeed, it made far more sense than the idea that Pemberton, who was besotted with his wife, would have ever done such a thing on his own.

It had been immature on his part to believe it was his father's infidelity that had seemed to so distress his mother, but Cam realized now that his understanding of the world—and everyone's, he supposed—was comprised of experiences and feelings beginning in childhood. It had taken hearing about the scene he'd witnessed in a different context to show him the effect his incorrect assumption had had on his views of marriage.

What, he wondered, would Gemma think of his change of attitude? She still believed their betrothal was a temporary thing that could easily be set aside once enough time had passed. Then, there was her belief that she needed to remain unwed in order to prove to the world, and perhaps to herself, that she took geology and fossil-collecting seriously.

That might prove to be a more difficult task than upending his misunderstandings about marriage, he thought grimly, lifting his forearm to cover his eyes.

He took a moment to question whether he was up to the task, Then realized with a laugh, that he had no choice. Gemma might not think their betrothal was real, but he was quickly coming to recognize that there was no other woman he wanted to wed.

And that, he reflected, was the real consequence of what he'd learned from Benedick. Not that he could contemplate marriage.

But that he could contemplate—and desire—marriage to her.

He'd simply have to prove to her that marriage between them wouldn't mean she'd have to give up her passion for fossils.

He wondered suddenly how the Duke of Maitland managed it. The Duchess was also one of the heiresses, and from everything Cam had heard was a brilliant mathematician and had not, as far as he knew, abandoned her field of study. Perhaps he should have a word with the duke and see if he had any suggestions.

If nothing else, he could speak to someone other than his brother—who could be a bit insufferably smug at times about the happiness of his marriage.

The matter settled, at least for now, he forced himself to empty his mind and sleep.

Chapter 15

Despite yesterday's excitement, Gemma awoke the next morning with a renewed desire to find her stolen fossil. She was also determined, no matter what happened, not to let herself get caught up in whatever it was that lay between her and Cam. She would keep her hands to herself, and if he tried to touch her, she would politely, but firmly, tell him she wanted no part of his seduction. At least until she found her fossil.

There would be time enough for carnality later. Thus it was that when Lord Cameron entered the library some two hours after she had risen and dressed and breakfasted, she greeted his bow with a polite but distant nod. That he too seemed to be a bit reticent should have pleased her, but instead made her chest tight.

It was all well and good to be the one doing the resisting, but not quite as pleasant to be resisted.

Still, she would try to be grateful for the lack of temptation. Though honestly, he had only to be himself to tempt her. She knew all too well now how soft his wind-swept dark curls were beneath her fingers, and just how enticing the scent of sandalwood and male skin was when he held her close.

"I see you have already started without me," Cam said, apparently oblivious to her Cam-inspired fever dream.

He gestured to the pages strewn across the wide oak library table. "Have you had any luck?"

Resuming her seat, and indicating that he should take one as well, she waited before responding. When he chose the chair next to hers rather than the one across the table, she sighed inwardly but outwardly ignored it.

"I've only been trying to put the different studies in order," she said, indicating the seven piles she'd formed thus far. "So far sorted out these individual essays, but without any sort of numbering it's been slow going."

He was once again dressed in country breeches and boots and looked far too well rested for someone who had endured the same day as she had yesterday. It had taken three cups of tea to truly awaken her and even that hadn't completely erased the circles beneath her eyes.

"I suppose we have whoever ransacked Sir Everard's rooms to thank for that," Cam said with a frown. "But you've made good progress."

Gemma shrugged at the compliment. It was hardly higher maths.

"I don't quite understand why he would travel with all of these scientific papers in his bag," she said aloud, trying to ignore the warmth of him sitting beside her. "Is that customary? And some of the papers are duplicates in differing hands."

"I don't know that it's all that strange," Cam said, lifting one stack to flip through the pages. "If he were planning to show them to one of the other men at the house party, for instance, it would make sense."

"But why the different hands?" she asked. "This essay for instance. It's word for word the same study. And both scripts are perfectly legible so it isn't as if he was recopying poor penmanship to be read more easily."

Cam frowned. "Let me see that." Wordlessly she handed the duplicate essays to him.

Silently, he scanned first one set of pages, then the other.

"There's something about this turn of phrase here," he said, pointing to a passage about the soil around a quarry in Northumbria.

"What about it?" she asked.

"I'm not sure," he said, thoughtful. "It seems familiar somehow."

"Maybe you've read it in a different one of Sir Everard's papers," she said. Then, with a speaking look, added, "When you published one of them in your scientific journal."

"Ha-ha," he said with a fake smile. Then, turning serious, he said, "For your information, I've never published him. But the quality of this is far better than the pieces he submitted and were rejected."

"Writers do improve," she said wryly. "Maybe he listened to your critique, or had someone else assist him."

At that he laughed in earnest. "Can you honestly imagine Sir Everard listening to anyone's suggestions for improvement?"

Gemma thought about the man she'd met a few days earlier. "No. Not remotely."

"I wish I could recall where I'd seen that phrasing," he said again. "I can't help but feel it will solve part of this particular puzzle."

"Let's put it aside for the moment," she said, taking the pages from him and placing them back where they'd been plucked from.

He nodded, though it was obvious that he was still troubled by his inability to recall where he'd seen the words.

By agreement, they split the rest of the disordered pages and began sorting them into their own individual stacks.

They worked in silence for nearly half an hour before there was a knock on the door.

Looking up, Gemma saw Serena in the doorway.

Was that relief in her eyes at finding them working rather than in one another's arms? Thinking back to their discussion the night before, Gemma realized it was. She'd confided her plans to keep from becoming further entangled with Cam this morning at breakfast, but clearly she hadn't been all that convincing.

Before she could say anything, however, Serena ushered in Lord Paley.

Gemma exchanged a look of alarm with Cam. They were elbow deep in stolen papers and it was quite possible Paley was in a position to recognize Sir Everard's writing.

She made as if to gather them up into one stack, but Cam shook his head slightly. Attempting to tamp down her nerves, she dropped her hands back down onto the table and tried to look innocent.

"Look who's come to call, Gemma," Serena said, entirely unaware of the distress signals her charge was sending with her eyes. "Wasn't it kind of Lord Paley to call to ascertain your well-being after yesterday's contretemps?"

In truth, yesterday had been such a disaster that Gemma had trouble guessing which of her embarrassments Serena could be referring to..

Then, she recalled that Lord Paley would only have known about the death of Sir Everard and her discovery of his body, and was somewhat relieved.

"Indeed," she said with what she hoped was a welcoming smile despite her nerves over the papers, "very kind."

Stepping forward, Lord Paley offered her a posy of violets. "I see I'm not your first visitor, however, Miss Hastings." His gaze flickered over to Cam, and she was surprised to read enmity there. Were not the two men friendly, then? It could hardly be jealousy. She barely knew the man.

Taking the flowers from him, she buried her nose in them to stall for time. "These are lovely. Thank you so much."

He must have found a shop that bought from a hothouse, Gemma thought. Which meant the man—or his valet more likely—had gone to a deal of trouble to secure these.

"Paley," said Cam, coming to stand beside her. He didn't touch her, or in any overt way indicate that they were anything more than what they seemed. Sister and brother-in-law. Or friends.

And yet, she felt the ownership he projected around her as clearly as if he'd marked a circle around her like a wolf in the wild.

Far from backing down, however, Lord Paley simply bowed. "Lord Cameron. I see that your familial concern has brought you here this morning as well. How admirable of you to look in on Miss Hastings."

"Not so familial as all that," Cam returned with a smile that showed far too many teeth.

Serena looked alarmed, and Gemma felt her worry about the newcomer finding the stolen papers was eclipsed by annoyance at both men.

"Perhaps we should call for some tea," Serena said with forced brightness, moving to the bellpull.

Resigned, Gemma raised her arm to indicate the quartet of chairs before the fire. "Why don't we have a seat.?"

She felt Cam following close behind her. So close she had to resist the urge to stop short just to make him bump into her.

Men were such absurd creatures, she thought in disgust.

Though on the bright side, she would have little difficulty resisting Cam in his present mood, which must be
counted as a positive.

"I heard about what happened with Sir Everard yesterday, Miss Hastings," said Lord Paley, taking Gemma's
hand as they came to a stop before the fire. "What a hor-
rific scene for you to come upon. I hope you are not too
overset."

"A dreadful business," she agreed stiffly, taking her
hand back and indicating that he should be seated. "I hope
we'll find out soon who is responsible for poor Sir Everard's murder."

She took one of the chairs, while Lord Paley sat opposite her. Cam meanwhile moved a third chair closer to
Gemma's.

When she turned to look at him with a frown, he ignored her and leaned back, stretching his long legs out before him like a king getting comfortable on his throne.

"Indeed," said Lord Paley said, perching on the edge
of his own chair so that he was only inches from Gemma.
His expression was troubled and she could tell that he
was genuinely upset. "I knew Sir Everard was frustrated
by the way we insisted he leave the fossil to return to the
next day, but I had no notion he'd come back in the dead
of night. It was a risk, both because of the inclement
weather and the mud, but also, as he learned to his detri-
ment, because of thieves."

"None of us could have foreseen what happened,"
Gemma said firmly. "Only the man who murdered him
knows why it happened."

"But Lord Cameron and I did ride back to Pearson
Close with him," the viscount continued, his mouth
twisted with dismay. "I wanted to assure you that he said
nothing in my presence about retur—"

Cam cut him off. "Nor in mine, Paley," he said with a scowl. "Of course if he had I would have told Miss Hastings at once."

Clearly reading the tension between the two men, Serena intervened from where she stood near the fire. "Of course, neither of you knew of Sir Everard's plans," she said smoothly. "I assure you, Lord Paley, we know who our friends are. And you may rest easy that none of us suspects you had any knowledge of Sir Everard's scheme."

The thought had crossed Gemma's mind, but she was hardly going to contradict Serena now. Especially not with Cam and Lord Paley at daggers drawn.

"Well, that is a relief, Lady Serena," Paley said emphatically. "I couldn't bear it if either of you suspected me of being in cahoots with a man like Sir Everard."

The footman came to the door then and Serena stepped aside to speak to him about the tea.

"It's interesting you should come in person to reassure Miss Hastings," Cam said once the chaperone was gone. "I should think a note would have sufficed."

"And I find it intriguing that you spend so much time in this house given that your brother lives only a few miles down the road and you are ostensibly still a guest at Pearson Close." Lord Paley didn't look away from Cam's steady gaze. "You didn't come back to Pearson Close last evening, did you?"

"Are you my keeper, sir, that you pay such close attention to my comings and goings?" Cam asked, with a tilt of his head.

"No," Paley said through clenched teeth, "but I do pay attention when a gentleman is careless with a lady's reputation. Especially when they are newly betrothed and he leads her into indiscretion in someone else's home."

Gemma's eyes widened. "What do you mean?" she

demanded. But she had a sinking suspicion she knew exactly what he meant.

When he turned to her, Lord Paley's gaze softened. "I do not wish to cause you alarm, Miss Hastings. On the contrary. But I, unfortunately, occupy the room next to Sir Everard's at Pearson Close and couldn't help but overhear some of what . . ."

Cam rose to his feet. "If you were a gentleman you would stop speaking right this moment."

"If you were a gentleman you would not expose your lady to such scandal," Lord Paley shot back, leaping to his feet, his fists clenched.

"You were goading me on purpose," Cam said bitterly. "You knew all along about our betrothal."

"I wanted to see if it was truth or a fiction you made up on the spot to excuse your bad behavior." Lord Paley's words were as sharp as cut glass.

"I'll show you bad behavior," Cam said, stepping forward with menace.

"No," Gemma hurrying to push between them. "Lord Paley, I appreciate the sentiment, however, I—"

"Stay out of this, Gemma," Cam said in a low voice without taking his eyes off Paley. "This is not your concern."

"Of course it's my concern, you nodcock," she said in a sharp tone. "Who do you imagine you're arguing about?"

If she'd expected Lord Paley to see more sense than Cam, however, she was very much mistaken.

"Miss Hastings, he's right," he said in an apologetic tone. "You have already suffered enough indignity and—"

"What is going on?" demanded Serena in a surprisingly authoritative tone.

As Gemma watched, her chaperone came rushing forward and, in a manner only the mother of a small boy could manage, ordered, "Gentlemen, I must insist that you both sit back down and stop this nonsense this instant."

When they didn't, Serena stepped over to where they stood nose to nose and tried to push in between them. When that didn't work, she turned to Gemma. "Go get George and William and tell them that we'll need them to bring the ash buckets."

Without waiting to ask why, Gemma began to hurry to the door.

She was almost there when she heard Cam. "Stop, Gemma. You won't need them."

Turning back, she saw that the two men had stepped back from one another and had relaxed their militant poses.

"I apologize, Lady Serena," said Paley, looking sheepish. "That was unforgivable of me. I should have discussed this matter with Lord Cameron somewhere else. Away from where we would disturb you two ladies."

Gemma put her hands on her hips. "So that you could fight over my honor without my involvement at all, you mean? I hardly think that's an improvement, my lord."

Lord Paley blinked at her vehement tone.

"Yes," she told him with a sour look. "Contrary to what men believe, ladies do not wish to be fought over like a bone between curs. And this lady most certainly does not wish it when the so-called scandal was of her own making."

"There's no need to—"

But before Cam could finish, she cut him off. "And you, sir. I don't know what makes you think that I am your personal responsibility, but you are not my blood relation and our connection is tenuous at best. Pray do not involve yourself in feuds with other men on my behalf. I am perfectly capable of taking care of myself, or if I wish it I will ask my sister's husband to intervene for me."

When he opened his mouth as if to respond, she held up a staying hand. Turning to Serena, she said, "I will go see what's become of the tea tray. While I am gone, I would ask that you see to it that these two cloth-heads reach some kind of peace. Otherwise I am perfectly happy for both of them to take themselves off."

With that, she stepped into the hallway and slid the pocket doors closed behind her.

Chapter 16

The only sound in the library after Gemma's departure was the popping of the fire.

Cam watched as Serena looked from him to Paley, then back again.

"Well, gentlemen," she said with a regal nod, "I'm going to see if Gemma needs my help."

And without bothering to give them any parting wisdom, she left the room, sliding the doors shut behind her.

When Cam looked up it was to find that Paley still stood with his feet braced apart, as if expecting to ward off a blow.

"Oh stand down, man." Cam strode to where the brandy was kept and poured two generous glasses. "It would cost more than my life is worth if I challenged you. I have little doubt Gemma would follow us onto the field and shoot both of us and leave without a backward glance. And we'd deserve it."

But Paley was still skeptical. "What's your claim on her? She doesn't seem particularly ready to claim you."

"It's complicated," Cam told the other man, handing him a glass. "I still have some persuading to do."

"An understatement, surely," Paley took one of the

fireside chairs and didn't seem particularly interested in leaving, much to Cam's dismay. "And it doesn't seem as if Miss Hastings is one who does anything not of her own volition."

That was certainly correct, Cam thought. But aloud he said, "In time, I believe we'll come to an understanding."

"Then why not let me take a run at her?" the viscount asked blandly.

"She is not a fence to be jumped, Paley." He was offended on Gemma's behalf. "We are betrothed. Let that put an end to your meddling."

"I suppose that will have to do," Lord Paley said thoughtfully. "But if anything should happen . . ."

"It won't," Cam ground out. He took the seat opposite and the two men sat in tense silence for a moment, sipping their brandy and thinking.

"I couldn't help but notice when I came in that you were looking at papers," Paley said. "I don't suppose those are Sir Everard's?"

Since Paley had admitted to knowing they'd been in the baronet's rooms, it wasn't too great a logical leap.

"Yes," Cam said. He wasn't going to volunteer information unless absolutely necessary—especially since they had no idea who had killed Sir Everard and stolen the fossil.

When Cam didn't say anything else, Paley made a noise of frustration. "I'm not your enemy. I ask because Sir Everard stole something from me and I wish to know if you might have found it."

At the mention of theft, Cam went on alert, though he was careful not to show it. "We only took papers," he said casually. "No objects or fossils or the like."

"It's papers I'm looking for," Paley said with a scowl. "Sir Everard stole several papers from my home and I have reason to believe he brought them with him to Sussex in order to give them to Roderick Templeton."

Templeton was one of the men at Pearson's house party and published one of the newer, more influential scientific magazines.

"What makes you think Sir Everard brought them?" Cam asked. Though Paley's stolen papers could explain why the documents from Sir Everard's room were in two different hands. It was possible, of course, that Sir Everard had hired an amanuensis to copy them out. But there was usually some mark from the scribe on the pages they wrote, and he and Gemma hadn't yet found any.

"As soon as the pages went missing I sent correspondence to the editors of all the major journals inquiring whether they'd received any proposals on these particular topics," Paley explained. "Templeton sent word a month ago that he'd received an offer of one such paper from Sir Everard. We arranged for Templeton to tell Sir Everard to meet him at Pearson Close with the paper."

"That's quite the supposition," Cam said thoughtfully. "Why would you imagine someone had stolen them? Perhaps you merely misplaced them?"

"Because my home was burgled," Paley said with a scowl. "That's when I noticed the pages were missing. And only someone with an interest in geology and fossils would have found them at all interesting. The papers were only valuable insofar as they could be published."

"What were the titles?" Cam asked, curious despite himself.

"One was called 'Thoughts on a Pebble from the Sandstone of the Tilgate Forest in Sussex'," Paley said.

It was a mouthful. Which was precisely what Cam had thought when he'd seen it at the top of one of the pages currently in a tidy stack on the library table.

"Would you be willing to write out something to prove the piece is in your hand?" he asked without confirming they had the essay.

The other man put his brandy down on a side table and sat up. "You've found it." It wasn't a question.

"There is one such paper amongst the items we found," Cam admitted. "But if you have someone else copy out your pages then I'm afraid I won't be able to give it to you without some corroboration from Templeton."

Paley laughed. "Oh, I write them out myself. Because I didn't trust anyone else with the task." He shook his head in disgust. "I was focused on the wrong thief, obviously."

There was a pot of ink, pen and foolscap on one of the other library tables and Cam watched as Paley wrote out the full title of the article he claimed he'd composed.

When he was finished, he sanded the page and handed it to Cam.

"Well?" Paley asked as Cam looked at the title page they'd found among Sir Everard's papers and compared it to the new version.

"I'm no expert, but I'd say these were written by the same person."

His relief evident, Paley crossed to where Cam was standing at the wide table with Sir Everard's documents on it. "May I?"

Cam indicated that he was welcome to study them, and took a moment to think.

It was not all that much of a surprise, given Sir Everard's attempt to steal Gemma's fossil, that he would have also stolen Lord Paley's intellectual work to publish as his own. He'd often found that once a man began to practice deception, it became a way of life.

But one thing puzzled him. "Surely Sir Everard didn't break into your home himself? He didn't strike me as the sort of fellow who could move about a house in the middle of the night on cat-feet."

Looking up from his study of the documents, Paley said with a scowl, "He hired a man to serve as my footman. I'd noticed some older pieces in my collection had disappeared a few months earlier. I thought I'd misplaced them until I caught the fellow at it. I made an inventory of my entire collection, and my papers, and discovered the Pebble write-up was missing."

"The footman told you who'd hired him?"

Paley shook his head. "He didn't know, but most of the major collectors in England are known to me, and it was hardly a leap to think it was one of them. Then I hit on the idea of writing to the editors."

"I'm the editor of a prominent natural science magazine," Cam challenged.

The other man shrugged. "To be honest, I didn't think you'd respond. You're well known for ignoring the magazine in favor of traveling to find fossils. I didn't want my suspicions in the hands of some underling who would gossip about it."

It was on the tip of Cam's tongue to argue that his personal secretary, who was in fact the one who did the most work on the magazine, would never gossip about such a thing. But then he realized how damning the other man's assessment was.

"I like to be there to find my own fossils," he said, hearing the defensiveness in his voice but unable to stop it.

"Which is admirable," Paley said with a raised brow. "But you must then accept that you will not be the best person to respond to letters like mine."

There was more he could say on the subject, but Cam chose instead to change it altogether.

"It's there, then?" He indicated the table of documents.

"It is," Paley said with a smile. "He was able to take some that I'd written years ago and decided not to publish, as well. The man was a fraud, pure and simple. I have little doubt that the rest of the publications credited to him are also someone else's."

"Why go to the trouble, though?" Cam asked. "If he wasn't interested in the work, why bother with it at all?"

"I don't know," Paley said. "It's hard to know what motivates others without knowing them quite well. And I certainly didn't claim friendship with the fellow. Though we did meet a few times over the years."

The doors of the library opened then and Serena and Gemma stepped inside followed by a housemaid carrying a large tea tray.

"Lovely," Gemma said with an approving nod as she looked them over—presumably to ensure that neither was injured. "It appears that you have worked out some sort of compromise."

Then as she realized that Paley had some of the documents in his hand, her eyes flew to Cam's.

"A compromise indeed," he said. "And some clarification on the extent of Sir Everard's crimes."

"You can tell us all about it over tea," Serena said in the voice she normally reserved for her son Jeremy.

Knowing to obey orders when he heard them, Cam moved to the seating area, Paley close behind him.

Though she'd left the two men together insisting they come to a compromise, Gemma had not, in fact, been at all sure one was possible. Especially once Serena reached her side in the kitchens.

"I hope they don't actually come to blows," the widow said with a troubled look.

"I'm sure they won't," Gemma assured her with a confidence she didn't feel. "If for no other reason than they both know I will be extremely put out if they do. And for the moment at least, they both are intent on pleasing me."

"Never say you are enjoying the fact that they're fighting over you." Serena only looked as if she were partly joking.

"No. Of course not." Gemma wasn't that far gone, at least. "But if their foolish rivalry keeps them from coming to fisticuffs then I am all for it."

"And what will you do when they expect that you'll choose one of them at some point?"

"Are you not the one who only last evening tried to convince me to break things off with Cam because of his temper?"

"That was before I realized he holds you in genuine affection," Serena said. "He was serious about fighting for you, Gemma. I think he really does l—"

Gemma put a finger over Serena's lips before she could finish. "Do not say it. I am already too close to abandoning all of my plans and deciding to take this betrothal seriously. I need no more encouragement. Especially not with the idea that he is thinking the same thing. One of us must be strong, And if Cam cannot be trusted to be the strong one, then it will have to be me."

"But if you lo—"

"Shhh." Gemma stamped her foot. "Do not say it. Please, Serena."

Her chaperone looked at her in amusement. "All right. I won't say it. But that isn't enough to make it untrue."

For the time being, Gemma thought firmly, it would have to be.

"Let's go tell cook to get the tea ready," she said, deciding a change of subject was necessary.

Some thirty minutes later, they were both seated in the

library again, enjoying the sandwiches and cakes cook had included along with a steaming pot of fragrant tea.

And to Gemma's relief, the men had settled their differences.

"It's wrong to speak ill of the dead, Miss Hastings," said Lord Paley apologetically, "but I fear you weren't the only one Sir Everard stole from."

Quickly, Lord Paley explained what he knew about Sir Everard's scheme to steal artifacts and papers from other collectors.

"At least, I'm sure he tried to," Paley assured them. "I spoke with a few of the others at Pearson Close last evening and they all reported having missed items from their own collections in the past year. No one had lost important papers, but they all intend to search their documents when Mr. Northman allows them to go home."

"It's extraordinary," Gemma said. "How can one person so utterly fool a group of collectors and scholars into trusting him? And not only that, but holding him up as some sort of model of wisdom? It would be laughable if it weren't so utterly deplorable."

"I suppose we're all too trusting," Cam said, taking a bite of cake. When he was finished, he continued. "We take men at their word and don't question them."

"Especially men," Gemma said scowling. It was really too frustrating to see how easily Sir Everard had fooled the major players in the world of fossil collecting. She had little doubt if Sir Everard had been Lady Evelina, there would have been a very different outcome.

"You aren't wrong," Cam said with a note of apology. "I daresay he'd not got as far as he did without the inherent trust of other men."

Gemma was taken aback. "Do you really believe that now?"

"I do," said Cam. "And you've opened my eyes to the uphill climb that ladies must face in the scholarly world."

She looked at him through narrowed eyes. Was he serious? she wondered. Or was this another way to score points over Lord Paley? He looked sincere enough, however, and she felt her heart melt a little.

"Thank you," she said, trying and failing to keep the admiration from her voice.

Lord Paley clearing his throat alerted her to the fact that she and Cam had been staring moonily at one another for several long seconds.

Dash it.

"Well, I mean to say," she said hastily, "that is most interesting, Lord Cameron."

"I see now I was mistaken earlier," Lord Paley said wryly.

Gemma frowned, not knowing what he meant. But before she could speak up, he was speaking.

"There is something else I thought you should know," he said. "In fact, it was my primary reason for coming here today, but we got a bit distracted."

Distracted. What everyone called almost getting into a duel these days, Gemma thought with an inward sigh.

"The evening before Sir Everard was killed," the viscount said, "after we'd returned from our tour of the collection here at Beauchamp House, and his false discovery of your fossil on the shore, Miss Hastings, he confided to a few of us that he was quite convinced that the skull was part of the Beauchamp Lizard."

He turned to Cam. "I believe you'd already gone to bed, Lord Cameron."

"What is the Beauchamp Lizard?" Gemma said, not waiting for Cam to comment.

To her surprise, Lord Paley looked at Cam.

Cam, whose jaw was set and whose cheekbones were tinged with red.

"What is the Beauchamp Lizard?" she repeated, beginning to feel a bubble of anger welling in her chest.

Lord Paley looked apologetic. "I thought Lord Cameron would have told you by now or I wouldn't have mentioned it, Miss H—"

"Someone had better tell me what the Beauchamp Lizard is," said Gemma angrily, "or I won't be answerable for my actions."

"It's not as dire as you imagine, Gemma," Cam said hastily. "I doubt the thing ever even existed."

She didn't miss the furious glance he gave Paley before he went on. "According to Sir Everard, Lady Celeste found a large lizard fossil on the shore just below Beauchamp House some twenty or so years ago. And it came to be known as the Beauchamp Lizard."

"And when, pray, did you learn about this?" she asked him coldly. "And when did you intend to tell me about it?"

She tried to tamp down the sense of hurt she felt at being kept in the dark about something that, by rights as the heiress who shared Lady Celeste's love of fossils, she should have known from her first day at Beauchamp House. She felt betrayed both by her benefactress and by Cam.

"To be honest, I haven't really given it much thought since Sir Everard turned up dead," Cam said, thrusting a hand through his hair.

She unbent a little at that. It *had* been an eventful couple of days.

Turning back to Lord Paley, she asked, "Where is it? And why would Sir Everard think that the skull I found had anything to do with the Beauchamp Lizard?"

"As to the first, I have no idea. And as for the latter, I asked him that very same thing, Miss Hastings, I assure you." Lord Paley was warming to his topic. "But he assured me that it bore all the hallmarks of the Lizard, which he claimed to have seen years ago when he and his father had come to Sussex to visit Lady Celeste."

"If he'd been to the house before," Cam asked with a frown, "why wouldn't he mention it when he came to visit this time?"

"I can only imagine because he didn't wish anyone to know he had some prior knowledge of the Lizard," Paley said. "And of course, it would have removed his reason for touring the collection if he'd been here before."

"So that's what he was looking for," Gemma said with a start. "I got the feeling the entire time we were examining the collections that he was searching for something in particular amongst the shelves. And he wanted to go through the boxes in the attics."

She turned to Lord Paley with wide eyes. "As did you, my lord."

Now it was Paley's turn to redden. "Sir Everard might have mentioned the Beauchamp Lizard on the drive here, and I became caught up in the fever to see it. Especially if it was as impressive as Sir Everard claimed it was."

Gemma shook her head. It would appear that she was surrounded by mendacious men.

Getting back to the matter at hand, she asked, "What made him think that my fossil was the Lizard?"

"He claimed that there had been several attempts at theft not long after she found it," Paley said. "And that his father suggested she bury it to keep it safe."

"But surely one whose sense of right and wrong was as flexible as Sir Everard's would have come here to retrieve it long ago." Cam said, his expression puzzled.

"He said without knowing where or if Lady Celeste had buried it, he hadn't the time or inclination to go digging for it. Of course, that was before he had the good fortune to come upon it after you'd done much of the hard work, Miss Hastings," Lord Paley said. "I don't know whether to believe the story or not, but the fact that he was murdered in the process of taking the fossil from where you found it tells me that someone among the guests at Pearson Hall he told did believe it was the Beauchamp Lizard. And likely killed him for it."

It was too fantastical to be believed, but Gemma had learned over the past year that when it came to Lady Celeste, the most outlandish turned out to be the most accurate. And she would be just the sort of person to hide a thing in plain sight.

"You will know far more about Lady Celeste's inclinations and actions than I will," Lord Paley continued, "but I do know that it was wrong for Sir Everard to steal your discovery whether it was the Beauchamp Lizard or not. And I knew I had to warn you that your benefactress's most celebrated fossil might very well be the same skull you'd unearthed."

"Now," he continued, "I must be off. I do apologize for our earlier contretemps, Lady Serena," he said with a bow to the chaperone. "I misunderstood the relationship between Miss Hastings and Lord Cameron."

Before Gemma could protest this last, he'd bid them both goodbye and had accepted Serena's offer to show him out.

When they were gone, Gemma was unsure which of her multiple annoyances with Cam to confront him with first.

"A penny for them," Cam said after a few moments of gathering her thoughts.

Deciding to start with the most troublesome, she said, "you should have told me about the Beauchamp Lizard. I had a right to know. Especially since Lady Celeste didn't see fit to tell me about it."

He sighed. "I know. I am sorry. I honestly didn't consider that the fossil Sir Everard told us about on the ride here that day could be one and the same as the fossil you'd found on the shore. I did know he was trying to determine if it was in the house during the tour. But when he didn't find it there, I thought no more of it."

She wanted to believe him. Really she did. But a fossil find as big as this particular one was said to be would go a long way toward elevating its finder's reputation in the world of collecting. And even someone as celebrated as Cam couldn't simply rest on his laurels.

Rather than discuss something she had no way of knowing for certain at the moment, she turned to the next most troublesome issue Lord Paley had raised.

"I don't know what he meant about our relationship," she said with a shake of her head. "Clearly, Lord Paley has a very active imagination. And even if—"

She broke off with a squeal as Cam leapt up from his chair, gathered her in his arms, and turned to sit in her chair. All in the course of a few quick seconds.

"What are you doing?" she demanded, though once he'd settled again she made no move to escape him. "I'm quite cross with you. I have no intention of allowing you to kiss me again."

"I'm taking advantage of your chaperone's absence," he said, nuzzling her neck. "It's what fiancés do. It's science, I'm sure of it."

She closed her eyes against the feel of his hot mouth against the sensitive skin. "It's not science," she said in a credibly schoolmarmish tone, considering the shivers coursing through her. "And I haven't forgiven you yet."

"Haven't you?" he asked, pulling back a little and looking into her eyes. "Because I am sorry, Gemma. Very, very sorry."

At the sincerity in his eyes, she felt her stomach flip.

"Are you?" she asked in a voice barely above a whisper. And suddenly she knew she was asking for more than just an apology.

"I am," he said, kissing her softly. "Please forgive me, Gemma."

Closing her eyes, she let him tell her without words that he regretted his actions.

When they were both breathless, she said with mock severity, "If this is your way of proving to me that our relationship is . . ."

She trailed off when she felt his hand close over her breast.

"Yes?" he asked, amusement in his voice. "If our relationship is. . . . what?"

"Whatever," she said on a moan as he stroked his thumb over her. "This isn't fair," she muttered as she found his mouth.

"I don't play fair," Cam said as he opened his lips to her. "I play to win."

Chapter 17

"To win?" Gemma shifted so that she was astride his lap. Then she could kiss him more fully, stroking her tongue into his mouth in the way she'd learned he liked best. Pulling away a little, she asked, "And what if instead of competition, we engage in a meeting of equals?"

While she waited for her words to filter through the lust, she stroked her hands over his chest, which she had to admit she was very curious to see without all of his coats in the way.

"What are you proposing?" he asked, his blue eyes suddenly suspicious.

It was a notion she'd come up with last night, thinking about how much she'd wanted to continue what they'd started in Pearson Close. She knew it wasn't precisely the most proper way to go about things, but then propriety wasn't something she'd ever been all that invested in. She'd ended up betrothed to Cam because of a few stolen kisses. All for propriety's sake.

When their temporary engagement was at an end, she'd realized, she would very likely never be this close to a man again. She had little doubt she would receive offers once it became widely known she was the sole heir to Lady Celeste's estate. But she'd made up her mind that she would not give up her inheritance to a man simply for the sake of being wed. Her plans to go through life alone, as her Aunt Dahlia had done, hadn't changed.

"After we go our separate ways," she said, leaning back on her heels so that she could look him in the eye, "I will have no other opportunities for these kinds of—"

One of his dark brows rose. "Interactions?" he supplied.

"Yes," she said with an approving nod. "I have decided that I'll model my life after those of my Aunt Dahlia and Lady Celeste. I'll live a solitary life of scholarship. Without the distraction of this sort of thing."

He made a skeptical sound. "While I admit this sort of thing can be very distracting," he admitted, "I do not think you can know what your aunt and Lady Celeste actually got up to. Their reputations were unblemished, but who's to say they didn't take lovers?"

This was a possibility Gemma hadn't considered. But it was true that one could never truly know how a person's private life was conducted. In truth, however, it was beside the point. "Whether they did or not," she said with what she hoped was dispassion, "I will endeavor to remain unentangled."

"And what has this to do with me?" he asked. To his credit, he was not looking at her as if she had maggots in her head. Which was another reason why she was certain he was the perfect man to assist her with her scheme.

"Once our betrothal is at an end," she explained, "I'll no longer have any opportunities like this. So I wish to take advantage of our proximity while I may. And I hope it will be agreeable to you as well. An experiment of sorts."

"So, we're back to this, are we? You wish to use me to

experiment?" he asked, brow furrowed now as if he were trying to understand her proposition.

"Yes," she said with relief. It was one thing to hit upon a notion, but it was another thing entirely to be forced to explain it. "I will have you as my lover for the duration of our betrothal but at the end of it, we'll go our separate ways as we agreed upon before."

Now he was frowning. "Gemma, it is no small thing for a gentleman to set aside the morality he's been brought up to follow from boyhood. Not for me, at any rate."

She felt the sting of disappointment. She had known there was the possibility that trying to formalize the caresses and pleasure they'd thus far engaged in as the opportunity arose would ruin things. But she'd never been one to find comfort in serendipity. She liked a bit of order and agreement in her world.

Unable to speak, she began to turn so that she might stand. But soon found herself held firmly.

When she wouldn't look up at him—how could she?— he lifted her chin.

"I haven't said no," he said in a husky voice. "But I have some conditions."

Another thing she hadn't considered was counterarguments.

"And they are?" she said, trying to sound unconcerned.

"I want your agreement that if there is a child, you'll marry me without argument," he said, his expression deadly serious.

Gemma blinked. "There are ways to prevent it," she said finally, knowing her face was scarlet. Ladies were not supposed to know about ways to prevent pregnancy, of course. It was another means to keep them in their place. But Aunt Dahlia had taught both Gemma and her sister about them.

A circumstance that suddenly had her reevaluating Cam's suggestion that perhaps Aunt Dahlia hadn't been as celibate as Gemma had imagined.

Cam must have considered it too because he didn't look particularly scandalized. "All right," he said with a nod. "If you need my help procuring them . . ."

She shook her head.

"Another condition," he said, "is that if at the end of our betrothal in a few months you find you've changed your mind, you'll let me know. I am not against the idea of a marriage between us."

"You aren't?" she asked with a frown. "But I thought—"

"Opinions change," he said with a shrug.

When he didn't elaborate, she pressed, "What else?"

So far, he'd surprised her with all of his conditions. She could only imagine the others would be equally as shocking and she wanted to get this part over with.

"You'll agree not to put yourself in danger while we search for your fossil," he said firmly.

"What has that to do with my proposal?" she asked, puzzled. "I consider the two to be entirely separate."

"I'm not foolish enough to think you'll follow my orders any other way," he said. "And I'm not finished with this one—if you should happen to endanger yourself, you'll agree to marry me. No arguments, no wheedling. As soon as I discover you've put your life at risk, the betrothal becomes real."

"That is most irregular," she objected.

"And proposing that we become lovers for the duration of a pretend betrothal is entirely aboveboard?" he asked. There was that brow again, she thought with a scowl.

"Fine," she said with a roll of her eyes. "But you must

promise not to lure me into dangerous situations so that you can force me into wedlock,"

"I am a gentleman, Gemma," he said. "I keep my word."

"So we're agreed then?" she asked. "I agree to all of your conditions, and you agree to mine?"

"It would appear that we are," he said, and she noted that his eyes had darted to her lips.

Leaning into him, she pressed those lips against his.

"Sealed with a kiss," she said softly. She made to pull away, but he deepened the meeting of mouths. By the time she pulled away, they were both a little breathless.

"I'll figure out a way to get to your rooms tonight," he said, allowing her to pull away and stand.

That brought her up short. "Here?" she asked, and realized it sounded rather like a squeak.

"You've given me a three-month limit," he said with a shrug. "I mean to use every day of them."

Gemma blinked. What had she got herself into?

She'd just smoothed out her gown, and Cam had patted down his hair, which looked just as if she'd been running her fingers through it, when Serena entered the room, followed by Sophia and Benedick.

"I hear you've had a bit of excitement," Benedick said. And Gemma couldn't help the guilty glance she turned Cam's way.

"Lord Paley, he means," Sophia said, reading far more into the exchange than Gemma had wanted her to. Her sister knew her far too well.

"Yes, of course," Gemma nodded. "It was quite the scene. But Lord Cameron did the right thing and he and Lord Paley came to an agreement."

"I agreed to let him live," Cam agreed with a nod.

At her scowl, he shrugged. "And we may have discussed some things about Sir Everard and learned a great deal of new information about that fellow's activities. I don't think anyone will be surprised to learn that he was just as much of a scoundrel in other parts of the collecting world as he was with Gemma's fossil."

Serena excused herself to check on Jeremy, and the two couples moved to the seats before the fire.

"What else had Sir Everard been up to?" Benedick asked, oblivious to the glances being exchanged between his wife and her sister.

Gemma, however, was very much aware of her sister's searching look. As Cam explained what they'd learned from Lord Paley, Gemma shook her head slightly to warn her off. The look Sophia gave her—lips pursed and brow furrowed—indicated that she would revisit the subject later.

Which was fine with Gemma. As long as they didn't discuss the fact that she and Cam had agreed to engage in an affair in front of his brother the vicar, she was content.

My, how her standard for contentment had changed this week, she thought wryly.

Then she turned her attention to the subject of Sir Everard.

But beneath her concentration on that matter, a little hum of excitement ran through her.

Tonight, it seemed to repeat. Tonight he would come to her.

Just then, Cam caught her eye. And she knew he was thinking the same thing.

Despite his distraction over his assignation later with Gemma, Cam was able to concentrate on the matter of Sir Everard and her missing fossil as soon as he saw that his brother wasn't as oblivious as he'd seemed.

This, Ben had conveyed with only a slight narrowing

of his eyes. Anyone else would have missed it, but Cam had spent his entire boyhood learning his brothers' silent cues. And if he wasn't mistaken, his brother the vicar had not missed the heated look Cam had just exchanged with Gemma.

Fortunately, Sophia was there too, and was more interested in discussing Sir Everard than her husband seemed to be.

"Do you believe Sir Everard's suspicion that your fossil was, in fact, this Beauchamp Lizard?" she asked Gemma, who also seemed able to concentrate on the matter at hand. "If he was a fraud about his own abilities as a scholar, I mean, who's to say he wasn't simply wrong and intended to pass off your fossil as Lady Celeste's?"

"I'm not as familiar with Sir Everard's work as Cam is, I fear," Gemma said with a shrug. "I do know that my first instinct on seeing the skull fossil was that it could be quite exciting. But I didn't have the time to examine it properly, or to compare it against other important finds in this area to see if it bore any relationship to them."

"I have been acquainted with Sir Everard for some years," Cam said, "but I never found him to be the scientific equal of some of the other prominent members of our circle. I had no notion he was such a fraudster but nor did I think him a genius. I think to know whether it is, in fact, Lady Celeste's lizard, we'll need to find some sketch or description of it."

"She never wrote about it in any of the scholarly periodicals?" Sophia asked. Cam supposed her knowledge of the natural science world came from being Gemma's sister. It spoke well of their relationship. His brothers, whom he held in great affection, had never bothered to learn any of the details of his passion for collecting.

"I have examined all of the scientific papers and

books in this library," Gemma said, gesturing to one wall of books and bound documents, "and I've never seen any mention of it. I suppose there may have been something in her diaries, but when we made a point of reading through them, we weren't looking for scientific things." As Cam understood it, when the heiresses had first come to Beauchamp Hall they'd undertaken to read through all of Lady Celeste's personal journals in an effort to find their benefactress's killer.

"It sounds as if we have some light reading in our future," said Ben, stretching out his shoulders as if in preparation for some physical endeavor.

But Gemma, who was wearing the expression Cam had come to recognize as the precursor to an outlandish idea, shook her head. "I don't think we'll need to go to the journals yet."

She turned to her sister, "Do you recall how I used to make you draw the items I found whenever I went fossil collecting?"

"How could I forget?" asked Sophia with a sigh. "I was never more pleased than when I stumbled on the idea to teach you to sketch them yourself. I know artists are supposed to enjoy drawing in and of itself, but stones are deadly dull as subjects go."

Cam knew at once what Gemma was getting at. "You think Lady Celeste must have some sort of collecting journal or sketchbook."

It wasn't a bad notion. Most collectors, wanting to have a way of showing their best finds without lugging them cross-country in a trunk or valise kept some kind of descriptive record. Lady Celeste's collection, as he'd seen on the tour, was quite extensive and if she'd been as active in the collecting community as she was said to have been, she would have had sketches.

"It's a logical idea," he agreed. "Especially if she intended to hide it. She'd want to know precisely what it looked like without needing to remove it from its hiding place each time she wanted to see it."

"I don't understand why she would have buried it, though," Ben said. "If Sir Everard's tale was even true."

Cam did, though. "Collectors are all a little mad about their finds," he explained. "And I've seen them do all sorts of things to stop other collectors, or worse thieves, from making off with their most prized discoveries. As schemes go, burying it in the cliffs where she found it wasn't all that bad. After all, she'd already found it there. Why would someone search there again?"

"But it's quite common to search the same place again if it yielded something important earlier," Gemma argued.

"Yes, but she owned that particular bit of beach," Cam said. "She would have no fear of someone else coming onto her property to dig there. At least, no one but you."

That made her eyes widen. "You don't think she buried it there for me to find, surely?" Despite the negative way she'd asked the question, it was obvious that she found the notion tempting. It must weigh on her that she'd not been left a specific quest as her fellow heiresses had been.

"You'll have to figure out if your fossil was, in fact, this Beauchamp Lizard," Sophia reminded them. "So you have to find the sketches. Then you'll know more about her motives."

"Agreed," Gemma said. "You don't happen to recall seeing anything like that in your studio, do you?"

"Alas, I do not," Sophia responded. "I should think you'd have the most luck in the collection, or the workroom."

But Gemma shook her head. "I've inventoried every-thing in both rooms and there was nothing like that. I'm afraid there's only one place where they can be. I feel foolish for not considering it earlier."

"The attics?" Sophia asked.

Gemma gave a quick nod. "I think that's our only option now."

"We'll discuss our strategy over luncheon," Ben said, rising to his feet.

"We wrangled an invitation as soon as we saw Serena," Sophia explained, linking arms with her sister. "It's too cold to go back to the vicarage without sustenance."

"Why do I get the feeling you pressed for that invita-tion so that you wouldn't miss any gossip," Gemma said with skepticism in her tone.

"You are free to draw whatever conclusion you wish," her sister returned tartly. "I get luncheon either way."

Walking behind the sisters, Cam glanced at his brother.

"How's your jaw?" Ben asked. "I may have hit you harder than I originally intended."

"Nice of you to say that now that the damage is done," Cam said, his hand going to the bruise.

But if he wanted an apology, he would be doomed to disappointment.

"I didn't say you didn't deserve it," Ben said. Though he was a vicar, he was still an elder brother with all the ar-rogance that came with it.

Cam didn't argue. But he felt Ben's gaze on him.

"What?"

They'd just reached the hallway in time to see Gemma and Sophia's skirts disappearing around the corner.

"Why do I get the sensation that I owe you another thrashing?"

Thinking back to his earlier discussion with Gemma, Cam reflected that he was probably owed more than a few thrashings for what they'd agreed to embark upon. But at the end of it, he had every intention of making said thrashing unnecessary. His brother could hardly fault him for touching his own wife.

He'd simply need to convince Gemma to take on the role.

"I don't know what you mean," he said to Ben, adopting his most innocent air.

"You're such a terrible liar," Ben said, shaking his head in disgust. "I thought we taught you better."

"I must admit, it never fails to amuse when my brother the vicar reminds me that he is a better liar than I am," Cam said.

"Don't change the subject."

To Cam's surprise, Ben stopped in front of him and looked him in the eye. "Let's speak frankly, shall we?"

At Cam's nod, he continued. "I want your word that if things go too far, you'll marry her."

"Of course I will." Cam was a bit offended that there was even a question of it.

"Do not look so put out," Ben said. "You're the one who told me you never wished to marry."

"Perhaps I've changed my mind," Cam said in a grudging tone. He hadn't had any intention of telling his brother that his revelations of the reasons for their father's infidelity had shifted something inside of him. Whatever impediment he'd harbored that stopped him from considering happy ever after for himself was gone.

That took Ben aback, he was perversely happy to see.

"Have you indeed?"

"I just said so, didn't I?"

Ben examined his face for a moment before, apparently,

satisfied by what he saw there, clapping him on the shoulder. "I'm glad to hear it."

"Don't be so pleased yet," Cam said. "I haven't convinced Gemma to go along with it."

But this didn't worry his brother in the least, it would seem.

Grinning, he grabbed Cam in a one-armed hug. "You're a Lisle boy, Cam," he said with all the arrogance that statement entailed. "I have every confidence in your powers of persuasion."

That made one of them, Cam thought wryly.

For now, it would have to be enough.

Chapter 18

Luncheon was a jolly affair, and Gemma found herself unexpectedly pleased at the fact that for once, she wasn't the only heiress at the table without a gentleman of her own there with her.

She also, much to her chagrin, was more concerned about how her friends felt about Cam. It wasn't that she needed them to approve of him. They'd met him when he was here in the summer and seemed to like him well enough. But they'd not seen him as a potential match for her then. And however false she might tell herself their betrothal was, her earlier conversation with Cam—and his insistence that if there was a child she'd agree to marry him—had her considering how he would fit into her world. And, far more than her parents, her fellow heiresses were important to her.

The thought of her parents gave her a pang of guilt over what Aunt Dahlia would make over all of this. Her insistence before she left Little Seaford that Gemma owed it to the female scholars who had come before her to use this opportunity to make her mark had been forgotten in the wake of what had happened since Sir Everard's murder.

But now, the memory of her beloved aunt's warning

gave her pause. No longer hungry, she pushed her plate back and took a sip of wine.

To her discomfort, it was Cam, seated beside her, who noticed her change in mood. "Not hungry?" he asked, in a quiet voice only she could hear.

"Just tired," he said with a smile she knew seemed false. She'd never been very good at hiding her emotions.

He slipped a hand beneath the table and took hers. "If you've changed your mind about . . . um . . . tonight," he said, "I won't hold it against you. It's been a hectic week. Perhaps we should take it a bit more slowly."

The relief she felt was profound and it must have shown in her expression because he squeezed her hand, then let it go.

"That would be for the best," she said. "I don't want it to seem like I don't know my own mind. Because I do, but . . ."

"You needn't apologize, Gemma," he said with a rueful smile. "I'm not an ogre."

The rest of the meal passed without any further chance for private conversation, and to Gemma's surprise, when the meal was concluded, rather than staying so that he might search the attics with her, Cam excused himself.

"I noticed that my gelding is having a bit of trouble with his right foreleg," he said easily, "so I need to see what your stablemaster recommends."

To Gemma's further surprise—though on reflection it shouldn't have surprised her at all—Kerr and Maitland, and even Ben, who was not known to be particularly horse mad, were at his side in seconds, offering up their own suggestions.

"Send word if you find something useful in the attics," Cam said with a nod. To Gemma's disappointment, his farewell was only verbal and if she wasn't mistaken, he had made it a point not to meet her eyes.

Was he really so upset that she'd rescinded her invitation to her bedchamber for that evening that he'd run away?

She stood staring at the door that had just closed behind them, dumbfounded.

"Is there a problem?" Ivy asked, stepping up beside her.

"Tea," said Daphne from her other side.

"We just had luncheon," Gemma said, laughing despite her mood.

"It will be dessert," Sophia said, taking her by the hand and leading her toward the library where they'd always done their best thinking.

Maitland had examined the foreleg of Cam's bay gelding, Romulus, for no more than a minute before he looked up at him in disappointment.

"There's nothing wrong with his foreleg at all, is there?"

"It was a ruse," Cam said sheepishly. "I'm sorry to deny you the torn ligament you were hoping for."

"Woman trouble," said Kerr with a nod. "I surmised as much. Especially given that tête-a-tête between the two of you at the luncheon table."

"What have you done?" Ben asked his brother in exasperation.

"Now, vicar, now's not the time for recriminations," said Maitland, clapping Ben on the shoulder. "It's obvious to anyone with eyes that the fellow is in love."

Cam felt color rise in his face. To his relief, Kerr spoke before he had to. "Don't put him on the spot. What this calls for is a pint."

"Too cold to walk," Maitland said with a shiver.

"Then isn't it convenient we're in a stable with more than a few carriages in it?" the marquess asked drolly.

"Come on," he told Cam and the others. "The sooner we get to the village, the sooner we can warm up and solve all of young Lord Cameron's romantic troubles in the process."

Having removed her slippers and tucked her feet beneath her in her favorite library chair, a cup of tea warming her hands, Gemma felt some of the tension that had threatened to overwhelm her earlier dissipate.

"It's good to be together again like this," she said aloud as she took in the sight of her sister and Ivy and Daphne similarly disposed in chairs of their own.

"Do you wish to talk about what it is that's bothering you?" asked Ivy gently. "I promise you whatever you say will not go farther than this room."

Before she could stop herself, Gemma looked at Sophia.

Her sister shook her head. "I know you think that I tell Ben everything, but if you tell me something in confidence, I keep it. I give you my word. You are my oldest friend, Gemma. As well as my sister."

Gemma felt a pang of shame at even questioning Sophia's loyalty. But that was an indication of just how much this business with Sir Everard and Cam and the Lizard had overset her. "Of course," she said. "I just don't know what to think. Of myself as much as anyone else."

"Has Lord Cameron done something to make you doubt yourself?" Ivy asked gently.

"Not as such," Gemma said with a sigh. "Not intentionally, I mean."

"How then?" Daphne asked.

"I just never considered before—not seriously at any rate—the idea that I would ever marry," Gemma said. "Indeed, I promised Aunt Dahlia that I wouldn't. So that I wouldn't squander the opportunity that being selected to come here has given me."

Three sets of eyes stared at her.

"Do you think that we've squandered our opportunities?" Sophia asked, aghast. "That by marrying we've thrown away what Lady Celeste gave us? Does Aunt Dahlia think that of me?"

"Of course I don't think that," Gemma said, frustrated that she'd worded her concern so badly. "Of course, you've all chosen husbands who will support you in your studies. But even you must admit that gentlemen like that are a rarity."

"Has Lord Cameron done something that makes you think he wouldn't be as supportive as our husbands?" Ivy asked.

"No, nothing like that," Gemma said with a shake of her head. "If anything, he's been as eager as I am to find the stolen fossil."

"Then what is it?" Sophia asked, gently. "Has he pressed you for more than you're willing to give him?"

It took a moment for her to get her sister's meaning but when she did, Gemma shook her head. "No! Not at all. If anything I've been more . . . that is to say . . ."

"Of course you have," Daphne said with a nod that seemed almost proud. "You're a healthy woman of child-bearing years with an interest in a handsome man."

Gemma hid her laugh behind a cough. "Yes, well, it's nothing about Cam's behavior that worries me. It's more my own fear of disappointing Aunt Dahlia, and I suppose myself, that is of concern."

"You can't make such an important decision as who to

love," Sophia said, "or even whether or not to marry, based on anyone's opinion but your own."

"But this is Aunt Dahlia, Soph," Gemma protested. "She is the one who took me to see my first collection of fossils. Who saw to it that our governesses had more than a passing knowledge of geology. Without her guidance I would never have considered it possible I could study fossils, much less make it my primary focus in life."

"Dearest," Sophia said with a sympathetic smile, "you must understand that however much you might wish to please Aunt Dahlia, she would never wish you to give up something you truly wanted just to please her. And, though I love and respect her, I think it's unfair that she put such a burden on you."

It was a relief to hear what she'd even feared to think to herself said aloud.

"I don't want to disappoint her," she said softly. "And though I do think I've grown very fond of Cam, how do I know if choosing to marry him will not do precisely what she thinks and keep me from making a place for myself in geology?"

"Have you tried asking him whether he would support your work?" Ivy asked thoughtfully. "Because it seems to me that some frank discussion between the two of you might set your mind to rest. Or at the very least let you know whether to continue with the betrothal."

"That would seem to be a sensible thing to do, wouldn't it?" Gemma asked wryly.

"Whatever you decide," Sophia said, "you must do it for you. Not for Aunt Dahlia. Not for me and Ben. Not for Lady Celeste. This is your life. If nothing else, Lady Celeste's bequest gave us each the independence needed to make decisions for ourselves."

Gemma nodded. "Thank you," she said with a smile. "All of you."

Suddenly she felt much less anxiety about all of it. She still had work to do, and a difficult conversation to have with Cam, but at least she knew now that her decision was her own.

The tavern in Little Seaford was not particularly busy at this hour of the day, and the Lisle brothers, accompanied by Kerr and Maitland, were soon seated in the taproom with tankards of ale before them while the icy wind whistled against the windows.

"So, young Cam," said Maitland after a generous swig of ale, "tell Uncle Maitland all about it."

Resisting the urge to roll his eyes, Cam reminded himself that he'd asked them for their help. Even so, he thought, seeing Kerr and Ben exchange gleeful looks, it was at a cost.

"I want to know," he said, deciding to just come right out with it, "how to go about reassuring Gemma that marrying me won't mean she has to give up her ambitions as a geologist."

Maitland frowned. "I should imagine you just tell her," the duke said with a shrug.

Cam sighed. "I thought perhaps, since the duchess seems to have kept up with her mathematics since your marriage that you might have some suggestions. Or perhaps you would, Kerr. I believe Lady Kerr is a classicist?"

Before Kerr could respond, Maitland guffawed. "If you think Daphne's maths work is anywhere in my purview, old man, then you know very little of marriage. Or Daphne."

When Cam turned to Kerr, the marquess gave him a sheepish grin. "Our wives have minds of their own, and we knew that when we married them. I don't know about Maitland, but it was understood that Ivy would continue to pursue her work."

Maitland nodded.

Benedick, who had been silent so far, added, "Sophia was afraid that her painting would affect my ability to move up in the church hierarchy. It took some persuading to prove to her that I cared more for her than becoming a bishop. But I did manage it."

Cam took a swallow of ale.

"If you don't mind my saying so," Kerr said with a twist of his lips, "perhaps it's not just marriage that's what frightens Gemma, but marriage to another fossil-hunter. The three of us are not in competition with our wives."

That was something that hadn't occurred to Cam. Which was foolish since it was what had caused their very first disagreement. He, a fellow geologist, had rejected her geology paper for his journal.

"Can it really be that simple?" he asked with a shake of his head. "She's just afraid I'll try to eclipse her?"

"You must admit," Ben said, "it's not easy for ladies in any area that's dominated by men to make a name for themselves. Perhaps she's afraid that marrying you will bring her under suspicion from the rest of the collecting world who might suggest she was trying to climb up the ladder by marrying someone on a higher rung, so to speak."

"That's ridiculous," Cam said, angry at the idea anyone would think such a thing.

"It's how the world works," Kerr said. "Like it or not, marriages are made every day for more mercenary reasons than professional acclaim."

"I suppose so," he admitted, thinking of Sir Everard's, and even Paley's, speculation about the Beauchamp fortune and how much Gemma was worth.

"Whatever misgivings she has," Maitland said, his normally sunny expression muted with sympathy, "you have to show her that you care more about her than your fossils and whatnot."

His words pierced Cam like a knife.

He couldn't remember a time when he hadn't been obsessed with collecting objects from the natural world.

"Don't look so morose," Ben said gently. "You don't have to give them up altogether. Just prove to her that she's more important than the fossils are."

"How do I do that?" Cam asked, relieved, but only just.

"Give her your most treasured fossil," Maitland said without batting an eye.

"My collection isn't here with me," Cam said with a scowl.

"You brought some with you though, didn't you?" the duke asked, with a gimlet eye. "You collector chaps can't leave the house without bringing your best bits along."

Cam thought about the highly polished cherry trunk in his bedchamber at the vicarage that held some of his more interesting fossils and other stones. "Yes, of course I did. I suppose I could give her one of those."

"Most of all," his brother said, "you must convince her that you're marrying her not because you want to stop her from succeeding, but because you can't succeed without her. That you're better together than either one of you is apart."

"That's damned eloquent, vicar," said Maitland raising his glass.

All four men laughed, and Cam, the tightness in his chest dissipated for the moment, drank the rest of his ale before requesting another round.

Chapter 19

Gemma didn't venture up to the attics until after breakfast the next morning. She felt more at ease about the situation with Cam thanks to her discussion with her friends and her sister, and she was able to concentrate more fully on the search for the missing skull bone.

One thing had marred her evening, however, and that was finding some of her own notebooks in the workroom next to the collection had been disarranged. She was all but certain she'd reshelved them after looking through them that morning. But there they were, scattered over the worktable.

It was possible she had been so distracted by other things that she was mistaken, but she didn't think so. When considered in context with the feeling of being watched and the threat left on Sir Everard's body, the thought that someone had been in her workshop made her shiver.

By breakfast she'd convinced herself that she'd been imagining things, however, and putting it out of her mind, she headed upstairs.

It had been some time since Gemma had explored the attics, and she was surprised all over again by their tidiness.

She'd only just lit the lamps nearest the door when she heard the sound of footsteps in the stairwell.

"I hope you didn't think we'd let you search up here without help," said Sophia as she stepped into the cluttered, but tidy space.

To Gemma's surprise, she saw not Daphne and Ivy behind her but Cam.

She tried to keep her expression neutral, but she felt a familiar jolt of awareness and relief at seeing Cam there. She might not be completely sure that marrying him would be the best thing for her, but she knew that more than just a small part of her wanted him to be.

"Where do you want us?" he asked with a lopsided smile that softened his blunt features and made her stomach flip.

She wished for a moment that he hadn't been accompanied by Sophia, but then decided it was probably better that he had. It was far too early in the day for the activity that smile inspired her to want. And they did have work to do.

"I begin to doubt we'll find anything of use," she said aloud as she turned to survey the room at large. "If there were something that seemed likely to be associated with Lady Celeste's collecting, I think we'd have discovered it by now."

"Since your letter was cut short by her illness," Sophia said, stepping up beside her, "perhaps Lady Celeste wasn't able to extract the information she needed for it from up here. And we haven't searched the attics thoroughly, you must admit. We looked at her personal diaries but that was all."

"She was so orderly about everything else, though," Gemma said, moving toward the far wall where she remembered she'd discovered a few items that might have gone into the collection room. "I don't know that I believe she'd have left anything to chance."

"She was quite ill, though, dearest," Sophia said, placing a comforting hand on her sister's arm. "She may not have trusted the task to anyone else."

Before they could continue, Benedick appeared in the doorway.

"I'm afraid I just got word that Mrs. Wallace has fallen ill," he said, his usual good humor replaced with concern. "I'll need to go see to her at once, but you may remain here, my dear—"

But Sophia shook her head. "Of course not," she said. "Her little ones must be frantic. And they do not care for her sister at all."

In just a few short months, Sophia had adapted to her role as a vicar's wife with an ease that made Gemma respect her even more than she had already. Far from dampening her enthusiasm for her art, her marriage had transformed her into a fuller, happier version of herself.

Still, she did wish her sister could remain here now.

Perhaps sensing Gemma's disappointment, Sophia kissed her cheek and said, "It can't be helped. I'll see you tomorrow if I'm not needed there."

"Of course." Gemma hugged her, then made a shooing motion. "Go, go. I'm sure poor Mrs. Wallace's children are worried sick."

When they were gone, she and Cam stood silently assessing one another until Cam said with a touch of amusement, "Do not look so frightened. I won't ravish you amidst the discarded furniture and disturbing dress forms of your attic."

She bit her lip. Of course he knew precisely what she'd been thinking. "I thought perhaps you were frustrated at my change of heart yesterday."

He stepped further into the low-ceilinged room and stopped just a foot away from her. "I won't ravish you at all, Gemma," he said softly. "If you're not willing, then I don't want you. Just say the word and we can end this betrothal now."

His words sent a stab of fear through her—whether it was the thought of dissolving their betrothal or his frankness, she wasn't sure.

"I meant what I said." She lifted her chin and met his gaze with a boldness she didn't feel. "I do wish to explore with you. It's just that yesterday was . . ."

"You needn't explain," he said softly, running a finger over her cheek. "I can wait. Until you're ready."

She lowered her eyes at the intensity of his gaze.

When she looked up again, though, he was smiling. "I will tell you, however," he said, his half smile revealing a dimple in his left cheek, "that exploration is my specialty."

She couldn't help her answering grin and she felt as if her heart would beat right out of her chest. Surely he could see it.

"Then perhaps we should—"

But he cut her off with a quick kiss. "We'll wait until tonight, in your bed."

"What if I don't want to wait?" she asked, growing impatient. "What if I want to get it over with?"

At that his eyes darkened. He slipped his arms around her and pulled her close. To her surprise, she felt him— one part of him in particular—pressing against her. "This is what you do to me," he said huskily. "And when I take you, I mean to take my time. You might not know it, but it makes a difference for a woman. The first time, especially, shouldn't be done in haste."

It was one area in which she was painfully ignorant. Despite having read as many of the books in the library on the subject, Gemma had no real experience, and even less understanding of the subtleties he described. And Sophia had been frustratingly vague, though Gemma was quite certain she and Benedick had anticipated their vows—in Sophia's studio, no less!

"I suppose in this," she said loftily, "I will have to trust you."

He smiled. "You'll trust me in more than this before it's all over," he said. "But for now, it'll do."

She shifted a little and he gave a hiss as she brushed against his arousal. Alarmed, she pulled away. "Did I hurt you?"

Huffing a laugh, Cam shook his head. "Not as such. I'll just need a minute."

He turned around and stared at the ceiling for a moment.

"How on earth do you manage to walk about like that?" she asked, curious now. She'd known of course about penises. Or was it penii? She'd have to ask Ivy when next she saw her. It wasn't the sort of thing one could write in a letter after all.

"I was exaggerating when I said I'd been like this ever since we kissed," he said. "But not by much."

"That still doesn't explain how—"

"Gemma?"

"Yes?"

"Perhaps you can begin searching now and we can save this discussion for later?"

She stared at his back for a moment. Well, if he didn't want questions, he ought not have brought it up.

Then she remembered distinctly his laughter when she'd said that precise phrase before.

"Brought it up," she said under her breath, understanding the double entendre now.

Stifling her laughter at the jest she moved to the trunk

where she'd found some of Lady Celeste's papers before and began her search.

Once he'd managed to lose his erection—thanks to a memory of a neighbor in the vicinity of his father's estate who used copious amounts of scent in lieu of bathing—Cam wordlessly moved to Gemma's side and began to sort through a trunk next to one she was looking in.

She'd said this area was where the items related to Lady Celeste's interest in fossils and collecting were to be found, and a cursory examination of the first few pages on top affirmed that assessment.

They worked in silence for some time, both of them removing the contents of the trunks they searched and placing item after item, document after document onto the floor beside where they knelt.

He was almost to the bottom of his trunk when a brisk knock sounded on the door of the attic.

"I thought you might be ready for a break," Serena said brightly, ushering the footman, William, into the room carrying a tray laden with sandwiches and the like. It had been a long time since luncheon.

"How did you know I wouldn't want to stop?" Gemma asked, standing and brushing her hands off on her gown.

"I have shared a house with you for almost a full year, Gemma," her chaperone said. "I think I should know your work habits by now."

Cam had risen as soon as he saw Serena, and moved over to where William, the footman, was setting up a small table and two chairs just inside the door.

"A picnic in the attic," he said dryly as he watched the servant place a small vase with what looked like one of Paley's hothouse roses on the table. "What a perfect setting for a newly betrothed couple."

He turned to eye Serena and she turned pink, confirming his suspicion. For whatever reason, she'd changed her assessment of him as a potential husband for her charge. He wasn't sure whether to be pleased or concerned.

It wouldn't make any difference in his own intentions, of course, but he did wonder what had changed her mind.

There would be no clues coming from Gemma, he thought wryly as she took her seat and impatiently gestured for him to be seated as well.

"I'm starving," she said, and her stomach gave a rumble then, as if to confirm it.

Seeing that they were not going to ignore the repast she'd arranged, Lady Serena gave a brisk nod.

"I'll be off and let you two eat, then," she said. "Enjoy your meal."

And before either of them could protest, she was gone, followed by the butler and footman.

Cam stared after her for a moment, then took his seat.

Gemma was indeed hungry, for she bit into a sandwich just then and sighed in a way that had him thinking of the scented neighbor again.

"Why aren't you eating?" she asked when minutes had passed without him selecting from the assorted food on offer.

"I am," he said, reaching for a bit of beef and cheese. "There, see?" he bit into it. And realized he was far more hungry than he'd realized.

Relaxing a bit, she continued to forage from the collation of cheese, fruits, meat and fruit tarts.

"You aren't one of those silly creatures who pretends no interest in food, I've noticed," he said with approval. He'd once thought—when he was fresh from university and full of himself—that a true lady would never deign to show interest in food or drink. No more.

"You know me too well now to have ever imagined that," she said with a shake of her head. "I shall never see the sense in pretending to be happy when I'm sad. Or pretending to be full when I'm still hungry."

"In some instances, pretending happiness might be necessary to prevent someone else from learning something painful," he said, thinking back to his father's behavior when the duchess had been ill.

"I suppose that's true," she said thoughtfully, "but I cannot imagine what—other than a need for gentlemen to feel superior—should make it necessary for a lady to pretend never to have human needs."

"It does become rather absurd when you see all the men at table stuffing their maws with every sort of delicacy while the ladies nibble small bites and never finish any of the dishes."

"Precisely," Gemma said with an approving nod.

Cam basked in the feeling for a moment.

"You've changed somehow," she said, tilting her head to really look at him. "It's as if you're—lighter. Less angry."

Had learning about the reasons behind his father's actions really wrought such a change in him in such a short time? Surely not.

She must have seen his skepticism, because she continued, "I don't know if it's something everyone would notice. But I see it."

That made him feel somewhat better. He'd never thought of himself as an easy read, but it made sense that Gemma, whom he'd spent the most time with, and been the most intimate with, would be the one to see it.

But was it something he was ready to share with her?

For once, the man who always knew exactly what his next move would be was uncertain.

* * *

As the silence between them lengthened, Gemma turned her attention back to the trunk she was examining. It was filled with the sorts of bits and bobs every collector of fossils and geological oddities gathered over a career of hunting for important finds. Too interesting to dispose of without a pang of guilt and too unimportant to place on display with the truly great pieces acquired on a hunt.

A glance at Cam revealed he too was poring over the contents of the trunk he'd opened.

They had worked quietly for nearly a quarter of an hour, however, when she realized that the floor of this particular trunk was not painted brown as she'd originally thought, but was lined with large, leather-bound books.

Her heart thumped as she recognized them as the same sort of notebooks Lady Celeste had used for her personal journals she and the others had looked through earlier in the year.

Hurriedly, but careful not to damage any of the fossils, she removed everything from the trunk.

Cam must have noticed her haste because he looked over, his eyes alert. "What did you find?"

"I don't know yet," she said, taking out the last large stone. "But I have a hope it's what we've been looking for."

She didn't name it aloud for fear of jinxing herself. She desperately wanted to find out if the fossil she'd discovered on the shore was actually the famed Beauchamp Lizard. She would accept the truth no matter what the outcome, but she could admit to herself, at least, that she'd be highly disappointed if it wasn't. Not only because it would mean she might have been wrong about the value of the stone she found, but also because it would mean that Lady Celeste hadn't, in fact, planted it there for her to find. The lack of her benefactress having made some kind of quest or plan for her enlightenment during the first year at Beauchamp House stung. And this seemed to be her last chance.

"Here," said Cam, as if sensing her fear, "I'll bring them out while you scan them."

Grateful for his lack of questions, she moved out of the way, and let him kneel down in front of the trunk.

While he worked, she moved closer to the lamp they'd hung on the wall just over where they'd been searching. There was an abandoned armchair there and she perched on the edge, scanning the pages.

The hand was one she also recognized from Lady Celeste's journals and the pages were lined with neatly inscribed dates, locales and descriptions of what she'd found there. In some cases, there were purchase dates and the name of the collector from whom she'd acquired the particular item or items, followed by a brief notation of where the items had been found.

The journal in her hands was dated some twenty years previous and contained five years' worth of discoveries and purchases as well as pencil sketches of the items. But nowhere in this particular volume, however, did she find a mention of any fossil that matched the skull fossil she'd discovered on the shore.

Cam finished removing all eleven remaining journals and offered them to her just as she set the first one she'd drawn out down on the table.

"You take these and I'll look in these," he said, not bothering to note that she'd obviously not found anything about the lizard in the first one.

Once more the attic was silent, though this time there was an air of excitement as they scanned the diaries for some mention of the stone Sir Everard had been convinced was the Beauchamp Lizard.

At last Gemma found it. The sketch was the only one in this volume Lady Celeste had rendered in any great degree of detail. The unimportant finds, Gemma had concluded, were only given cursory drawings. This one, however, was as finely rendered as any pen-and-ink drawing on display in the great museums. And there was no question it was the fossil they were looking for.

"Here, Cam," she said, her voice ringing with excitement. "A particularly fine fossilized skull of a marine lizard, found Beauchamp House cliffs, Little Seaford, Sussex, Ldy C. Beauchamp and Lrd Crutchley. 4 Sept. 1813."

"Crutchley?" Cam frowned. "Doesn't he have an estate near Lyme?"

Lord Richard Crutchley was not a particularly renowned collector, but he was known to have a small collection of finds he'd purchased from Mary Anning. He'd also written a few notes and letters to the various geological magazines.

"Yes," Gemma said thoughtfully. "I do recall Lady Celeste mentioning him in her personal diaries, at social gatherings and the like, but this seems more friendly than those entries did."

"She clearly had a large circle of acquaintances," he said wryly. "I suppose working for the Home Office can expand one's reach like that."

While Sophia and Benedick had been investigating a local art forgery ring, they'd discovered, among other things, that Lady Celeste had been an agent for the Home Office for a time. It had not come as a shock to the heiresses, who had come to understand that their benefactress was not only intelligent and kind, but also had her finger in far more pies than they could ever have imagined.

"How did you know about that?" Gemma asked with

a frown. She'd thought the heiresses had agreed not to spread word of Lady Celeste's work for the crown.

"I overheard Sophia telling Ben," he said ruefully. "But I promise not to say anything to anyone. I'm quite good at keeping secrets."

Turning her attention back to the notebook, Gemma considered what they'd discovered. "It would appear that we've found evidence that here was a Beauchamp Lizard, at the very least."

"Whether the specimen you found was the same fossil, however . . ." Cam said, trailing off at her glare. "I admit the signs are all there," he said, holding up his hands in a gesture of surrender. "It's just a matter of corroborating that information with someone who's seen the one Lady Celeste unearthed."

Rising from her chair, Gemma began marching toward the attic doors.

"Where are you going?" he asked, climbing to his feet.

"To change into something warmer," she told him over her shoulder. "You should call for your curricle. We've got a long journey ahead of us."

She felt the reverberation in the floor as he jogged to catch up with her.

"You might ask me if I wish to drive nearly to Lyme first," Cam complained as he reached her side. "Perhaps I'm tired."

"My dear Lord Cameron," she said with a raised brow. "If you are too tired to drive to Crutchley's estate then I fear you are too fatigued for any other activity."

He paused, then shook his head a little. "Point taken. I'll meet you in the entrance hall in thirty minutes."

"Fifteen," she said, "and don't be late."

Chapter 20

Normally, Cam would wish to spend some time planning a journey like this. Not because Lyme was particularly far, but because the weather at this time of year was unpredictable and one look at the skies as he lifted Gemma into the curricle was enough to have him seriously considering an attempt to put her off.

They'd secured hot bricks and his curricle was already equipped with blankets and furs, but he had a pang of conscience about taking her out on the road in the cold with the possibility of rain on the horizon.

"I've sworn George to secrecy," she said as she arranged a blanket around her and rubbed her hands together. "Serena was, fortunately, with Jem in the nursery, so there's little danger of her discovering we've gone until we're at least into the village."

They drove in silence for a long while, Cam lost in his thoughts, while Gemma all but vibrated with excitement about the coming interview with Crutchley.

"You do realize that as soon as Lady Serena notices we're gone, she'll assume we've eloped," Cam told her just as they reached the far side of Little Seaford.

If he'd expected Gemma to be cowed by the notion of Serena's assumptions, however, he was grossly mistaken.

"Of course she won't," Gemma explained. "I told George we were going to speak with Lord Crutchley and that we would be back not long after supper."

"Gemma, do you have any notion how far it is to Lyme?" he asked, bemused at her blithe disregard for the limits of time and space.

"Of course I do," she said with a shake of her head as the curricle hit a stone and she had to cling to his arm. "Why are you so cross about this?"

He had to admit, he thought as her violet scent teased him, being this close to her in a confined space would be no hardship.

"I'm not cross," he said with a huff of disbelief. "But why do you assume our trip to Crutchley's estate will only take a couple of hours. At this time of year, Lyme is at least three. And that's in excellent weather, which this is not."

She stiffened beside him. "What do you mean?" she asked. "I distinctly recall the day you came to rip up at me over the article for your benighted journal that you said you'd come from Lyme. It was early afternoon, so I assumed it was a trip to be made in a few hours."

"It is," he said patiently. "In late summer. But in late autumn, when the roads are in poor conditions thanks to rainstorms like the one that made it possible for you to find your skull fossil, it takes longer. Not to mention that the horses must rest."

Gemma was silent as she pondered this information. "She'll think we've eloped. So will Sophia and Benedick."

"Yes," he said. "Do you wish me to turn around? We can just as easily set out tomorrow. It was foolish of me to let you talk me into traveling today."

She snorted. "Yes, it's all my doing. Good heavens, Cam, do you not have sense enough to tell me when a plan is ill conceived? You seem to have opinions enough on every other matter."

"You were very obviously excited about finding Lord Crutchley's connection to the Lizard," he said defensively. "I got caught up in it. And I've been thinking about other things."

"What other things?"

"You know what other things," he said with a glare. She had him so tied up in knots he didn't know which way was up.

"Oh, you mean the—" she gestured with one hand.

"Yes," he said glancing at her, then turning back to watch the road. "That."

"Well, it's hardly my fault that you cannot concentrate on anything else," she said with a shrug. "I wonder that men are allowed to conduct business at all if they're so incapable of prying their thoughts away from carnal matters."

He ignored the slight, and turned back to the subject at hand. "Do you wish to go back?"

They were already well over a third of the way to Crutchley's estate, but if they were to return without Serena any the wiser, they'd need to go now.

When she didn't respond, he directed the horses to a roadside clearing.

"Why are you stopping?" she asked, frowning.

"Because I wish to know what you've decided," he said, feeling more than a little frustrated with her. Gemma wasn't normally given to behaving like a flibbertigibbet, but today was a marked exception.

"We have to continue," she said with a slight shake of her head. "I hadn't thought to alarm Serena, but knowing how long it will take us to reach Crutchley's home doesn't change my mind about the necessity for the trip. We need to know who stole the fossil. And who killed Sir Everard. He may not have been a particularly good person, but he didn't deserve to be murdered."

Cam leaned back against the padded seat of his curricle. The wind had begun to pick up and the horses were impatient to be on the road again if their huffs of white breath were any indication.

"You are the most maddening lady, Gemma," he said, his own breath a visible vapor in the shelter of the curricle roof. "I thought you were intent on exploring whatever this is between us without the risk of being forced into marriage."

At his words, understanding dawned in her eyes. "Oh, I see now. You're worried this will mean we have to wed."

"Not worried," he said hastily. "Or, perhaps on your behalf. You're the one who wishes to make a life for yourself alone."

He'd told his brother he would try to convince her to change her mind about her plan for a solitary life, but he didn't wish to win her over by default. He wouldn't marry her unless it was of her own free will. He'd seen too many arranged and forced marriages end in unhappiness for both parties.

"I'm embarking on this journey of my own volition, Cam," she told him, putting a gloved hand on his arm. "If it turns out that this hasty trip ends up causing me to abandon my plans, then I'm willing to live with the consequences."

He wanted to protest that he didn't want her that way, but it would be a lie. He wanted her any way he could get her. And the rapidity of his change of heart on that matter was something that frightened him. Only last week, he'd considered her to be one of the most difficult and uncomfortable ladies of his acquaintance. Now he was becoming certain that a life without her would be dreadfully dull.

"If you're sure," he said, placing his hand over hers. And when he caught her gaze going to his mouth, he gave in and leaned forward to kiss her.

It was just a brief meeting of warm mouths, but the contrast with the cold air around them made it that much harder to pull away. But he did so, despite wishing he could wrap her in his arms and keep out the cold. This was a public thoroughfare, however, and he wouldn't expose her to that sort of damage to her reputation, at least.

Still, when he pulled away, she smiled at him and he was almost lost.

"We have to go," she said firmly, before slipping her arm into his. "It looks as if it might rain."

Now she noticed, he thought wryly, "Yes, it does," he said aloud. "If we're lucky it will hold off until we reach Lyme."

But they weren't lucky.

Not long after they had gone another mile, a fat raindrop plopped onto the rump of the left leader. Then more followed that and soon they were experiencing that most uncomfortable of circumstances, driving against the wind into a rainstorm.

Cam's coat and hat were enough to protect him from the worst of it, but Gemma's clothing was made for fashion and not practicality. Thus, her jaunty hat, while pretty, did little to protect her from the shower. Nor did her coat.

Fortunately, they reached a village not far from Lyme a short while later. The inn there, which Cam had had occasion to stay in before, was not particularly luxurious, but clean and comfortable. But its proximity to Lyme meant it was a favorite with tourists visiting the seaside, and even at this time of year it did brisk business.

As he drew the horses to a stop, Cam leapt from the vehicle and when he crossed the wet inn yard to Gemma's side she was already being assisted to the ground by a familiar figure.

"Lord Cameron," said Lord Paley briskly as he slipped his arm through Gemma's and led her into the taproom. "You'd best get out of the rain."

Cam felt the man's presence like a punch to the gut. Of all the people to encounter on this benighted journey, it had to be Paley.

He didn't mistake the way the blackguard's hand rested on Gemma's as they walked, either.

Paley might have agreed to leave her be but it was obvious he found her attractive. What's more, why was he here at all? Wasn't he meant to remain at Pearson Close until Northman gave him permission to leave the area?

He'd just stepped into the interior of the inn when he heard Paley say, "What a surprise to find the two of you here so close to Lyme, Miss Hastings."

Gemma glanced at Cam before responding. "It was an impulse on my part, Lord Paley. I simply had to come to see Mary Anning's collection. Especially after learning that Lady Celeste purchased some things from her."

"So you were able to learn more about Lady Celeste's collection, then?" Paley asked, looking far too avid for Cam's comfort.

"Indeed," she replied, her mouth a little pursed at his obvious curiosity. "And Lord Cameron was kind enough to drive me here."

"What a dreadful bit of luck to encounter such bad

weather, then," Paley said, his eyes narrowed at Cam. "I would have thought Lord Cameron would take better care of his betrothed."

And something about the fellow's air of disapproval, coupled with the knowledge that Gemma's reputation was in real jeopardy thanks to this happenstance meeting, Cam pinned Paley with a glare. "Indeed, she is no longer my betrothed, Lord Paley."

At a gasp from Gemma and a frown from Paley, he continued. "She is now my bride. You may wish us happy."

The sight of Lord Paley at the entrance to The Fish & Fowl had caught Gemma by surprise. Especially since she hadn't considered the notion they'd see anyone of their acquaintance on their journey. It was foolish, she realized now, but she had genuinely been so focused on meeting with Lord Crutchley and questioning him about the lizard skull, and then on arguing with Cam, that it hadn't occurred to her.

For someone who prided herself on her intellect, she was behaving remarkably foolishly these days.

But she noted that Cam seemed far more put out by Lord Paley's presence than she was. If ever there were a man staring daggers, it was Cam and his eyes were, metaphorically at least, stabbing Lord Paley to bits.

"What a dreadful bit of luck to encounter such bad weather, then," Lord Paley was saying. "I would have thought Lord Cameron would take better care of his betrothed."

This ruffled Gemma's feathers on Cam's behalf. Especially given that she'd been the one to insist on making the drive today.

She was about to say so when Cam, looking like a man who was about to lay down a trump card on the table, said with a smile that didn't reach his eyes, "Indeed, she is no longer my betrothed, Lord Paley."

His words surprised her, but they also gave her a sense of foreboding.

Because rather than moving away from her, as would a man who was ending an engagement would do, Cam pulled her to his side, and away from Lord Paley's grasp.

"She is now my bride," he said, his voice ringing with triumph. "You may wish us happy."

Gemma stood as still as a stone for a moment while she watched Lord Paley's eyes narrow on them both. Recognizing that whatever game Cam was playing at there must be a reason for it, she filed away her sense of outrage to be examined later, and turned what she hoped would be interpreted as a smitten gaze on Cam. He, meanwhile, looked genuinely pleased with himself.

"I . . . that is a surprise," Lord Paley said with a puzzled frown.

"Nothing was planned. I hoped, but I was biding my time, you see," Cam told him, squeezing Gemma's hand in warning. "I came to Little Seaford with a special license in my pocket. I just had to convince Miss Hastings—that is, Gemma—to go through with it. My brother performed the ceremony."

To Gemma's relief, Lord Paley seemed to believe the story. And to Gemma's surprise he pumped Cam's hand in an enthusiastic handshake before asking if he could kiss her hand.

Bemused, she extended her hand to him and he bent over it. "I wish you both every happiness," he said with a mix of wistfulness and congratulations. "I do wish I'd met you earlier, Miss Hastings." Then correcting himself, he said, "Lady Cameron, I mean. You're a lucky man, Lord Cameron."

"I well know it, Paley," her false bridegroom responded with a loving glance in her direction. Really, if she hadn't known it was all a hum, she'd have been fooled completely. Cam was a far better actor than she'd first supposed.

Just then, someone opened the door of the taproom and a breeze came in and Gemma realized she was cold and wet and desperately uncomfortable.

"I'll leave you to it, then," said Lord Paley, with a sudden expression of discomfort.

He thinks he's interrupted our wedding night, Gemma thought with a start.

And Cam, who had likely read the other man's expression in the same way, gave him a brisk nod and, keeping her close by his side, moved to where the proprietor had been standing aside waiting until their business with Paley was concluded rather than interrupting.

"Milord," said the man with a deep bow. "I couldn't help but overhear. I'd be happy to offer you our best room. But I'm afraid there's only the one. The rest are full up thanks to the mail coach, which came in just an hour ago."

Gemma bit back an exclamation of frustration. She might have been planning to welcome Cam into her bedchamber at Beauchamp House, but that was before he put himself into her black books by declaring them wed before Lord Paley. He would be lucky if she allowed him to kiss her hand tonight, much less sleep with her in the large bed looming before them. And besides, she had no intention of remaining here tonight. The weather would no doubt turn and they could get to Lord Crutchley's home in time for an evening call.

She said none of this, however, just waited for Cam to reply to the proprietor.

"My—ah, wife," her "husband" said with the air of a man who is not used to the notion of having a bride yet, "will need a hot bath and we'd also like supper in our room."

"Of course," he said with a nod, leading them up a wide staircase to a corridor of doors.

The room he ushered them into was, as Cam had told her, comfortable, but not particularly lush. But the floors were swept and the counterpane and windows looked newly cleaned.

Once the innkeeper left them, and shut the door behind him, Gemma turned to face Cam.

To his credit, he didn't shy away from her scowl.

"You may rip up at me once you're out of your wet clothes," he said firmly. "I may be a liar and a rogue, but at least I won't countenance you catching your death."

She lifted her brows, but untied the ribbons on her hat and removed it. "It seems as if catching my death has been a real possibility in your company of late," she said as she placed the straw confection, now sadly drooping with moisture, on the mantelpiece.

Meanwhile, Cam had shrugged out of his many caped greatcoat and blue superfine. His neckcloth was as limp as Gemma's hat, and though it must be uncomfortable, he didn't remove it.

"Do not give up your comfort for my sensibilities' sake," Gemma said as she began unbuttoning her pelisse. "After all, we're as good as married now."

Cam looked up from an examination of his boots—he was clearly trying to figure out if he should remove them or not—and was arrested by the sight of the bare skin above her bodice. It had been covered by the pelisse, which was long-sleeved and high-necked. As Gemma watched, his eyes darkened and she felt an answering flush run through her.

"I meant your cravat," she said moving her gaze to rest on the knotted linen at his neck.

Wordlessly, he began to loosen the knot that someone—his valet?—had spent a great deal of time perfecting.

It was dreadfully intimate, Gemma realized, just this simple act of watching him unknot his neckcloth. She felt a flutter in her belly and her breath quickened at the realization. This was far more intense than she'd imagined it would be.

When he was finished removing his tie, he stepped closer to her.

She'd never seen a gentleman in shirtsleeves before. Never even seen one with his neck bare. His fine lawn shirt opened into a vee at the hollow beneath his throat, dark curling hair drawing her eye there like a bit of shale in a bed of lime.

"Are you very angry?" he asked softly, reaching out to touch her cheek. His hands were rough. Rougher than those of most gentlemen she guessed. Very likely because he spent much of his time digging in the soil and cleaning fossils and stones. The thought reminded her that she had far more in common with this man who had the ability to bring her to all sorts of strong emotions within the space of a moment.

And yes, anger was one of them.

"A bit," she admitted, but she didn't object as he pulled her against that broad chest she couldn't take her eyes off of. With a sigh, she leaned into his warmth and allowed him to hold her. "You must admit it was a scurvy trick."

To his credit, he didn't laugh at her turn of phrase—an

epithet she'd picked up from the footman, William, who had a brother in the Royal Navy.

"It was, indeed," he said, kissing her on the top of the head as he pulled her closer against him, so that her softness was flush against his solid strength. "I couldn't let Paley leave with the kind of gossip seeing us here together alone would have started, though," he said, his breath warm against her ear. "I'd have had to call him out in truth, this time."

"I know," she said, her own voice sounding breathy to her own ears. "But, without warning. I wasn't ready. I mean, I'd come to the realization that this trip was taking a risk. But . . ."

"There's no way I'd have let you go after you let me into your bed, though, Gemma." His voice sounded apologetic, but there was a hint of steel there that she recognized for what it was. Determination.

She pulled away a little so that she could look him in the eyes. "But you said you would let me go," she said, frowning. "Did you lie?"

He sighed. "I didn't lie. Let us instead call it a temporary agreement about which I hoped to change your mind."

His mouth curved into a sensual smile.

Despite her annoyance with him, she laughed. "Do you really think you're so skilled at this lovemaking business that you'd be able to sway me from my life goals?"

When he only grinned, she laughed again. "You are incorrigible," she said breathlessly. He pulled her close again and took her mouth in a kiss that told her just how confident in his skills he was.

When a knock signaled the servants bringing up the bath, they pulled apart, but Gemma couldn't help but touch her swollen lips.

She watched the play of muscles beneath his shirt and waistcoat as he directed them with the hip bath.

If he was as good as he thought he was, she mused, perhaps it was a good thing they were away from Beauchamp House for this.

Chapter 21

Before she left, the maid, who'd come up with toweling and borrowed nightclothes from the proprietor's wife, asked tentatively, "Would you like me to assist you, milady?"

Cam had been preparing to put his coat back on, as well as his soggy neckcloth, so that he could go down to the taproom while Gemma bathed, and was startled to hear her tell the girl no and send her on her way.

When they were alone again, he turned from looking at the door to find her watching him.

He hadn't been this overwhelmed by the prospect of bedding a woman since he was a lad. And just having her gaze on him was almost enough to send him over the edge.

"I'll need your help with my gown," she said, her nerves betrayed only by a hint of color in her cheekbones. It had taken some degree of bravery for her to say it so calmly, and he realized he was behaving like a halfling.

She turned her back to him as she stood beside the steaming tub, and wordlessly he crossed to where she waited. When he brushed his fingers over the nape of her neck, he heard her intake of breath, and watched as goose pimples rose on the soft skin there.

The pearl buttons that ran down to the dip just above her heart-shaped bottom were tiny, and not particularly easy to slip through the wool of her gown. So he took his time, unfastening them one by one, allowing himself the luxury of a touch here, a brush of his fingers there, as button by button, the soft creamy skin of her back just visible through the think chemise she wore beneath, revealed itself to him like a flower opening to the sun.

It was impulse that made him kiss her as he went. He let his fingers follow the line of buttons as he concentrated his mouth on the gentle slope of her shoulder, the gossamer place below her ear.

He could feel her shiver at his touch, and it wasn't from cold.

But he wanted her to know that he did nothing that she didn't want too.

"Is this agreeable?" he asked, as his fingers stole their way down her back, unfastening as they went.

She giggled a little, and he paused. "What's funny?"

Turning to face him, she held up the bodice of her gown, which was now gaping in the back.

"I hadn't expected you to be the sort of man who asked permission," she said with a raised brow.

He blinked. That was rather a lowering thought. "You think I take without asking?" he asked, tilting his head to look at her. He supposed he hadn't always been the picture of kindness in her presence, but nor had he expected her to assume he was the kind of fellow who would ravish a lady without gaining any kind of agreement from her.

His dismay must have shown on his face because her brows knit. "I didn't mean it as a criticism," she said, her expression troubled now. "Only that you surprised me. I thought asking you to share my bed at Beauchamp House was a sort of blanket permission."

"That was before I set the cat amongst the pigeons by telling Paley we were wed," he said with a shake of his head. "I should have thought you might at the very least need to revisit the issue, given that not very long ago you seemed as if you wanted to toss me bodily from the window."

She glanced at the window, which was rather small, but would have done the job if she had the strength of anger on her side.

"I do not understand you, Cam," she said finally. "One moment you seem to want nothing more than to hold me in your arms, and the next you're almost diffident."

"Because I'm trying not to ride roughshod over you," he said, pulling away and thrusting a hand through his hair. "I know you think I'm a . . . a bully, but I am trying not to be for your sake."

He heard her gasp and then felt her hand on his back. "Cam, I don't think you're a bully," she said firmly. "No more than I am. And I know quite well that I can be as stubborn as they come."

"I . . . regret that first meeting between us, Gemma," he said on a sigh. "More than you can ever know."

"Well, I don't," she said, and he had to turn to see her face because her words were so jarring.

"You despised me that day," he said frowning. "I despised me that day."

"But we've got past that, haven't we?" she asked, still grasping her gown to her chest. "There's more to a person's personality than one moment."

"Of course there is," he agreed. "But I want to be better for you. I was so angry then. At everything. I misunderstood some things about . . . life. And I'm not that bitter man anymore."

"I know you're not," she said softly. "I wouldn't be here

with you otherwise. No matter how much I wanted to learn the truth about this business with Sir Everard."

He had no time to respond because she let go of her gown then and she was standing before him in nothing more than her shift and stockings. With the fire behind her, he could see her sweet curves outlined in the light. Unable to stop himself, he reached out to touch her where her waist dipped in.

But she danced away from him. And moving to the side of the tub, she looked him in the eye then reached down and unfastened her garters, then rolled down her stockings. She took her time, just as he'd done with her buttons and by the time she was finished he was in danger of losing his control entirely.

When he reached down to lift her chemise, he knew he should turn away but a team of oxen couldn't have pulled his gaze away from his first sight of her gloriously naked.

Without a backward glance, she stepped into the hip bath and sighed as she sank into the warm water.

He was in danger of pulling her out of the bath and onto the bed when a knock sounded on the door. He made sure the screen was blocking the view of her, and opened the door to reveal the innkeeper and a couple of footmen with a table and trays of food.

The man seemed to wish to chat about everything from the weather to the state of the roads, but Cam finally had to cut him off in mid-sentence and send him on his way.

Gemma had left the bath and was rosy cheeked and dressed in a very practical flannel nightdress and dressing gown by the time he turned back to her. He felt a pang of disappointment before remembering he'd be taking off those prim garments before much time had passed.

"That smells divine," she said, padding over to the table in her bare feet. "I hadn't realized I was so hungry."

His senses once more in control, Cam took the seat opposite her. He had to admit that the food—fish stew, crusty bread and small beer—was delicious, and like Gemma he was hungrier than he'd thought.

As if by agreement, they talked about inconsequential matters while they ate. She told him about a recent encounter she and Sophia had with Squire Northman's wife, who still hadn't forgiven the ladies of Beauchamp House for an ill-fated dinner party when they first arrived. Cam related an amusing story about his brother Freddie and his angst about the prospect of his infant daughter ever being of an age to have gentleman callers.

"But why should that bother him," Gemma asked, tearing off a bit of bread. "I should think it was something that fathers took for granted."

"Freddie is the one of us who—before he was wed, mind you—had the most rakish reputation," Cam explained. He'd always found Freddie's ability to charm the wings off a ladybug a bit annoying if truth be told. It all seemed so easy for Freddie. Cam didn't hurt for female company, but he certainly didn't have the gift for easy conversation that his brothers did. Aloud, he continued, "I suppose he's afraid that his baby daughter will one day meet the latter day equivalent of . . . himself?"

Gemma laughed at that. "Poor Freddie. But at least he'll know what to look out for. It takes one to know one, after all."

It was a good point. "I'll tell him you said so," Cam said with a nod. "Though in fairness, he's been as straight as an arrow since he married Leonora. He's desperately in love with her."

Even as he said it, he wished he'd kept his mouth shut. He might be hellbent on marrying Gemma at this point, but love hadn't really entered into their conversation thus far. And he didn't wish to force it there just now either.

But, Gemma had no such reservations. "Will you be disappointed to be the brother who didn't marry for love?" she asked softly. There was something tentative in her tone, as if she knew it would be a sore subject. But his Gemma wasn't one to shirk difficult conversations.

He reached across the table to take her hand. "There might be love between us," he said seriously. "I hope there will be. There is certainly passion. And affection."

"I see how it is between my sister and Benedick," she said with a smile. "I hope it will be like that with us."

"For now, let's see how it is with us there," he nodded to the bed, which had been looming in the background throughout the meal.

With a nod, she rose. He did too, and crossed to where she stood.

Before things could become awkward between them, he pulled her against him and kissed her with all the passion he'd been holding in check.

"Yes," she said against his mouth. "The answer to your question is yes."

Without replying, he took her in his arms again and carried her the short distance to the bed.

Chapter 22

Gemma felt her heartbeat jump as he carried her to the bed, but rather than laying her down on it, he set her on her feet beside it.

"What are you doing?" she asked, puzzled.

"Removing this chastity belt of a nightdress," he said with a wry look.

But when he began to remove the dressing gown, she shooed his hands away and said primly, "You remove your clothes, sir. I will manage my own."

And without argument, his hands went to the buttons on his waistcoat and she shrugged out of the dressing gown and then began unbuttoning what really was the most unenticing flannel nightdress she'd ever seen. She paused, however, when he pulled his lawn shirt over his head.

The hint of hair she'd seen earlier when he uncoiled his neckcloth proved to trail down the center of his chest, and she took in the sight of his broad, muscled chest—the skin slightly tanned from some time spent out of doors in the sun. She'd felt its firmness with her own hands, but the sight of it, and the trail of curly dark hair that disappeared into his breeches was enough to make her mouth dry with wanting. This was what it meant to be intimate, she realized. Knowing what a man looked like out of his clothes as well as in them.

He tossed his shirt to the floor, and turned back to find her watching him.

"You seem very well made," she said, trying to maintain some dignity even as she felt her cheeks heat. Then, realizing what she'd said, she felt her ears turn red as well.

But to her relief, he didn't laugh, only said gravely, "Thank you. As are you."

And gently, as if he were trying not to spook a nervous horse, he moved his hands to where hers clutched the buttons of her nightdress and finished unbuttoning it for her. The enormity of what was to come sent a wave of emotion through her then, and she was grateful for the care he took with her. She looked down when the idea of meeting his eyes became too much, but she saw the bulge in his breeches there and looked up and focused on a freckle on his bare shoulder instead.

But then she was looking into his eyes again because he'd pushed the flannel gown off her shoulders and it fell with a shushing sound to the floor.

"My bosom is far too small," she said as she felt his eyes roam over her. "And I'm too fleshy around the middle."

She was about to continue with a critique of her legs, but he stopped her with his mouth. His voice husky he said to her, "You are the most beautiful thing I've ever seen."

He pulled away, and cupped her breast. "See how it fits perfectly in my hand."

She glanced down and the sight of his dark hand on her pale skin sent a wave of heat through her.

"And in my mouth," he said lifting her onto the bed, then following her up.

Just his words were enough to send a stab of sensation to her core.

And then he suited his words to deed and took her rosy nipple into his hot mouth and she thought she would combust. "Oh." She clutched at his shoulders as if she could pull him closer. Then he stroked a thumb over her other breast and she felt another jolt of fire run between her breast and her center.

"Perfection," he said, his deep voice vibrating through her as he kissed his way down her breast and over her ribs. "As soft as silk and so responsive."

A restlessness was taking over her, however, and she wanted him back with his mouth on her.

"You're as well formed as one of Elgin's marbles come to life," he said opening his mouth over the dip of her waist and then kissing his way further down.

Gemma was awash in desire at the sensations he roused, but when she felt his hand grip her hip, she realized what lay at the destination his mouth seemed intent on visiting. "Wait, Cam, where are you . . . ?"

She felt his laugh softly against her lower belly. Pushing himself up a little, he looked up at her and she was taken aback by the view of him looking up her naked body at her.

"Do you trust me, sweet?" he asked, his eyes dark with passion. "Because I very much want to kiss you here. And I think it will make your pleasure when I take you better."

"You think?" she asked, suddenly very aware of the fact that this was the strangest conversation she'd ever engaged in.

He had the decency to look abashed. "I'm afraid I don't have any experience bedding virgins," he said with a slight shrug. "But the last thing I want is to give you pain and I know there can be pain the first time . . ."

His expression betrayed his concern about causing her discomfort and Gemma felt her chest constrict at the knowledge. He was so much kinder than he revealed to the world.

"Very well," she said with a small nod. "If you think this will help with . . ."

And without waiting for her to finish her statement, he shifted so that her knees were over his shoulders. Her complaint, however, lodged in her throat as she felt his hot tongue slide up the center of her, right where she hadn't even known she needed him.

It was as if her body came alive at his touch, each new stroke of his tongue stoking the fire within her to higher flames. When he added his fingers, stroking then gently pressing inside of her, she cried out. That was what she needed. There, his fingers filling her. Of their own volition, her hips bucked against his staying hands, and she felt an overwhelming rush of excitement as she spiraled over some imaginary precipice into darkness.

When she came back to herself, she was slightly embarrassed, but her limbs were far too limp to do anything about it.

She felt Cam kiss her thigh before he moved up her body. Somewhere along the line he must have shed his breeches because she felt his strong legs slide against hers as he shifted to kneel between them.

His kiss was remarkably tender as he slid her knee over his hip, placing his arousal at the heart of her, and the press of him, when it came, was uncomfortable but not painful. She waited for him to be fully seated, and when he stopped, she exhaled slowly.

"All right?" She could feel the tension in his body, and knew his patience was not without cost to him. But he made no complaint.

She reached up a hand to stroke her thumb over his fur-rowed brow. "Yes," she said softly, memorizing his expression in this moment so that she'd remember it always. And before she finished the syllable he began to withdraw.

This was different from the anxiety of that first stroke, and Gemma felt bereft as he left her.

"Can't go slow," Cam said, in a voice both strained and apologetic, as he began to move faster and Gemma thought she would weep with relief. With each thrust, she struggled to hold on to him, and of their own volition her knees clasped him to her. His movements sent her into another frenzy of sensation, and she began to spiral up, up, up into the ether once more, even as she heard the sound of their breaths, and felt every touch of skin and sweat between them.

"Come for me, sweet," he said as his movements became more desperate and unable to hold back, she let herself fly.

As she let the feeling of bliss overtake her, she heard him cry out her name.

Not wanting to crush her, Cam flipped them so that she was lying on his chest, though it took every ounce of strength he had left to do it.

Never in his life had he felt more inclined to sleep than at this moment.

"Just a few minutes," he promised her, kissing the top of head as he struggled to get his breath back.

As it happened, however, a few minutes turned into a few hours and when he awoke again it was to find she'd moved to settle at his side, her gloriously naked leg entwined in his and her hair a tangle of curls.

He let his gaze drift lazily over her as he considered the consequences of what had been, all things considered, the most important act of his adult life.

He knew she'd been intent on ending their betrothal once the year was over. He'd been intent upon it too. But once he'd made the decision to wed her, it had become a goal he had no intention of giving up. And now that she'd lain with him, there would be no ending their betrothal. Especially not with the possibility of a child.

"You're thinking quite hard, I believe," she said, and he saw that she'd been watching him.

Her lips curved into a mischievous smile as she stretched her arms over her head.

"Thinking about you," he said, pulling her up onto his chest. Gemma gave a slight shriek at the manhandling then she sat with her knees on either side of him.

"You're going to rouse the inn with cries like that," he chided, brow raised. "Though I suppose they've already decided we're shameless newlyweds."

To his amusement, the unfazeable Miss Gemma Hastings looked abashed. "Do you think they heard us?" she asked, looking worried.

"You were quite loud at times," he said with shrug. "But," he added, "so was I, if it comes to that. I feel sure this inn has heard worse than the pair of us."

That must have relieved her concerns because she nodded, then leaned forward to kiss him. "I had no idea you had such a gift for tender talk," she said as she stroked her thumb over the stubble of his jaw. "In fact, you were much more considerate than I'd have imagined."

He let her control the kiss for a moment, letting her tongue stroke his until it was impossible to tell who was leading. When she pulled her mouth away, he stayed her torso with a hand. "Why should it surprise you I'm a considerate lover?" he asked softly.

He wasn't sure why it mattered, but he didn't want to

think Gemma had thought he'd be an inconsiderate lout either.

"Well, I have no one to compare you to," she admitted with a shrug. "But, given our tendency to rip up at one another, I had thought perhaps you'd be—I don't know—more demanding, I suppose."

"And what did you find?"

She grinned. "That you were gentle and sweet," she said, laying her head on his chest, and stretching her legs out over the top of his. "But also, forceful when I needed you to be."

"Forceful, eh?" he stroked a hand down her spine to the soft roundness of her bottom. "You liked that?"

"Very much," she said, toying with his chest hair.

"Gentle and sweet and forceful," he said. "Quite a combination."

"But you can change them up when the mood suits," she said with equanimity.

"Thank you so much, my dear," he said wryly. "And what of my wishes?"

"Of course you must tell me what you like too," she said, and she sat up again and looked down at him. A long lock of dark blonde hair fell down to cover her breast and he couldn't help but reach out and wrap it around his finger.

"Cam," she said, calling his attention back to her face. "I mean it, you mustn't feel as if you can't tell me what you want. I can assure you that I won't hold back from telling you."

He heard the note of concern in her voice and let go of her hair and took her hand. Kissing her palm, he assured her, "I will. Though I'm sorry to say that my wants are quite uncomplicated. I want you, however I can get you. The ways and iterations aren't all that important."

Her brow furrowed and he watched in amusement as she considered that there were likely more iterations than she'd previously imagined.

"Do you mean to say you do not wish to take me bent over a chair?" she asked, with a frown. And suddenly he could think of nothing in the world he wanted more. He glanced at the wooden chairs they'd sat in for supper and considered if it were feasible.

She must have read his expression right because she laughed. "So, perhaps your wants aren't quite as uncomplicated as you'd thought," she said wryly.

He shrugged. "Perhaps not," he agreed. "I will amend my statement and say that I very much want you in every way possible. You are the part of the equation that cannot vary."

"I feel sure Daphne would have something to say about your arithmetic," Gemma said.

And having decided they'd talked enough—especially given that his prick had very much liked the chair idea and wanted to be appeased, he flipped her onto her back again.

"You cannot keep doing that," she scolded, though it was evident from her wide smile that she wasn't as unhappy as she seemed. "What if I wished to control things?"

"Later," he told her, "you told me you liked it when I'm forceful."

He pressed her hands above her head and held them there with one hand while his other stroked over her straining breast, and down her belly.

"Yes," she said in a husky tone. "I do like it."

"Good," he said against her neck.

And when his hand reached the wetness at her center, he stroked over her once before guiding himself into her. With one swift thrust he filled her and they both cried out with relief at the joining.

"Let me touch you," she said, pulling her hands. "Oh please, Cam."

But he lifted her knee over his hip and thrust again. "Not yet. Trust me, sweet." He leaned down to kiss her.

And as he built up the fire between them, using the friction of her nipples against his chest to stoke them both, she began to twist beneath him.

"Cam," she exhaled as she followed his strokes with her hips and they began to move in tandem. He felt her inner muscles clutch him and he quickened his pace bringing her toward an edge that both of them longed to go over. When he felt the telltale tingle in his spine, he let go of her hands and she cried out again, the sudden freedom spurring her climax. And then they were both soaring over the edge into pleasure's abyss.

Chapter 23

When Gemma awoke the next morning, feeling sated and a little sore, she was disappointed to find herself in the bed alone. But, much as she would like to remain here forever, there were still important things to be done outside of their cocoon of bliss. So when the maid scratched on the bedchamber door and entered with hot water for washing, she welcomed the girl in and set about putting herself to rights.

By some miracle they'd managed to brush out her gown and pelisse and she'd be able to wear it to Lord Crutchley's without fear of disgracing herself.

She was putting the final pins into the simple chignon she'd managed with her hair—thanks to pins borrowed from the maid since she couldn't find where hers had gone the night before—when Cam returned. He too had had his waterlogged coats from the day before brushed and dried out and his cravat was even snowy white again.

"I thought we'd set out after breakfast," he said, clearly mindful of the maid's presence.

When the girl was gone, and Gemma had turned to face him, he stepped forward and kissed her properly.

"Good morning," he said, pulling away, though he did take her hands in his.

"I missed you," she said simply. It was the truth, and if she were going to be in this with him she wouldn't suppress her feelings.

"I wanted to let you sleep for as long as you could," he said with a smile. Then, ruefully, he added, "And I wasn't sure I could keep myself from reaching for you again."

"But I wouldn't have minded," she told him, her heart beating faster at the thought.

"That's precisely why I had to leave," he told her firmly. "You might not care about your poor, ill-used body, but I do."

"Your being the sensible one is very tedious," she complained. "Though I will admit to some soreness, so perhaps you were right."

He pulled her arm through his, but not before kissing her hand. "If we are to find your lizard then you need to be in fighting shape."

At the mention of the Beauchamp Lizard, Gemma sighed. "Right again. So let's be off."

It took nearly an hour for them to breakfast in a private dining room, and by the time Cam lifted her into his curricle, it was almost mid-morning.

They made good time, however, and since yesterday's rain had all but passed, leaving in its wake the same cloudy skies and brisk winds that had come before it, they remained dry if chilled.

The innkeeper had given Cam the direction of the Crutchley estate, and when the curricle turned into the evergreen-lined drive, Gemma sent up a tiny prayer that he'd have the information they needed.

Grooms were at the ready to take the reins from Cam and when he helped Gemma down, they were greeted by a dour-looking butler flanked by bewigged, liveried footmen.

"You're expected, Lord Cameron, Lady Cameron," said the butler as he gestured them into the imposing wide doors of the sandstone manor house.

Gemma's eyes widened at the words, and a glance at Cam revealed him to be as surprised as she was.

How did anyone at Lord Crutchley's estate know about their ruse at the inn? Besides the innkeeper and his staff, only Lord Paley had . . .

As if conjured by her thought, that gentleman himself stepped forward and took her hand. "Lady Cameron," he said with a silky smile, "How good to see you again."

"Paley," said Cam from beside her. She hadn't noticed the way he held her against his side, as if to protect her from the urbane gentleman before them. "What a surprise."

"Only if you think it a surprise to find me at my godfather's estate," said Lord Paley with a charming smile that didn't meet his eyes.

"Godfather?" Gemma shook her head. The possibility of a connection between the men hadn't even occurred to her.

"But let's not discuss it in the hallway," said Paley with a welcoming gesture. "Come into the drawing room. Lord Crutchley is quite eager to meet you both."

Not as eager, Gemma guessed, as she was to meet him. There were many things she wished to question the man about, not least of which was more about what Lord Paley might have told him about the goings-on at Pearson Close and Beauchamp House.

Feeling Cam's strong hand at her lower back, she followed the viscount up the double-sided staircase and into a lushly carpeted hallway.

The drawing room was a lavish chamber with brightly colored wall hangings and floor to ceiling windows that looked out over what was, at this time of year, a rather dour landscape.

Before the fire sat an elderly gentleman, who rose upon their entrance.

"Miss Hastings," he said as they neared him. "What a delight to finally make your acquaintance."

She curtseyed before him, then offered him her hand, which he kissed.

Behind her, she heard Cam clear his throat before saying, "I'm afraid she is no longer Miss Hastings, Crutchley, but Lady Cameron Lisle."

And as Cam stepped forward to exchange bows with the older gentleman, Crutchley laughed. "Too right, my boy. If this were my lady I'd be quick to claim her as my own as well. Especially if, as Paley has told me, she's the gift of knowing wheat from chaff."

Before Gemma could respond to that, Paley gestured for them to all be seated and once he was also in a chair, he said, "I wish you'd confided in me when we met yesterday that you intended to visit my godfather. But I suppose you had other things on your mind."

The insinuation hung in the air between them for a moment before Lord Crutchley spoke up, apparently oblivious to his nephew's gaffe. "I must admit, I have wished to make your acquaintance, Lady Cameron, ever since I learned Lady Celeste had chosen you to be one of her heiresses. That lady had as good an eye for fossils as anyone I've ever known and it wounded me dreadfully to know she was taken from this world so prematurely."

"But I don't understand," Gemma said with a frown. "How did you even know who I was?"

"Oh I didn't, I didn't," he assured her with a wave of a gnarled hand. "But I did know Celeste, and if she chose you to be the keeper of her collection, well, then that was endorsement enough for me. I may not move about in local society much anymore but I do have my ways of learning about the goings-on in the area. Paley, for instance, has been most informative about the goings-on at Beauchamp House and of course the gathering of fossil hunters at Pearson Close."

"Imagine my surprise," Lord Paley said before Gemma could respond, "when I learned that the collection at Beauchamp House I'd so recently toured was one which he'd played a role in shaping with Lady Celeste."

"You're overstating it, boy," said the older man with a frown. "I merely accompanied Celeste on a few of her fossil-hunting expeditions. That collection was all Celeste's doing. Especially once we had our falling-out."

This was the first Gemma had heard of a rift, and she risked a glance at Cam to see if he too was surprised. His answering nod told her he was.

"I had seen some mention of you in her collection note-books," Gemma said, trying not to appear too eager for information lest Lord Crutchley should regret his confidences. "But nothing about an argument."

"Oh it wasn't really an argument, my dear," said the old man. "It was really more wounded pride on my part."

He shook his head at the memory, then continued, "You see, she found a fossil skull that she was convinced held the key to some major understanding of the way that animal life developed on the Sussex coast. Found it right there on the bit of shore beneath Beauchamp House. And despite her trying to keep quiet about it until she was able to do some investigation into it, word spread among the collecting circles. Well, since I was there with her when she found the blasted thing, she thought I'd been the one to spread the news. It wasn't me, of course, and she even went so far as to take measures to hide the thing away because she became convinced someone would try to steal it from her."

"And did you know where she hid it?" Gemma asked, her breath catching.

"No," Lord Crutchley said with a mournful shake of his head. "And what's more, I didn't ever talk to her again after that dustup between us. I was stubborn in those days, and that bit of doubt on her part was enough to make me storm off in a huff and never go back. But I always regretted it. Always."

To Gemma's surprise, he wiped away a tear. "I'm a sentimental old fool, you see, and I thought we'd make it up again some way. But she was gone before someday ever came."

"I feel sure she would have liked to see you again," Gemma said quietly. Having read her benefactress's journals and other writings, she knew that while proud, Lady Celeste had been a loving person and she didn't doubt that if Lord Crutchley had initiated contact with her, Lady Celeste would have welcomed him with open arms.

"So you have no idea where she might have hidden the fossilized skull?" Cam asked, changing the subject back to the fossil.

"I don't," said Lord Crutchley. "Though we did have a mad conversation once about the best place to hide one's valuables. I thought of it because Paley, here, mentioned that you'd found a particularly impressive skull on that same stretch of shore, Miss H—er, Lady Cameron."

"And what was that?" Gemma held her breath, not quite daring to hope what he was about to say. They'd come here to ask the man about his dealings with Lady Celeste, but if he could give them some way to secure the provenance of the skull, they'd be that much closer to finding the person who stole it.

"Well," Crutchley said with a laugh, "we decided the best place to hide a thing was in plain sight, and for a thing dug up from the earth, that would be back in the same place where you'd found it."

At Lord Crutchley's confirmation that Gemma's fossil and the Beauchamp Lizard were one and the same, Cam saw Gemma's eyes light with triumph for a split second before she shuttered her gaze.

"Of course," Crutchley continued, "I would have no way of knowing if Celeste followed through on the scheme. For all I know, she locked the Beauchamp Lizard away in a safe place. But I must admit when Paley told me about the fossil you'd found, Lady Cameron, I did wonder."

"The business with Sir Everard does make it seem even more likely that the fossil is one and the same," Lord Paley added with a shrewd look. "Though I do wonder how he could possibly have known where to search for it. I only found out about my godfather's involvement with Lady Celeste last evening, so it wasn't me."

"And you've never met Sir Everard yourself, Lord Crutchley?" Gemma asked, frowning. Cam could all but hear the theories spinning through her head.

Then, another possibility occurred to him.

"Was there anyone else who might have heard your discussion with Lady Celeste about possible hiding places, Crutchley?" Cam asked. While he thought it was more likely Sir Everard had merely stumbled upon Gemma's work, there was something a bit too coincidental about the blackguard's boasts that it might be the famed Beauchamp Lizard.

"Or," Gemma added, "someone she might have confided in?"

Crutchley's lined face twisted into an expression of distaste. "There was one person who spent a great deal of time around her that year, but I never thought she trusted him enough to confide something like that in him. And if she had told him, he'd have stolen it long ago."

"Who was it, Lord Crutchley?" Gemma's impatience was beginning to show, Cam thought, noting her white knuckles on the arms of her chair.

"I suppose there's no harm in telling you," the old man said with a frown. "Though I know she was dreadfully embarrassed about the whole matter at the time."

Cam was beginning to understand Gemma's impatience.

Finally, though, Crutchley continued.

"I always understood that Celeste had decided at a certain point that she would never marry," he explained. "Especially as by that time she'd built up the estate at Beauchamp House on her own and was known as a scholar in her own right on many subjects including fossils. But there was a man who wanted desperately to marry her. I always suspected it was more because he wanted to own her, like a specimen in his collection."

Cam saw Gemma shiver at the description. He'd certainly known men like that—who saw women not as their own persons but instead as objects to possess. He was glad, suddenly, that Lady Celeste, who by all accounts was an independent and strong woman, had managed to evade this scoundrel.

"You may be wondering why I am so slow to reveal who this man was," Crutchley said with a rueful shake of his head. "But it's because in the years since Lady Celeste discovered the Beauchamp Lizard, he's come to be well known in the world of fossil collecting, though he himself has never once been the one to dig up his own specimens."

Something about the description made the hair on the back of Cam's neck stand on end.

It couldn't be.

But Crutchley's next words confirmed it.

"I believe you both are well acquainted with him," he said, with a nod to both Cam and Paley. "I'm speaking, of course, of Maximillian Pearson."

"Pearson?" Gemma asked, her shock evident. "But how is that possible? He cannot be old enough to have courted Lady Celeste twenty years ago, for one thing."

"Oh he was a stripling at the time," Crutchley assured her. "Barely twenty years old and yet he thought himself cock of the walk. He didn't care if Celeste wanted him or not. He wanted her and that was what mattered."

"But surely his parents," Gemma protested. "I cannot imagine any young heir's father being sanguine about his son marrying a lady so many years his senior."

"His father died when young Max was barely fifteen," Crutchley explained. "And his mother was no match for his strong will. Though Celeste did try to speak to her about the way he wouldn't take no for an answer. It was no help, obviously."

"Since she didn't marry Pearson," Cam said, "then I can only assume something managed to convince him to let her be."

"I'm afraid, Lady Cameron, that it might be a tale too delicate for your ears."

Cam almost laughed when Gemma tried to control her impulse to scoff at the notion.

Instead, however, she said simply, "I am a married lady,

Lord Crutchley. I'm sure it will not scandalize me over-much."

When the elderly gentleman turned his beseeching gaze to Cam, he shrugged. "I will not make up my wife's mind for her," he said. Though it did amuse him to note how quickly he'd come to think of her as his wife in the twelve hours or so since their pretend marriage.

"If you insist, Lady Cameron," said the elderly lord. "One afternoon, not long after Celeste found the lizard skull, we were . . . ah . . . behaving amorously on the shore below Beauchamp House when Pearson came looking for her. He had become suspicious of the amount of time we spent together, and made it his practice to simply show up without invitation at odd hours, in an effort to ensure that he had no serious rivals."

Gemma's cheeks turned a bit pink, but other than that, she remained unfazed by the confession. "And what did he do?" she asked, frowning. "I cannot imagine how dreadful it must have been for Lady Celeste to be spied on in such a manner."

"Oh, she was furious," Crutchley confirmed. "As was I. I wanted to call him out but she wouldn't let me. Pearson himself was more shocked than angry. He was, after all, little more than a lad. He'd put her on a pedestal and hadn't considered that she might be, as a woman some two decades older, someone with desires that he knew nothing about."

"And that ended things for him?" Cam asked. It was a bit difficult to believe that a man who was so covetous would simply give up at the first sign of difficulty.

"It was the beginning of the end," Crutchley said. "He called on her the next day and informed her that he was disappointed, but would forgive her if she promised she would agree never to see me again. Of course she refused."

"Of course she did," Gemma said with a scowl. "The nerve of the man."

"He took that badly, but he spent a few more weeks trying to bully her into accepting him. But gradually, he became more and more withdrawn. By the time she and I parted ways, he no longer left his estate. And, I'm quite sure it was the beginning of his hatred of all women. It wasn't until his mother's death some ten years later that he was able to eradicate all women from his life—even the servants. From what Paley has told me, he's become a total recluse now."

"You mentioned, Lord Crutchley," Gemma said, bringing the conversation back to their reasons for being here, "that you thought Pearson might have known Lady Celeste had hidden the lizard skull where she found it. Why is that?"

"That day he spied on us," Crutchley explained, "was the same day we discussed her fears that someone would steal the fossil. It was also not long afterward that Pearson became a fossil collector himself."

That was a bit of news Cam hadn't expected. "You mean to say Pearson had no interest in stones and fossils until Lady Celeste rejected him?"

"I think at first," Crutchley said, "the boy considered it was a way to take something from her. She wanted to add to her collection, so he wanted to ensure that the fossils she most coveted she didn't get."

"That's certainly mean-spirited," said Lord Paley with a frown. "I must admit, I had no notion that Pearson knew Lady Celeste at all, much less that he'd once been fixated on her. He must be livid that Lady Celeste left her collection to you."

It was news to Cam as well, and he couldn't help but wonder if Pearson's vendetta against Lady Celeste went beyond the lady's death.

"But if he knew that she planned to rebury it," Gemma asked, brows furrowed, "then why did he not go dig it up himself ages ago?"

"Perhaps he didn't put two and two together," Cam offered. "He was likely far more focused on the—happenings—on the beach. Remember it was Celeste he wanted then, not her fossils. It was only later that he decided to compete with her in that arena. And by then, the lizard had become an unseen legend. No one knew where it was. And after a time, it was forgotten."

"For all that he began to fancy himself an expert," Lord Crutchley offered, "it was always quite clear to me that Pearson wasn't particularly gifted in the brain box. He was far more about spending his coin to acquire things than in learning about why they mattered."

The visit had been even more illuminating than Cam could have imagined. He was about to rise and usher Gemma back out to his curricle when they all heard a disturbance downstairs.

"So many visitors," said Lord Crutchley with ill-disguised excitement. It made Cam feel a pang of pity for the old gentleman, who clearly craved company.

But when the butler appeared at the door to the drawing room, his words made him switch his pity from Crutchley to himself.

"The Reverend Lord Benedick Lisle and Lady Benedick Lisle," the servant said as Ben and Sophia entered looking travel-worn and somewhat harassed.

Well, perhaps only Ben. Sophia looked happy enough.

"What a relief it is to find you are both safe," Sophia said with a smile. "You must forgive us, gentlemen. We were expecting them back—"

"Dear Sophia," Gemma interrupted her, and Cam noticed that she was trying to communicate something to her sister with her eyes, "we did tell you that we would be paying a call at Lord Crutchley's estate after our wedding night in Lyme."

At the words "wedding night" Cam noticed a muscle in his brother's jaw jump.

Still, to his relief, Benedick smiled indulgently and said, "You know how your sister worries about you, Gemma. I fear she is having a difficult time—and I admit, I am as well—believing that you and my brother have married. It seems only yesterday we were discussing the surprise of your betrothal."

Cam was grateful for his brother's going along with their ruse, but he knew with the surety of a lifetime as Ben's younger brother that he would pay dearly for it later.

Chapter 24

Gemma watched the interplay between the Lisle brothers as Viscount Paley introduced Sophia and Ben to his godfather.

Benedick, it turned out, was a far better actor than she'd supposed because it was obvious to her, at least, that he wanted nothing more than to drag his brother out of the drawing room by the ear.

For his part, Lord Crutchley just seemed delighted to have more visitors.

"It's delightful to see you both again so soon," said Lord Paley as he rang for refreshments. It was clear to Gemma, at least, that he spent a great deal of time in Crutchley's house, which made her feel somewhat better for the elderly man's situation. It had bothered her once she learned of his connection with Lady Celeste that he seemed to be lonely for company.

"It's certainly a surprise," Benedick agreed as he moved to stand with his back to the fire. "Though you mustn't allow us to burden you with unexpected visitors. We merely wished to assuage my wife's worry for her sister's welfare. Now that we've done that, we will all leave you to your peace and quiet, of course."

"But that's absurd," Lord Crutchley protested. "You cannot mean to make the drive back to Little Seaford without a meal at the very least."

And that was how the party from Beauchamp House ended up partaking of the midday meal at the home of Lord Crutchley.

It felt somewhat absurd, Gemma thought, considering that she and Cam were pretending to be married, while her sister and brother-in-law pretended to believe it. And Lord Crutchley and Lord Paley believed the pretense to be the truth.

Sheridan couldn't have written a more absurd farce.

The delay of their departure, however, allowed her and Cam to explain what they'd learned from Lord Crutchley about his time spent with Lady Celeste and just how much they'd not known about Maximillian Pearson's history with her.

"What a dreadful time Lady Celeste must have had with him watching her all the time," Sophia said with a frown. "I am no longer surprised that she chose not to marry. I wonder that she ever entertained the prospect at all."

"Oh, she was made of stern stuff," Lord Crutchley assured her. "Your benefactress was one of the most intelligent and strong-minded ladies I ever had the pleasure to meet."

He gave a wink in Gemma's direction. "Though I believe your sister may be the first I've met in years to hold a candle to Celeste. If I were twenty years younger, and I'd met her first, I'd have given Lord Cameron a run for his money."

Gemma blushed at the elderly gentleman's blandishments. "I'm quite sure I don't deserve such praise, my lord."

But Cam surprised her by agreeing with their host.

"Gemma is the cleverest lady of my acquaintance, Crutchley. But I must admit to a bit a relief at having won her before she made your acquaintance, for I feel quite sure I'd have had a time convincing her I was worthy."

"If you would believe it, Crutchley," said Ben drolly, "these two were at loggerheads with one another only a week ago. I still can't quite believe they're wed."

Gemma suppressed her desire to kick her brother-in-law in the shin. But Sophia must have done it for her if his sudden yelp were anything to go by.

The meal passed without further incident, and soon enough, the sisters and brothers were taking their leave of Crutchley and his godson.

"Thank you all for giving an old man a chance to relive happy memories," their host said as he took Gemma's hands in his. "I know without a doubt that Celeste would have been pleased as punch to know she'd left her collection in the hands of such a special lady."

"Thank you for sharing your stories," she told him, then kissing him on the cheek. "I feel as if I know Lady Celeste even better now. And I hope we'll be able to find her Beauchamp Lizard and put it back in her collection where it belongs."

When Lord Paley took his leave of them, Gemma noticed that he pulled Cam to the side and they talked quietly for a few minutes while the carriages were brought around. She filed that bit of information away to query him about later.

It was decided that since Benedick and Sophia had brought the brougham from Beauchamp House, Gemma and Cam would ride in the more comfortable closed carriage with them while one of the grooms drove Cam's curricle back to Little Seaford. She couldn't have imagined a less congenial prospect than a four-hour drive with her angry sister and brother-in-law—because she was under no illusion that their sunny conversation at Lord Crutchley's had been anything but a polite fiction for the sake of their host—seated across from them.

And once the carriage pulled away from Crutchley's house, the fireworks began.

"Of all the mutton-headed, arrogant, reckless things you have ever done, Cameron," Ben said, his voice eerily calm despite the tenor of his words, "this is by far the worst."

Something about the way he immediately blamed their situation on Cam made Gemma's hackles rise. "I am not a young innocent being led into misbehavior, Benedick," she argued. "It was my idea for us to travel to meet Crutchley in the first place. And we couldn't have accounted for what would happen with the weather. So, you may keep your sharp words to yourself."

"Do you know what could happen to you if word gets out that the two of you spent the night together in an inn, Gemma?" Benedick asked, not backing down from his position one bit. "If you thought the risk from what happened in Pearson Close was great, then this escapade is far worse. You were even seen by Paley, for heaven's sake."

"But Paley thinks we're wed," Cam said, squeezing Gemma's hand as she slipped it into his. "And we will be as soon as I can procure a special license."

She felt a pang of conscience over the rift she'd caused between the brothers. She'd never considered that Benedick would take his role as her pseudo-guardian so seriously. A glance at Sophia revealed her sister was concerned about his anger over the situation as well.

"That's not the point," Ben was saying in response to Cam. "And lying about your marital status is hardly the way to begin your life together."

"Dearest," Sophia said, placing a hand on her husband's arm. "You must remember that none of us at Beauchamp House has precisely followed the usual order of things when it comes to marriage. Even you and I didn't wait until we—"

"But that was different," Benedick said with a frown. "We didn't go about telling people we were wed when we were not. And I dashed well knew I intended to make good on my promise to marry you."

As soon as he spoke the words, Gemma felt Cam stiffen beside her. A glance in her sister's direction told her that she'd also realized just how far over the line Benedick's words had been.

"What. Did. You. Say?" Cam asked, his tone as deadly quiet as his brother's had been.

"I'm sure he didn't mean it like it came out, did you, Benedick?" Gemma clung to Cam's arm as if she feared he would launch himself across the carriage at the vicar.

To his credit, Ben sighed and rubbed a hand over his face. "I don't know, damn it. I don't know anything anymore."

"You just suggested that I seduced and intend to abandon your sister-in-law," Cam said coldly, "so I think if you didn't believe it, you were being just as reckless as you accused me of being."

"It was badly worded," Ben said with a shrug, "but you must admit that you've never shown any inclination to marriage. And you certainly had no particular fondness for Gemma before this business with the Beauchamp Lizard."

"Nor did you show any particular desire to marry before you met Sophia," Cam protested. "And relationships change. Gemma and I may have argued a great deal, but that doesn't mean I didn't want her."

At that confession, Gemma wanted to tell him she'd wanted him too, but decided that might be too intimate a conversation for the present moment.

"I didn't say you didn't want her," Benedick said. "Just that you didn't want to marry her."

"Perhaps we can save this conversation for later," Sophia said before Cam could speak up. "After all, you may both wish to speak more freely and that doesn't seem possible while Gemma and I are here, does it?"

Ben had the grace to look abashed. "I hadn't considered your feelings, Gemma," he said with a look of apology. "Perhaps we had better save this until later, as Sophia suggested."

But Cam shook his head. "I have no secrets from Gemma. She knows that we've both undergone a change of heart over the last week or so. And I freely admit that I had no intention of marrying last week. This week is different, however."

"Is that what you want, Gemma?" Ben asked her, his sympathy now making her want to throw it back in his face for the way he'd hurt his brother. "For us to speak freely, I mean."

"Yes," she said. "Don't hold back on my account."

Sophia made a sound of dismay, but didn't speak up.

"Very well," Benedick said with the air of a man who was doing his duty but not with any kind of relish, "didn't you tell me just a few days ago that you preferred to marry someone entirely different from Gemma?"

Since this confession on Cam's part had been one that Gemma herself overheard, she should be inured to its power to hurt her. And yet, it still stung.

"That was a stupid thing said in the heat of the moment," Cam said, and he brought Gemma's hand up to kiss her palm. "Gemma and I discussed it and she knows I regretted saying it."

She had forgiven him the slight days ago, but she could feel from the tension in his body that Cam still carried the guilt of it.

"I think perhaps rather than calling your brother to account," she said to Benedick with a scowl, "you should consider that I am the one who was more against the notion of marriage. If anyone is likely to run away before we are married, it will most certainly be me."

She felt three sets of eyes on her.

"What?" Cam demanded, turning to face her. "Why would you do that?"

She patted him on the hand. "I didn't say I would do it, just that of the two of us, I would be the one more likely to scarper off. You know it's true. If you are stubborn, I am positively a brick wall of will."

Sophia laughed. "My money would be on Gemma as the one to run as well."

Ben looked at his wife in disbelief.

"What?" she asked with a shrug. "I know my sister. She's quite correct about her stubbornness."

Her husband pinched the bridge of his nose. Gemma had no doubt that he was regretting his decision to bring up the matter at all.

Cam, meanwhile, was still concerned about the possibility that Gemma would follow through on her hypothetical plan to run away. "You won't leave before we marry, though, right?"

She was touched to hear the tinge of worry in his voice. "Of course I won't," she said, hugging his arm. "It was just a silly comparison. I have no intention of leaving before you marry me."

He relaxed a little. And mindless of the presence of the other couple in the carriage, he kissed her.

Then, realizing exactly what she'd just said, she pulled away and added, "Nor *after* you marry me either."

They all laughed, and the mood inside the carriage lightened considerably.

"Good," he said, lifting her hand to his lips, "because I love you."

The rest of the drive was far less eventful, though Cam felt as if he'd run naked through the streets of Little Seaford after confessing his love to Gemma in front of his brother and sister-in-law.

It was not lost on him that she didn't say she loved him too, but of course that wasn't something he required. After all, it had only been a few days—as had been pointed out to him multiple times today—since they'd even come to like one another. He could hardly expect her to tumble head over ears into love at the same rate he had.

Still, the ease with which she took his decision that he would return to stay at the vicarage when the brougham drew up before Beauchamp House was troubling.

"I'll see you in the morning," she told him as he handed her down from the carriage. "We need to pay a call on Pearson to question him about the fossil but I am far too fatigued to do so now."

Her knowing smile reminded him of the reasons why she was so tired, and he felt a bit better at her sending him away.

But only a bit.

Her next words, however, made some degree of sense.

"I wish you could stay here," she said as she leaned into him, "but I don't wish to add more reason for strife between you and your brother. I'm quite cross with him already."

At her defense of him, Cam smiled. "Do not be too angry with him," he told her. "Ben has had to endure years of my selfishness and I think he genuinely doesn't want to see you hurt."

"But what about you?" she asked, still not convinced. "I could just as easily hurt you."

He kissed her quickly. "You could, at that. But I hope you can find it in yourself to forgive him. For my sake as well as Sophia's. Because I think it would be very uncomfortable for her if you loathed her beloved husband."

She lifted her chin. "I don't loathe him."

"Good." He grinned at her. "Now, you'd better get inside and show yourself to Serena. I have a feeling she will have a few words for you."

At the mention of her chaperone, she sighed. "I cannot wait until we are wed in truth so that I need only answer to myself."

Cam considered telling her that she would have to answer to him, but he'd had enough arguments for one day.

He escorted her up the steps of Beauchamp House then jogged back down them and climbed into the carriage with his brother and his wife.

Soon, he thought as he watched the house fade from view. Soon he would be entitled to go inside with Gemma and shut the door behind them.

Chapter 25

Gemma had no sooner stepped through the door of Beauchamp House when she was waylaid by Serena, who, rather than scolding, simply enveloped her in a fierce hug.

"I thought you'd be furious," Gemma said with a startled laugh once her chaperone had let her go.

To her further surprise, Serena was wiping tears from her eyes.

"I guessed you were with Cam, of course." The lady, who was most often as calm as her name implied, shook her head a little. "But after the dangers that the others faced when they began digging into my aunt's past, I feared that you both might have been kidnapped or worse."

That possibility hadn't even occurred to Gemma and she suddenly understood why both Ben and Sophia had been angry as well as relieved upon finding them.

"I am so sorry," she said, grasping her chaperone's hand. "It didn't occur to me that you'd worry on that score. I did tell George that we'd be back last night but we were delayed because of weather and—"

"—and now will be married by special license as soon as Cam can obtain one, I'll wager," said Serena with a twist of her lips. "I will go down in the annals of chaperonage

as the most incompetent ever. That will make four of you
who managed to slip past my ruthless attempts to preserve
your reputations."

Though she said it with a bit of a laugh, Gemma knew
she genuinely felt the sting of her failure. "And four who
have married happily," she reminded her. "That is no
small thing, I believe."

"Come, let's go upstairs and you can tell me what you've
discovered in your search for your fossil," Serena said.

Once they were in Gemma's bedchamber, Serena
called for tea and a bath for her charge and while they
waited, Gemma filled her in on the details of the journey—
minus the pretend marriage and night in the inn—and
when she began to tell of the relationship between Lady
Celeste and Lord Crutchley, Serena looked thoughtful.

"I think I remember that," she said with a faraway look.
"Kerr, Maitland and I were children, but I do remember
one summer in particular when my aunt had one gentleman friend who brought along his . . . godson, I think it
was? My cousins will perhaps remember more of the time
than I do. I was only Jeremy's age, but I do remember the
godson because he was a bit of a terror. He broke my favorite dolly, you see and that was the most—"

Gemma interrupted her. "Godson? Are you sure of it?
Do you remember his name?"

She was furious with herself for not realizing it sooner.
Had Paley been following their every move with them
none the wiser?

"Toby?"

"Topher?" Gemma asked, with a rising sense of excitement remembering that Topher was sometimes used as a
diminutive form of Christopher—as in Christopher, Lord
Paley.

"Yes," Serena said with a nod. "I knew it was something I'd never heard before because I remarked upon it. I think that's why he retaliated with my doll, if I recall correctly."

Serena's maid arrived then with the tea tray, and despite her earlier fatigue, Gemma moved to the wardrobe and removed her cloak.

"Where are you going?" Serena asked. "You just returned. What about your bath?"

"I need to speak to Cam," Gemma explained as she pulled the hood of her cloak over her head. "And it can't wait until morning."

"Gemma, you just apologized for running off with him yesterday."

She paused in the doorway. "I know, but please trust me. I think I know who killed Sir Everard. And we have to alert Mr. Northman."

Not waiting to hear Serena's reply, she hurried down the hall toward the cellar entrance to the tunnel.

Cam felt at loose ends almost as soon as he entered the vicarage with Sophia and his brother.

It felt wrong to have left Gemma at Beauchamp House.

They'd spent the past two days in one another's pockets and her absence was a physical ache. An ache that had nothing to do with the intimacies they'd shared and everything to do with the love he'd professed for her.

He closed the door to his bedchamber in the vicarage, having decided to allow his brother and his wife some time alone without his interference. He had little doubt that Sophia would have some choice words for Benedick after his accusations in the carriage.

The knowledge that his brother thought him capable of

seducing and abandoning Gemma had stung. How could it not have? But not as much as it would have if he hadn't known, deep down in his bones, that the accusation was dead wrong.

He knew better than anyone what his intentions had been when he entered that inn with her, and there was nothing for him to be ashamed of.

And Gemma knew that too, if her leave-taking kiss had been anything to judge by. It did bother him that she'd not returned his sentiment, but he knew better than to rush his fences. Especially in such a delicate situation as this.

Tomorrow he would travel to London and get a special license, and when he returned they'd be married. Gemma's feelings would catch up to his. He was confident of it.

He began to unravel his cravat, and realizing the curtains were still open, he moved to close them against the already dark night. But as he did so, a flash of light caught his eye.

This side of the house faced west, toward the shore below Beauchamp House. Another flicker shone then and he swore under his breath.

Had the killer returned to the scene of the murder? Or was someone searching for more fossils where the famous Beauchamp Lizard had been recovered?

He made haste down the stairs, not caring if he disturbed his brother and sister-in-law. If someone was there, it could be the key to finding Sir Everard's murder. And getting the Beauchamp Lizard back for Gemma would be the perfect wedding gift.

Retrieving his greatcoat from the butler, he told the man not to lock the cellar door to the secret passageway, and with a lit lantern in hand, he stepped into the darkness.

* * *

Because the secret passageways to the beach weren't linked, Gemma had to step out onto the shore before she could locate the door leading into the vicarage tunnel.

Thus, when she stepped out onto the shore, she was hit by a brisk, cold wind that made her pull her cloak closer.

Then, almost as suddenly, a dark figure moved closer and she was suddenly in the grip of very strong arms.

"Convenient of you to bring a lantern, my dear," said Lord Paley as he pulled her out onto the rocky beach, one gloved hand covering her mouth so that she couldn't cry out. "It will make my search that much easier."

Why was he here? she wondered. He already had the Beauchamp Lizard, she was sure of it now.

"If you'll promise not to scream," he said coldly, "then I'll remove my hand. But if you renege, I'll kill Lord Cameron."

The threat against Cam sent a jolt of fear through her, and despite her wish to thwart the man holding her, she nodded.

He removed his hand, but then began to tie her hands behind her back with rope he must have had on his person.

"What are you doing here?" she asked, thinking to distract him with talk as he shoved her along toward the chalk cliff where she'd found the skull fossil. "No one would be foolish enough to hide the same fossil here a third time."

He laughed softly and she heard a note of disgust there. "I have the Beauchamp Lizard, you dolt. I want the rest of it. There can't be just a skull with no body. There has to be a full skeleton there beneath the chalk. And I intend to find it."

"But, it was a fossil," she said, puzzled. "If it were an actual bone, perhaps, but there's no guarantee that the entire lizard . . ."

"I'm not a simpleton," he snapped. "I know the chances are slim, but I need something to set me apart. And I won't be able to declare I've found the Beauchamp Lizard for decades thanks to Sir Everard and his blasted boasting. It will mark me as his murderer as surely as if declared it on the front page of the *Times*."

"Then why kill him for it?" she asked, genuinely curious. It made little sense if he'd only wanted the fossil.

"Because the blackguard intended to cut me out of our arrangement," Paley said with a scowl. "I'm the one who told him about the Lizard in the first place. And where I thought it was hidden."

"Because you were there," she said softly. "When Lady Celeste and your godfather found it."

"Lady Serena remembered, then," he said with a sour smile. "I knew it was a risk, but I assumed that enough time had passed and I'd grown enough that she would have forgotten."

"You broke her doll," Gemma said simply. "Of course she remembered."

"She was too young to play with us lads, anyway," Paley said with the pique of a remembered childhood anger. "I thought it would make her leave, but it just made her cousins angry. I went out to the shore because they shunned me."

"And saw your godfather with Lady Celeste," Gemma guessed. Not particularly appropriate viewing for a child, no matter how nasty he grew up to be.

"Actually," he said with a shrug, "I was surprised to learn that from Crutchley this morning. I'd guessed, of course, but I'm grateful I missed that bit. But I did come upon Pearson. He was furious, and brushed past me as if the hounds of hell were on his heels. I don't even know that he saw me, he was so incensed."

"What did you see, then?" Gemma asked.

"The Lizard, of course," he said as if she were stupid. "They were obviously excited about it. Lady Celeste held it up in the light and it was glorious. And then I heard my godfather tell her that she'd be famous for it. *She* would be famous."

He shook his head in disgust. "It was just as much his find as hers. He was there too. But he was giving her the credit."

"Because she unearthed it," Gemma said before she could stop herself.

Paley glowered. "Of course you would think like that. Women have no business putting their names on artifacts. If it were up to me, they wouldn't be involved in the collecting world at all. In that, at least, Pearson and I are in perfect agreement."

"So Pearson had nothing to do with Sir Everard's death, then?" Gemma asked.

"Of course not," he said with a smile that didn't reach his eyes. "But he made the perfect scapegoat once I heard the story of his unrequited youthful passion for Lady Celeste. What better person to blame for the murder of the man who stole her most famous find?"

The wind was picking up, and Gemma couldn't stop the shiver that ran through her. She was beginning to lose feeling in her fingers.

"What will you do with me?" she asked, realizing that Serena thought she was at the vicarage and would very likely not search for her if she didn't come back tonight, thinking she'd just chosen to remain at her sister's house.

"You'll keep me company while I dig," said Lord Paley. "And if I don't find anything I will find . . . other ways to amuse myself with you."

Gemma swallowed. "But it's so cold," she said in a

plaintive tone. "Won't you at least let me use my cloak?" He'd removed it before tying her hands.

"If you think yourself a man's equal, Miss Hastings," he said with a cruel smile, "then you can manage a few hours in the cold. I have endured far worse in the quest for evidence of our natural history."

"That's Lady Cameron Lisle to you," she said with equal coldness. Perhaps reminding him that she was not without a champion would give him pause.

But Paley laughed. "You don't really think I believed that charade at the inn?" he asked with a shake of his head. "My dear Miss Hastings, you were both as transparent as a pane of glass. It comes from being truthful most of the time, I would imagine. Though I did enjoy it when your sister and brother-in-law arrived at my godfather's house looking just like what they were—angry relations searching for a couple on the run."

"If you knew, why didn't you say anything?" Gemma asked, genuinely wondering. "You might have sent us on our way."

"Because I needed to hear the whole blasted story from my godfather's perspective," he said with a shrug. "He never would tell it to me. I think because he suspected I would resent him for his weakness in the matter. Which he was perfectly correct about. But being faced with Lady Celeste's chosen collector, he couldn't resist."

"You really hold him in no affection at all?" Gemma asked.

"Why should I?" he asked sullenly. "He might have taken me under his wing when I showed an interest in geology, but instead he claimed it was too painful for him because it reminded him of her. Simpering fool."

She'd been standing the whole while they spoke and

suddenly, she felt a tremor run through her as the cold wind
hit her.

"Oh sit down, you foolish child," Paley said as he saw
her wobble. Before she could brace herself, he placed a
hand on her shoulder and shoved her into a sitting position. The rocks were hard on her bottom and back, but
Gemma didn't make a sound.

He was shuffling back up to where he'd been digging
when Gemma saw movement at the other side of the little
crescent of shoreline.

As she watched, Cam crept soundlessly across the
rocks. He held a finger to his lips, indicating that she should
keep quiet and she clenched her teeth so that she wouldn't
cry out her relief at seeing him.

Some sixth sense, or perhaps some sound of boots on
stone, alerted Lord Paley to his presence, however, because
he turned suddenly.

On seeing who was creeping up on them, he stood up
and opened his arms wide.

"Oh look, it's the debaucher of innocents come to rescue his false bride," he said with a sneer. "Do come closer
so that I may greet you properly, Lord Cameron."

And to Gemma's horror, she saw that in one of those
outstretched hands Lord Paley held a pistol.

Chapter 26

As soon as Cam stepped through the door leading to the beachhead, he saw that the light he'd glimpsed from his window was a lamp. The next thing he noted, and what made his heart leap into his throat, was Lord Paley, shoving Gemma, her hands tied behind her back toward the sloping chalk cliff where she'd found the fossil they knew now was the Beauchamp Lizard.

Not wanting to alert the other man to his presence, he waited while Gemma questioned him about his role in Sir Everard's murder. He wasn't sure if she was stalling until someone came to save her, or if she simply sought to understand the man's motive.

Either way, he used the time to his advantage, searching for and finding a large enough stone to cause the other man damage if Cam were to strike him with it. He clutched it in his hand while Paley continued to talk, until he saw him shove Gemma to the ground. And he knew he had to act.

As quietly as he could, he walked across the rocks toward the far side of the shore, and when Gemma saw him, he indicated that she should remain silent. She gave a slight nod, and he continued.

But something must have warned Paley because he turned around, and to Cam's horror, when he rose to his feet he was holding a pistol in one hand. A pistol he aimed at Gemma.

"Oh look, it's the debaucher of innocents come to rescue his false bride," Paley said with a sneer. "Do come closer so that I may greet you properly, Lord Cameron."

"Don't hurt her, Paley," Cam said, suddenly wishing he'd gone back for Benedick's help when he saw Paley had Gemma. "If you hurt someone, make it me. Don't hurt her. You haven't harmed a lady yet. Don't start now."

"How would you know?" Paley scoffed. "Just because I murdered Sir Everard, that doesn't mean he was the extent of my criminal career. Not all of us are bound to some outdated code of honor where women are concerned. I had hoped you were one of us, but then you fell prey to this hussy's charms. It will never cease to amaze me that otherwise intelligent men so often find themselves tied up in knots over something that can be had for a few bob on the nearest street corner."

"Either I'm an innocent or a hussy, Lord Paley," Gemma said boldly. "Make up your mind. I cannot be both."

Cam bit back a curse at her taunt. She was going to get herself killed.

"She's not worth it, Paley," he shouted, desperate to take the man's attention off Gemma and onto himself. "Don't waste your shot."

But Paley had already turned to face his prisoner. "You are bold for someone on the other end of a pistol, Miss Hastings," he said coldly.

"Because I have more courage in my little finger than you ever will, you murderer," Gemma shouted. "If you were any sort of collector you wouldn't have to steal to get what you wanted. In fact, you would have—"

To Cam's horror, Paley made a growling sound and raised his hand to fire.

Even as he watched, Cam ran as fast as he could toward the other man and a shot rang out in the night, followed closely by another.

By the time he reached where Gemma and Paley struggled on the ground, he found them both covered in blood.

Furious, he pulled Paley off her and raised his fist to punch the man, but somehow Gemma's voice penetrated the red fog of his anger.

"Cam! Cam! He's hit already."

And to his shock he realized that Paley was indeed the one who was bleeding.

He turned to Gemma. "Are you hit as well?" he asked as he shoved the other man to the side. "I heard two shots."

"No, I'm not hit," she said with a shake of her head. "But I don't know who fired the other shot."

"That was me, I'm afraid," said a voice from the stairs leading from the top of the cliffs to the beach.

They looked up to see Maximillian Pearson coming toward them, followed close behind by Serena.

Not waiting to greet the man, Cam turned Gemma so that he could remove the ropes binding her hands.

Mindless of the blood on her gown, he pulled her to him.

"I thought you'd be killed, you stubborn girl," he said as he held her against him with trembling arms. "What were you thinking to taunt him like that?"

"I was thinking that I very much wanted him not to shoot you," she said against his shoulder. "What were *you* thinking?"

"Perhaps you can carry on this conversation indoors?" Serena asked from where she stood beside Pearson.

"We'll need to make room for the footmen to remove Lord Paley into the house."

"Of course," Cam said, then much to Gemma's chagrin if her squeal was to be believed, he swung her into his arms and carried her toward the door leading to the tunnel into Beauchamp House.

Though her bath from earlier was cold by now, Gemma washed quickly in the water and changed into a clean gown before she made her way to the drawing room, where she found Serena, Mr. Pearson, and Cam.

The latter two were sipping brandy, and when Serena offered her a cup of tea, Gemma declined it and turned to the sideboard to pour herself a bit of brandy too.

Not caring about the propriety of it—on a night like this she would do what she pleased—Gemma took a seat beside Cam and curled up against his side, welcoming his arm around her shoulders.

"Lord Paley is being seen to by Dr. Holmes upstairs," Serena said without commenting on her charge's boldness. "I've sent for Mr. Northman as well so that he may hear the full story of Lord Paley's misdeeds."

"I must confess, Lady Serena," said Pearson with a frown, "I blame some of this on myself. If I hadn't been so unwilling to speak about what I knew about the Beauchamp Lizard, I feel sure that Paley wouldn't have felt it necessary to kill Sir Everard over it."

"What did you know, sir?" Gemma asked, curious now whether, as Lord Crutchley had told them, Pearson had been there the day Lady Celeste found the fossilized skull.

"I was here the day Lady Celeste found it," he said with a pained expression. "I was . . . infatuated, I suppose is the word . . . and I was watching her. I saw her unearth it, with Lord Crutchley by her side. I saw more as well—"

He broke off and Gemma knew he was speaking of the intimacy he'd also seen that day.

"I decided, and I'm not proud of it, but I decided to steal the fossil from her." Pearson shook his head. "If I couldn't have her, I would have that damned fossil she was so proud of."

"So it was your theft attempt that made her decide to hide it?" Gemma asked.

"Yes," he said with a look of shame. "I did many things I'm not proud of. Then, as well as now."

"How did you come to be here tonight?" Cam asked. He was grateful for the man's shot that saved Gemma, but wondered why he'd been here at all.

"I received a note from Lord Crutchley," he said with a bemused look. "I hadn't thought of the man in decades. Not since those days when I was so taken with your aunt, Lady Serena. But he was concerned that his godson might be about to do something foolish. He spoke specifically of danger to you, Lady Cameron."

He turned to Gemma and Cam. "Felicitations on your marriage, by the way."

Gemma didn't have the heart to tell him that she and Cam weren't married just yet, so she simply said, "Thank you," and Cam echoed her.

There was an awkward silence before Serena leapt into the breach with her usual social aplomb. "Why don't you tell them what happened when you received Lord Crutchley's note," she said kindly.

As if surprised to find her still there, Pearson nodded. "I set out for Beauchamp House at once. I had found Paley to be interested to the point of obsession about the

Beauchamp Lizard over the course of the gathering at Pearson Close. And when Sir Everard turned up dead, after boasting about having found it, I had a suspicion that Paley might have been involved."

He took a deep breath. "I should have said or done something, but you must understand. Tonight is the first time I've left my estate in decades."

Recognizing true contrition when she saw it, Gemma placed her hand over his. "And I am so grateful for it. I have no doubt you saved my life tonight, sir."

His cheeks colored and he looked at the floor. "Thank you, Lady Cameron."

The drawing room door opened then to admit Sophia and Benedick.

Unmindful of the others, Sophia hurried to her sister's side and knelt beside her. "Are you trying to give me an apoplexy?" she asked, taking Gemma's hands in hers.

Ben, meanwhile introduced himself to Pearson and said, "We had word from Serena that my services might be needed here tonight. Little did I realize that when we ate luncheon with Paley and his godfather he'd attempt to murder Cam and Gemma later in the evening."

"If you ask me," Gemma said with a scowl, "Lord Paley doesn't deserve last rites. He's already murdered one person and intended to murder me and Cam as well."

"But that's the thing about the lord's forgiveness, Gemma," her brother-in-law told her gently. "It's there for everyone. Even the murderers among us."

He came forward and kissed her on the cheek, though to take the sting out of his words. "I'm glad you're unharmed."

As she watched, he placed a hand on Cam's shoulder. "And you, as well. I would have spent the rest of my days regretting it if our quarrel in the carriage were my last words to you."

Cam moved to clasp his brother's hand in his. "But it wasn't. So you'd better go say some holy things over Paley before he dies of his wounds."

The brothers exchanged grins and Gemma knew that whatever animosity had been between them was healed now.

When Benedick was gone, Pearson stood. "I will be off then," he said, clearly a little uncomfortable with the family scene before him.

He was interrupted, however, by the appearance of Squire Northman in the doorway. "I think not, Pearson, if you were here when Lord Paley was shot."

Realizing that they had a long night ahead of them, Gemma turned to Serena. "I think I will have that cup of tea after all."

Chapter 27

When Cam finally slipped into Gemma's bedchamber some two hours later, he was bone tired. But he'd been almost constitutionally incapable of returning to the vicarage with his brother and sister-in-law. After almost losing Gemma to a madman's shot, he had to hold her in his arms or he'd never get a moment's rest.

She'd gone up a half hour before and when he shut the door behind him, he saw that she had left a lamp burning on the bedside table.

Despite that, she was fast asleep, her hair glinting around her like a halo as she lay curled beneath the blankets.

As quickly and quietly as he could, Cam shucked off his boots and coats and stripped down to his smallclothes before slipping beneath the covers with her.

She murmured something as he pulled her warm body against him, but didn't wake up. And for the first time since they'd left the inn that morning, he relaxed and breathed in the violet scent of her, then fell fast asleep.

When he came awake again the first rays of light were peeking through the narrow gap between the curtains, and a warm mouth was working its way down his neck.

"Who is this intoxicating creature?" he asked, his voice still thick with sleep.

"You're dreaming," she said, crawling up his body to kiss him on the mouth. "I'm a mere figment of your imagination, Lord Cameron."

"If that's the case then I don't know what I will tell my intended," he said, sliding his hands down to cup her bottom. "Because I fear she's a very jealous lady. She won't like your being here with me at all. In fact, I think you'd better go, imaginary lady."

"And what if I told you she wouldn't mind?" Gemma took his lower lip in her teeth, and Cam felt himself harden against her.

"Would she not?" he asked, moving his hands to grasp the fabric of her nightdress and slide it up her body. "I don't think you know her as well as I do."

She shifted to let him remove the gown completely, and sighed against him as her bare breasts brushed against his chest. "I think I do," she said, moving her hips to tease herself against his hardness. "She likes this very much, I think."

"Does she now?" Cam asked, grasping her hips and moving her so that he was right where she wanted him.

Gemma breathed out a sigh of pure pleasure before shifting to brace her hands on his chest. Then in one fluid motion, she sat up, seating him fully inside of her.

Cam looked up at her, naked and glorious as she sat impaled on him. He moved one hand to cup her breast, while the other guided her hip as she began to move. There were no more words, then, only sensation as she experimented, finally finding a rhythm that they both found pleasing. And he watched her for as long as he could, her eyes closed and her mouth wide with ecstasy as she rode him to completion.

When he felt her quiver around him, Cam held her tight, and flipped them so that he was on top and let himself go, taking her, claiming her, loving her with his body as he whispered words of love against her neck until he felt himself fly over the edge into bliss.

He came to himself again with the soft stroking of her fingers in his hair. He'd collapsed on top of her, he realized with a start, before he began to roll to the side.

"Don't you dare move, Cameron Lisle," she said, clasping him to her with her ankles locked around him. "You're perfect just where you are."

"I don't want to crush you," he protested, moving a little so that he could see her face.

She moved her hand to brush an errant lock of hair from his face. "I like it. You may be sure that if I ever find you are doing something I dislike, I will tell you."

He laughed. "I suppose that's right."

"Now," she said firmly, "lay your head back down so that I can stroke you."

"Your hair," she said in response to his raised brow.

Laughing again, he laid his head on her breast while she continued to toy with his hair.

"We'll have to marry soon," she said conversationally. "If only so that we don't have to sneak around in order to do what we just did,"

"There's also the small detail that we've already passed ourselves off as a married couple," he said wryly. Though he too would like to marry so that they could enjoy one another without fear of being caught.

"But there is one thing we haven't talked about," she said thoughtfully. "The matter of where we will live."

"We haven't discussed it, of course," Cam said, moving so that he was lying beside her where he might see her face. "But I do have a tidy little manor house just down the coast on the other side of Brighton."

She frowned. "Do you, indeed?"

"You didn't think I'd wed you without having something to offer you besides a collection of fossils, did you?"

Her expression was sheepish. "Well, I had thought since it was so sudden—" she began.

"Gemma," he said with a shake of his head. "Did you really believe I had nothing more to my name than fossils? That I wished to marry you so that I might lay claim to Beauchamp House?"

He wasn't sure whether to be annoyed or amused.

"Not to get Beauchamp House, no," she corrected him, sitting up with her back against the ornately carved headboard. "But if it were necessary, I would not have objected to our living here. I am the last of the heiresses after all, so . . ."

"But we've a full month before the year ends," he reminded her, kissing the end of her nose. "So, last or not, you too will be wed before the first year is up. You'll all have to share joint ownership."

"About that," she said with a look of embarrassment. "What if we waited until after the first of the year to marry?"

He stared at her. "Are you serious?"

She stared back. For so long that his heart began to beat with alarm.

Gemma watched as his eyes shone with real alarm, and she couldn't punish him any longer.

"Of course not, you madman," she said as she threw her arms around his neck. "I am in love with you. I don't want

to wait, and I wouldn't wait even if it meant full ownership of Beauchamp House."

He breathed out a sigh and she realized she'd held out
a little too long for his comfort.

"Just for that," he said pettishly, "I won't give you the
present I brought you."

She pulled back to see his face, to determine whether
he was jesting.

His response was raised brows. "Yes, I have a present
for you, but I'm not sure I wish to give it to someone who
would toy with my feelings like that," he said in mock-
pique.

Deciding she'd have to win him back no matter the cost,
Gemma began peppering his face with kisses, until, that
is, he caught her face between his large hands and stilled
her so that he could kiss her properly.

When they were both breathless, he pulled away and
lifted her off him.

She watched with great appreciation as he strode naked across the room to where his greatcoat lay draped
over a chair.

"I wondered why you brought that up with you," she
said, sitting up and fluffing the pillow behind her.

He kept his back to her as he removed something from
the inner pocket of the coat. To her great disappointment,
he hid whatever it was behind his back as he came back
and slid beneath the bedclothes and sat beside her against
the headboard.

She turned to look at him, and to her wonderment, he
actually looked a bit nervous.

"Before I give this to you," he said solemnly, "if you
think it's foolish you need only tell me and we'll forget it
ever happened."

Gemma blinked. She never thought she'd see Lord Cameron Lisle so shy. It was a side of him she'd never thought to see. And her heart seemed to flip over at the knowledge he'd trusted her enough to show it to her.

As she watched, he proffered his closed fist and, in one fluid motion, opened it.

There, nestled atop his palm was one of the brightest blue banded agate stones she'd ever seen. With a shaking hand she took it from him and traced the bands of different hues of blue that surrounded the asymmetrical triangle of lighter blue in the center.

"It's beautiful," she breathed, too moved to say more. She knew without him telling her that this was important to him.

"I found it on the shore near Lisle Hall when I was a small boy," he said softly. "It was my first find. My father helped me polish it, and he found a man to shave off the side so that the striations would be revealed. It was the beginning of a lifelong love."

"It's lovely," she said, leaning forward to kiss him. "But I can't take it from you."

But Cam shook his head. "I need to give it to you. To show you how much you mean to me, Gemma."

He cupped her face in his hands.

"You mean more to me," he said fiercely. "More than this stone. More than geology. If it takes me giving it up to make you happy, I will do it. I love you that much."

Gemma felt tears fill her eyes. All this time, she'd been afraid that somehow marrying Cam would mean she'd have to give up some part of herself. The scholar, the fossil-hunter, the bluestocking.

Aunt Dahlia was wrong. Marrying this generous,

loving, wonderful man wouldn't diminish her. It would make her stronger.

They would make a formidable team.

"Thank you," she said, kissing him again. "But I could no more ask you to give up fossils than you'd ask me. I love you, you see. I'm not quite sure how we will manage it, but I do know that I can imagine no one else I'd rather comb beaches and quarries for specimens with."

As she spoke, she watched as his smile transformed his entire face. There was joy there, and relief, but also love. "Are you sure?" he asked, though it was clear from his expression that he believed her.

Still, she couldn't help but say, "I think I've loved you since that day that we fought over your silly geology magazine. I simply didn't know it yet."

He pulled her against him. "But why didn't you say? I poured my heart out in the carriage yesterday and you never said a thing. I could have kept my prize agate."

She gave him a playful punch in the shoulder.

"I wasn't sure of it," she told him honestly. "I've never felt this way before and I didn't want to tell you I loved you when I might discover later it was . . . I don't know, indigestion."

"So now you know it's not indigestion?" he asked, his mouth curved into a smile.

Her heart clenched. "I knew it when I saw Lord Paley holding that pistol."

She clasped him to her and held on tight.

"I love you so much, Cam. More than I can ever show you."

He whispered a suggestion of how she might do so in her ear.

"You, sir, are a tease," she said before kissing him.

"But you love me anyway?" he asked, pulling back a little.

"Of course I do," she said with a serene smile. "How could I possibly resist such a rogue?"

Epilogue

"I can hardly believe almost a full year has passed since we arrived here," said Ivy staring out at darkened parkland beyond the window. "I didn't know any of you, and now I can't remember life without you."

"I feel the same way," said Sophia, slipping an arm round her friend's waist.

Gemma, who had married Cam only a few days after the incident with Lord Paley on the cliffs, sat with Daphne at the library table where they'd spent many happy hours in quiet study punctuated by the occasional laughter and sometimes tears.

"I can," Daphne said dryly, "and it was much less pleasant."

"And we hadn't met Serena either," Gemma said. "I hope she'll be amenable to our scheme. Without her, it will be difficult. Not impossible, of course, but I'm not sure I could trust anyone as I do her."

It was hard for Gemma to believe that it was nearly time for them to go their separate ways.

They could come and go as they pleased, of course.

The house belonged to all of them equally. But marriage meant that their comings and goings couldn't always be dictated by their wishes. And once children came, even with the best intentions, they would not be able to live in one another's pockets. Not as they had here at Beauchamp.

In the month since Gemma and Cam had discovered that it had been Lord Paley who murdered Sir Everard and stole the Beauchamp Lizard, the four Beauchamp House heiresses had been hard at work on a scheme that would see to it that even once they were all departed to live with their husbands, the house itself would remain a haven for lady scholars.

"You did ask Serena to meet us here, didn't you?" asked Sophia with a frown. "I haven't seen her since luncheon."

The four heiresses and their husbands had spent the holidays in the house together, along with their chaperone, Lady Serena, and her son, Jeremy.

"Of course," Gemma said. "I think she's tucking Jeremy in. She said she'd come up to see us as soon as she was finished."

"I still can't believe you managed to find the Beauchamp Lizard," said Ivy with a shake of her head as she stepped over to one of the other chairs at the table. "With only an unfinished letter from Lady Celeste and those odious men trying to steal it from you."

Gemma had been sad, at first, that she alone of the four heiresses hadn't had a full letter and quest from their late mentor. But the truth of the matter was that she felt as connected to the bluestocking leader as she would have if she'd left her a whole trunkful of personal letters. Because she alone knew the same excitement Lady Celeste had when she saw the fossilized skull emerge from the chalk cliffs only a few hundreds of yards from where she sat now. And she'd been able to restore it to its rightful place in Lady Celeste's collection.

"It wasn't easy," she said aloud. "But I had help from Cam, and I feel a certain degree of satisfaction knowing that Lord Paley wasn't able to enjoy the fruits of his evil deeds."

Once he'd recovered from his gunshot wound, Lord Paley had been taken to London to await his trial by the House of Lords, which wouldn't happen for another month or so. But Gemma had little doubt that even if they didn't sentence the man to hang, he would, at the very least, spend the rest of his life in gaol.

"I was a little surprised we were able to tear you away from polishing the Lizard," said Sophia wryly. "I don't believe any of the other pieces in the collection is afforded that kind of treatment."

"It's a very important find," Gemma protested. "Once I hear from Cuvier in Paris I'll know more, of course. But I am fairly certain this fossil will shed some light on how life developed in this part of England. In fact—"

She broke off when she realized her sister had been teasing her. "Well, it's important," she ended lamely. Then spoiled her vehemence by sticking out her tongue at Sophia.

"Ladies," said Serena as she came into the room. "Must I remind you what constitutes good behavior? One does not stick out one's tongue, no matter what the provocation."

Her wide smile took any sting from her words, and the four heiresses welcomed their chaperone for the past year into the room by offering her a chair at the mahogany table and putting a glass of brandy in her hand.

"You were all so secretive about this little gathering," she said after she'd taken a sip. "I couldn't even persuade

Maitland to tell me, and you all know my poor brother is hopeless at keeping secrets."

"It's one of his most admirable qualities," said Daphne with a grin. "I was able to winkle every last one of my Christmas gifts from him."

"But in this case, he held firm," Serena said with a shake of her head.

"You don't have the same sorts of persuasive tactics at your disposal," Gemma said dryly.

"There is that," Serena said with raised brows.

"Now," she continued her blue eyes sparkling, "you'd better tell me what you're plotting before I die of curiosity."

Ivy looked round at the other three and with their nods of agreement, she said, "First of all, we would like to know if you've decided where you'll go once you've decided to leave Beauchamp House. Or, rather, if you truly wish to go at all."

Serena looked from one to the other of them. "I had thought to return to the Maitland estate," she said carefully. "Though if that is no longer agreeable to you, Daphne—"

"If you wish it," Daphne said carefully, "then I am agreeable. But we have another offer."

"We, the Beauchamp heiresses," said Gemma with a smile.

"For you, and Jeremy if you wish it," Sophia added.

"We-would-like-to-turn-Beauchamp-House-into-a-school-for-bluestockings-and-we-would-like-for-you-to-run-it," said Ivy in one long breath.

When the other three heiresses stared at her, the classical linguist shrugged. "I made up my own compound word."

Serena blinked. "What did you say?"

"In a slower fashion," said Gemma wryly, "we would

like to turn Beauchamp House into a sort of haven for lady scholars like ourselves, and we would like you to serve as chaperone to them. And perhaps oversee a few scholars we employ to live here and instruct them. Like a school, but without all of the strictures and silliness that are emphasized at ladies' schools. More like university learning for ladies."

"You wouldn't need to interact with them on a daily basis if you didn't wish it," said Sophia hastily. "Since I'll be only a few miles away at the vicarage, I can come and manage things for you from time to time if you become overwhelmed."

"Or we could hire someone to be the headmistress," said Ivy quickly. "You needn't do it at all if you don't wish it. I know being forced to stay here for the past year must have been tiresome at times, when you wished to visit friends, or see family. We simply thought that since you'd done such a good job of it with us. And there's no one we'd trust to protect Beauchamp Hall than you."

At that Serena began to laugh. And laugh. Until tears were streaming down her face.

"You needn't make fun of us," said Daphne stiffly. "If you don't want to do it, you need only say so."

"Oh my dears," said Serena, wiping her eyes, and reaching across the table to take Daphne's hand with her free one. "I'm not making fun. Truly, I'm not. It's just that, I think I can say unequivocally that I have been the most inept chaperone ever to hold the title."

"Of course you haven't," Ivy protested. "You were quite cross when I had to marry Quill after only a few days' acquaintance."

"And you were most firm when you overheard Maitland and me in the wine cellar," Daphne added with a nod.

"You looked properly upset when you caught Benedick

coming into the breakfast parlor that time," said Sophia solemnly.

Gemma shrugged. "I think by the time I disappeared overnight with Cam you were used to misbehavior. But you did call the magistrate when Lord Paley tried to shoot me, which cannot be overlooked."

"My dear girls," said Serena beaming at all of them. "You cannot think I am the right person to head up this endeavor. I cannot believe it."

"But you're the perfect person," Ivy protested. "You are kind, you are a paragon of good behavior yourself and therefore a good role model."

"And you never fail to say and do the right thing," said Daphne. "I know, because I've watched hoping you would fail, but you never do. It's most frustrating."

"But I know nothing about running a school," Lady Serena protested.

"That's the perfect part," Gemma said with a smile, "it wouldn't be a school as we all understand schools to be. It would be more of a house of learning where the female scholars we choose—we've decided they needn't come from the gentry or the aristocracy, because why should education be only for those with money—would be afforded the tutelage they need to become proficient in their fields of study. They could go on to become teachers or governesses themselves, or time in Beauchamp House would give them the propriety and manners they need to rise in society."

"But that sounds like a finishing school," Serena argued.

"A finishing school with scholarly learning too," Sophia said. "And the arts, of course. I would be happy to come once a week and teach painting, for instance."

"And what is the mission of this endeavor to be?" Serena asked. "To turn out intelligent wives?"

"To turn out educated women," Gemma corrected her. "Who can mix in whatever society they like, and pursue their scholarly endeavors with the confidence needed to hold their own in a world of men."

"I'm not a scholar, though," Serena insisted. "I've only ever been a wife and mother. I haven't one ounce of the scholarly learning the four of you have."

"You're a scholar of society," said Daphne. "You know more than I ever will about the rules of precedence. Or how to properly address the wife of a baronet's younger son."

"You know what month it's best to air out the linen closet, and what dishes might be made from a goose," said Ivy.

"Your needlework puts all of ours to shame," Gemma said wryly.

Serena couldn't argue with any of that. Because she'd found almost as soon as the four heiresses arrived at Beauchamp House that what they knew about household management paled in comparison with what they knew about their fields of study.

"Even if one knows all there is to know about maths," Daphne said, "it is still necessary to speak to the housekeeper about the dashed menus."

Menus were a particular trial to Daphne now that she'd spent some time at the ducal estate.

"I have been wondering if it might be possible to remain here," Serena said slowly, and knowing they'd won, the heiresses cheered.

"You won't be sorry!" cried Ivy as she clapped her hands.

"I knew you would agree," said Gemma as she pulled Serena into a hug. "You've enjoyed this year, admit it."

Tears shone in Lady Serena's eyes as she welcomed the

hugs of her former charges. "It's been the happiest year of my life, you scapegraces, and well you know it."

"I say this calls for a toast," said Gemma, suddenly needing to pay tribute to the woman whose brilliance and generosity had brought them all together.

Raising her brandy glass, she waited until the others had done the same.

"To Lady Celeste Beauchamp," Gemma cried with a glance toward the portrait of their benefactress, which hung above the fireplace. "May we never forget her generosity of spirit."

And almost at the exact moment they touched glasses the candles in the chandelier flickered.

The quintet were silent for a moment, exchanging wide-eyed glances.

"You saw that too, did you not?" Daphne asked, her blue eyes wide.

"I believe my aunt approves of your toast," Lady Serena said with a nod toward the portrait.

Gemma lifted her glass again. "Thank you, Lady Celeste. Thank you for everything."

The candles didn't flicker that time, but Gemma was quite sure she saw the portrait wink.

Catch up on the Studies in Scandal series

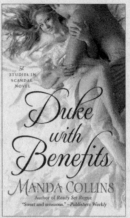

Available now from St. Martin's Paperbacks